FIGHTING BLIND

INSPIRED BY A TRUE STORY

R Y A N   B O W

KAMINARI
ENTERPRISES

Published by Kaminari Enterprises, L.L.C.
Email: info@kaminarienterprises.com

ISBN 979-8-9874558-4-5 (Paperback)
ISBN 979-8-9874558-7-6 (eBook)
First Edition

Contents

Chapter 1

T he boy stands transfixed, his Coke-bottle eyeglasses reflecting the floor-to-ceiling shop window. He holds his father's hand, standing a head taller than the man's belt. His thick specs slide down his nose, and he pushes them up to get a better look, totally uninterested in the swirl of life around him on the city street.

The boy and his father stand on a short avenue in a run-down section of Grand Rapids, on their way home from picking up a few groceries. It's the kind of low-slung sprawl, with storefronts below and apartments above, found in urban areas everywhere. Cars park parallel to the curb. Delivery trucks clatter by with a waft of diesel. Yesterday's newspapers and burger wrappers blow down the sidewalk in the light breeze. Posters on the steel staging of a construction site advertise an upcoming R&B concert at the Intersection night club.

In his early thirties, the man has a handlebar moustache, soul patch, Afro, and the build of an aging athlete. He looks down at the boy, smiling. He can't remember the last time his son had shown this much interest in anything.

"Ryan," the man says. The boy ignores him.

The kid's scrawny, wearing loose-fitting jeans, a pair of beat-up sneakers, and a white striped shirt. He has an orange padded helmet on his head, bright against his warm brown skin, and he's absolutely entranced by what he's seeing. The boy absently sets down the bag of chips and loaf of bread he's carrying and stares.

Painted on the window in action-style lettering: Chi Yiu Judo School.

The kids on the other side of the glass wear baggy martial arts uniforms. Several are so small their white cotton pants drag on the floor and the tops hang below their wrists, like they're wearing their parent's bathrobes. The boy doesn't notice any of this. He's just mesmerized by what they're doing. Which is throwing each other over their hips and onto the thin tatami mats that make up the floor. They stand in pairs, one facing the street, the other with their back to it. The student standing closest to the window grabs the other by the waist and levers them over onto the mat.

They can't be any older than him, thinks the father, amused. The man's parents named him Amen. The story went that, as the youngest of fifteen kids, his mother said: "Amen," when he was born – that was enough children for her. Like his wife, Diane, Amen is a teacher. She teaches French at the high school across town; he, English, at the one just down the street that his son would one day attend. He looks down at the boy.

2

"Ryan," Amen says again.

The boy continues to watch, intent on the action. He's amazed to see the kids who'd been heaved onto the floor, hop right up as if nothing happened. They resume their place at arm's length from their partners and do it again. And again. Always seeming happy to get up and go back for more, occasionally even high-fiving their opponents.

Finally, the boy looks up at his father.

"You wanna to try a class?" Amen asks him.

He nods, taking his father's hand.

***

The light of the TV glows on Ryan's glasses. He sits cross-legged a few feet from the small set, his eyes wide. On the screen, a young black martial artist pursues the transcendent state known as "the Glow" in *The Last Dragon*. Ryan is totally engrossed as "Bruce" Leroy Green battles Sho'Nuff, the "Shogun of Harlem." When either of the fighters lands a punch or kick, there's an electric spark, and Ryan can't take his eyes off the screen. He doesn't even hear the tinkling piano emanating from the next room, where his mother Diane is practicing. The music comes to an abrupt halt.

"Ryan." Diane, a shapely woman with large glasses beneath well-manicured black hair, leans against the doorway. The boy watches Sho'Nuff deliver one kick after another, not hearing or not caring to hear his mother.

"Ryan," she says, a little louder.

He ignores her, completely captivated.

3

"Ryan!" she yells, striding over and switching off the TV.

"Hey!" He looks up, his eyes darkening.

"Don't you hey me," his mother says. "It's time to get ready for bed." He opens his mouth to say something and thinks better. He knows it's futile to argue, especially when she smells like medicine. She notices.

"You better listen when I'm talking to you." Diane points toward the ceiling. "Get your butt upstairs, now."

"Yes, mom," he says.

"C'mon, Ry," Amen says, sticking his head around the doorway behind Diane. "I'll take you up."

Ryan climbs the carpeted staircase slowly, holding on to the railing as he takes each painstaking step.

His dad pats his back, encouraging him upwards. He leans down and says into Ryan's ear: "I got you some new, PJs. Wait'll you see em."

Who cares. I wanna finish my movie.

Ryan steps into the bathroom to brush his teeth and then pads down the hall to his small bedroom. His father hands him some pajamas still on a blue plastic hanger, new from a store. Ryan sets them down on a chair without looking at them.

"Hey, check those out," his dad says, picking them back up and holding them out to him. "I think you're really gonna like them."

Ryan lifts them in front of him to have a look. His eyes widen, taking on a sparkle behind his thick black plastic frames – they are pajamas, but they look like a kung fu uniform. The black long sleeve top has fake closures printed on it, a mock collar, and white cuffs. The black pants taper to a tight ankle.

Just like the ones Bruce Lee wore in Fists of Fury!

Ryan immediately puts them on and begins to fight imaginary enemies, throwing kicks and punches around his bedroom.

"Thanks, Dad!"

"I thought you'd like 'em," Amen grinned. "You're going to have to save the world tomorrow, though. Time for bed, before your mom comes up."

Ryan hooks the hanger on a dresser drawer, so he'll see his new kung fu jammies when he wakes up. Then climbs under the covers of his twin bed, looking over at the outfit one last time before Amen pulls the blankets up to his chin.

"I love you, son." Amen kisses him on his forehead and turns for the door. "Sleep tight."

"Dad?"

"Yeah, Ry?"

"Is mom going to be alright?"

"Your mom feels some powerful feelings inside, sometimes. And sometimes they get the better of her. We just have to support her as best we can."

Ryan nods.

"Is that why she takes so much medicine?"

Amen's mouth tightens and his head falls a moment. Then he nods.

"And Dad?" Ryan says, pulling the covers around him. "Yeah?"

"I want to be a fighter when I grow up. Like you."

Amen blinks. He pauses a moment, before he understands.

"Son, I'm just a wrestling coach. I'm not even a wrestler anymore."

"I know, but you *were*."

Amen stares off for a second before bobbing his head. "I guess I was," he says quietly. Amen sits at the side of Ryan's bed, propping himself up on one arm and looking down.

"Son, there's something I have to talk to you about." Amen glances around the room, thinking about how to say what's on his mind. "Your mom and I were talking."

"Yeah?"

"I know you want to be a fighter. You've been talking about it as long as I can remember. So, we've decided to let you try judo class."

Ryan nods. "Can't wait. Going to go to the Olympics one day."

"Well, careful with those hopes son."

"What do you mean?"

"You can never really fight, fight, Ryan. Full contact. Punches and kicks."

"Why not?"

"Well, you know it's not safe, right? When you were born you were really sick. That's why you wear your helmet."

Ryan looks down at his lap.

"And you have to wear those glasses. Can you see well without them?"

"No, but. . ."

"How could you fight someone without being able to see?"

"Well, I could. . ."

"No, you can't. That's the point. We have to protect your head."

Ryan stares at the Bruce Lee poster on the wall a minute and then pulls the covers up over his face and rolls over.

Amen sits with his hand on his son's shoulder.

"I know it's not what you want to hear, son. But you'll understand one day."

"No, I won't," Ryan says with a sob.

Amen rubs his shoulder and then gets up and turns off the light.. As he closes the door, he can hear Ryan weeping.

Amen shuffles down the hall to his bedroom. Diane is sitting up reading. Several pill bottles sprawl across her nightstand. Prozac. Zoloft. Others with hard to read labels.

"I told him."

She puts her book down in her lap.

"How'd he take it?"

"Crying when I closed the door."

Diane frowns and interweaves her fingers in her lap.

"Well, there's no getting around it," she says.

"When we were in town today, I told him he could take a judo class," Amen. He leans back, wincing.

Diane sits up and glares at him. "Are you out of your mind?"

"It's judo, not karate. We're not talking about punches and kicks and head shots. It's more like wrestling. And he'll be wearing his helmet."

"Wrestling," she shakes her head, inhaling sharply. "Wrestling!" Diane's lips go tight and her brow furrows. She shakes her head. "Amen, you need to stop trying to relive your glory days through your son."

"I'm not. . ."

"I swear to God, if anything happens to him, I will never forgive you. . ."

Diane stares at him for a minute, eyes ablaze, and then rolls over onto her side, turning off the lamp on the nightstand.

***

The place seems much different inside than it did from the street. The first thing Ryan notices is all the trophies, lining a shelf next to a large mirror. The rest of the wall is covered in photographs and a long banner: Chi Yiu Association. The fighting room, so big from the outside, is much smaller than he expected. On the far side is a narrow office and another doorway. Though floor-to-ceiling windows look out onto it, the street seems a world away, and the room is quiet. Ryan had never been anywhere where the sounds of the city totally disappeared.

He leaves Amen's side and steps over to look at the pictures. Most show smiling people holding trophies or posing in brightly lit arenas. One simply has an Asian boy about his age alongside a man Ryan guesses is his father. The kid smiles broadly and holds a medal out toward the camera, his dad's arm around him.

"That one's me," he hears over his shoulder.

Ryan turns to find a trim young man smiling down at him. Asian, with tape over his ears, he has forearms that look like tensed wires underneath his karate suit.

"I'm Sensei Kong Chan," he says, holding out his hand.

"You must be Ryan."

Ryan nods and takes his hand, which is firm and dry.

"Amen," says his father, shaking the man's hand.

"I must have been about your age when that was taken," Sensei Chan says, gesturing at the image. "So proud to be learning judo from my father. He was the sensei then. Let me show you around before the others get here."

"This is the dojo, a Japanese word that means school for self-defense. But it means so much more than that. It is also a place of honor, respect, practice." He turns and points toward a room with a desk and filing cabinets. "That's the office. I'm hardly ever in there. Over here," he says, pushing open the other door, "is the changing room. Come Ryan, I have something for you."

Sensei Chan leads them into the changing room, which is tiny, about the same size as the office. He walks to a row of white cabinets, opens one, reaches in, and withdraws a package wrapped in plastic. He holds it out to Ryan, one hand above and the other below.

"This is your gi," he says, kneeling down to look Ryan in the eyes. His eyes narrow. "Every time you put it on, do so with respect. For the school, your sensei, and your fellow students."

Ryan nods.

He eagerly pulls the white uniform from the plastic. It is much sturdier than it looked from the street, the lapels almost as heavy as the bag his father carries his books to school in. Ryan puts his arms through the sleeves and pulls the two sides of the top together. He steps into the pants, which almost reach the floor, baggy like some of his old pajamas. Sensei Chan wraps a bright white belt around Ryan's waist.

"White is for the beginner," he says. "It shows you are on the path."

"Mr. Bow, you are welcome to observe," he says to Amen as they leave the locker room.

A handful of kids are now in the training area, most older and bigger than Ryan. He doesn't recognize any of them, but that's no surprise. Grand Rapids has about fifty schools besides the one Ryan attends, and kids come from all over.

"Everyone," the sensei says clapping his hand, "this is Ryan, he will be joining our class." The kids walk over, each one bowing slightly at the waist toward the newcomer. He nods back, his glasses slipping down his nose. He notices several of the kids looking at his orange helmet with curiosity.

His father sits in a row of chairs under the photographs, watching.

By now, a few additional kids have come in. The class has eight students in all, unless someone's absent. A couple of boys seem much older than the rest, probably high school age, and there are two girls who might be a grade higher than Ryan in school. They all give him the same polite bow, even the ones wearing colorful belts.

"Let's begin," sensei says with a clap.

***

Judo becomes all he can think about. School, homework, TV, friends – nothing else matters. He starts off with a class on Wednesday after school and another on Saturday mornings. Soon he's asking his father if he can practice on Tuesday and Thursday as well. He never brings it up with his mother, because she's made her feelings about it very clear.

Talk about it too much, and I won't get to go at all.

It was the first throw that hooked him. He'd been paired with a kid who was bigger than him, a tall boy a few years older with gangly arms and legs. Name was Nick. He went first, looking over his shoulder to watch Sensei Chan demonstrate proper form, and then turning back to Ryan.

"Not sure about this," he said. Nick's belt was as shiny white as Ryan's.

He watched Sensei Chan, then let out a long sigh. He turned back and took hold of Ryan's lapels and then spun, rolling Ryan over his hip to the floor. The throw didn't go at all like the sensei described, and Ryan hit with a flop. He pounded the tatami mat the way Sensei had shown him, and he was astonished he felt no pain. Ryan hopped to his feet and smiled at Nick.

"Nice one," Ryan says.

They switched positions. Ryan watched the Sensei.

He's way too tall, how can I possibly throw him? How is this ever going to work?

He grabbed Nick's lapels in his fists. Turned his back into the bigger boy and used his leg muscles, hips, and forward motion to leverage him into the air. Nick flew over Ryan onto the mat. Ryan was amazed. He'd hardly felt Nick's weight. It was so simple. Nick seemed so much taller, so much heavier. But it was so simple.

"Well done, Ryan," Sensei Chan said. "Now again."

He'd always felt so small at school. Powerless. No recourse against all the kids that teased him about his glasses and his helmet.

Not anymore.

***

That night he tells his parents about it over chicken and mashed potatoes. His father seems intrigued. His mother eats quietly, her hand quivering from her medications.

"It's really just physics," he says. "When you think about it. You use your opponent's weight against them."

His father smiles.

"Sensei Chan calls judo the soft form of combat."

"How can fighting be soft?" Amen asks, liking the idea of Diane hearing the answer. Though he's a teacher and a coach, he believes in sticking up for yourself. In wrestling, that meant being assertive on the mats. When a couple of bullies started a playground tussle with Ryan a year ago, he was disappointed his son didn't fight back.

"If you walk away," Amen said, "they'll just keep coming back."

Because of Ryan's issues, Amen has mixed feelings. He's pleased to see Ryan interested in learning to stand up for himself, doubly so when he discovered the sport builds confidence, respect, and responsibility. But he worries the boy will become too interested and want to follow this fighting dream.

"They call it that because it's about subduing your opponent by using their own weight against them," Ryan says between bites of veggies. "Judo doesn't have the punches and kicks and strikes of the hard martial arts like kung fu and karate. It's really about physics more than anything." He glances at his Mom.

"Physics?" This, too, his father likes.

"Yeah, leverage, weight shifting, stuff like that."

Diane has nothing to say to all of this, except: "Don't talk while you chew." She sits there looking concerned, her hand shaking as she uses her fork.

"Sensei Chan says judo helps us realize that worrying is a waste of energy," Ryan explains. "Even when your opponent is bigger and faster. He says judo helps us overcome anxiety and control our emotions."

"Really? That doesn't sound very martial at all," Amen says. "That sounds like what I'm always saying to you."

His father puts down his fork and puts his elbows on the table.

"Sensei Chan seems a very wise man, to me," Amen says. "I'm liking what I'm seeing."

Diane just looks out the window.

Chapter 2

Amen mumbles in his sleep, flipping over onto his side, then rolling on his back, troubled by the same dream. It's recurred at least once a month since the day it happened.

Nurses rush Diane into the Emergency Room. She's gasping and staggering, and the nurses take her by each arm, supporting her onto a table. A towering, clean-shaven black man in a white jacket strides in and says, "Not here. Surgery 3." They place Diane into a wheelchair and whisk her out the door.

"Wait, where are you taking her?" Amen asks.

"We need to induce, sir," says the lanky physician, pausing at the door. "I'm Doctor Burton." He extends his hand. The doctor gives Amen a quick shake and turns to leave.

"I don't want to take any chances." He strides down the hall, leaving Amen standing there.

"Why, what's happening?" Amen calls after him. He waits a moment, unsure whether he should follow. He's heard of men in the delivery room but isn't sure about emergency surgery. Nobody gives him any direction in the rush of the ER, so he trots after the doctor.

They wheel Diane into an operating room, and nurses scurry about, hooking her up to various machines.

"Dear Lord," Amen says seeing the staff whirling about, hearing all the monitors sounding. The room is beeping like a plane in freefall.

"Oh, God."

"Not now, Amen!" Diane barks. She starts to breathe in and out rhythmically, her chest rising and falling above her enormous belly. She glances up at her husband, eyes on fire. Then she softens.

The medication dripping into her IV is working.

"I'm sorry," she says, putting her hand on his.

Suddenly, she's sleepy. Her head droops, lolling off to one side.

"My baby," she says, beginning to lose consciousness. "My baby. . ."

"It's gonna be all right, baby," Amen says to her. He looks at the doctor.

"Right doc?"

The doctor ignores him and says to the nurses: "Prep for immediate C section."

"Doc, talk to me. . ." Amen says.

The doctor pauses and turns to him.

"Sir, we need to deliver this baby. Because it's so early, the baby is struggling. There's a possible intrauterine stroke. Your wife has a history of blood clots, and . . ."

"A stroke?" Amen grabs the doctor's arm. "My wife's having a stroke?"

"Not your wife. The *baby*. The vitals are not where they should be."

"Oh, my God," Amen puts his hands to his head and starts to pace. The nurses work around him, prepping trays of tools, getting Diane ready for the procedure. They are a wonder of precision and orchestration, each knowing just what they should be doing at what time.

Amen clutches his elbows to his side as he walks around the room, staring at the floor.

"No," he says. As he paces, he repeats it over and over. "No. No. No."

A tall, heavyset nurse walks over to him. She bends her face down to look into his.

"Sir, she needs you," she says quietly, gently steering Amen to a chair she's moved bedside.

Amen drops into it, taking Diane's hand as the doctor begins working behind a sheet.

***

Diane has a hard time focusing, lost in a fog of medication. Amen sits next to her bed, sprawled in a chair. A petite blonde nurse enters smiling, with the baby boy wrapped in light blue linens. The little guy starts to wail, pumping his fists and feet out from the swaddling.

"Well, he's come out swinging," says Amen, beaming.

The nurse rocks the child, his head cradled in her arm. "Shh shh now."

"He's beautiful," she says, handing the baby to his mother. "Do you have a name?"

"Ryan," says Diane. Amen sits on the bed, and the couple look down at the infant. He stops crying and stares up at them. One of his eyes wanders off to one side, looking past them at the wall. Doesn't matter. He's alive.

"My beautiful boy," Diane says. She looks up at Amen and gives him a weak smile. Her eyes flutter, and she grimaces. She leans down and kisses the boy and hands him to Amen.

"Don't feel right," she says.

"He'll be fine, baby," Amen responds. "I'm sure it's just. . .

"No." She puts her hand on him. "*I* don't feel right."

She leans back against the pillows and looks up at the ceiling. And then she slumps sideways, passing out.

"Nurse!" yells Amen, sliding his legs off the bed onto the floor. He carries the baby to the door. "Nurse!"

With his father shouting, baby Ryan starts to cry again.

The nurse takes the little bundle back, returning him to the NICU, others rush in to check on Diane, who is logy and weak.

"She'll be fine, sir," one nurse says to Amen. One on either side, the nurses settle her in to bed, where she rests, her eyes closed. Amen sits in a nearby chair with his hands on his knees and pumps his leg up and down.

***

They're allowed to take Ryan home after a week. The infant spent several days in the intensive care unit before moving to the neonatal ward, Dr. Burton pleased with his progress. The little guy takes to nursing and sleeps well for a newborn. Diane and Amen do their best to settle in to their small home, the baby sleeping beside his mother in bed, relegating Amen to the couch. Other than the wandering eye, Ryan seems to be developing fine and is happy and healthy.

So, the couple are surprised when the phone rings and a nurse summons them back to the hospital for a meeting with Doctor Burton. The woman on the phone refuses to answer any questions, repeating:

"The doctor will fill you in when you get here" to everything Amen asks. He grows increasingly annoyed but agrees to head back to the clinic.

They leave Ryan with Amen's mother across town and make the short trip to the doctor's office, where they're let in to see Doctor Burton.

The rangy physician sits behind a narrow mahogany desk. He leans forward, elbows on the desk calendar, hands folded together. In his 40s, with a low fade that is beginning to gray. He looks at Amen and Diane, sitting there holding hands, perched on the edge of their padded office chairs.

"Your son had a stroke in the womb."

Once again, Amen's nervous knee bounces up and down. He tries hard to concentrate on what Doctor Burton is telling him.

"Come again?" Amen says. "A stroke? I thought strokes were for old people. . ."

"Strokes happen when the blood supply to a region in the brain is cut off temporarily, often due to blood clots," the doctor says. "Can be a baby or a grandfather. When denied oxygen, cells in that area begin to die, which can cause a variety of problems. In the case of a child, it might result in cerebral palsy, epilepsy, or learning difficulties. Ryan seems to have been spared the worst of it, but he's suffered damage to his eyes. We won't know what other problems he might face until he gets a little bit older and his brain develops. I want you to watch him closely. Any questions, issues, let your pediatrician know."

And that was it.

Doctor Burton takes a few questions from Amen – is the damage necessarily permanent, what should we look out for, is there anything that can be done to repair it? – before he stands and sweeps his arm toward the door, ushering the couple out. Amen and Diane leave, countless questions remaining between them.

***

The two boys hurry down the stairs as fast as they can, plopping onto the floor in front of the TV. A Sega Genesis sits on top of a green Michigan State University rug, Amen and Diane's alma mater.

"Hi Mr. Bow!" Larry says.

"Hey Larry. No hats on in the house, please."

"Yes, sir." Larry takes off his cap revealing stylish waves beneath, laying it down on the floor beside him.

Ryan takes off his protective helmet and sits beside his friend. He pops open the Blockbuster case and inserts the video game they rented into the console, firing up the machine. The two boys battle it out on the screen, ferociously squaring off in *Mortal Kombat*.

Ryan's Liu Kang versus Larry's Sub-Zero, trading punches and kicks. The blue-and-black clad fighter gets the upper hand.

"Finish Him!" commands the machine.

Larry fires a sheet of ice across the screen, freezing Ryan's character solid.

Sub Zero stands next to Kang. He crouches and lunges upwards with a powerful uppercut, leaving Kang's bloody body in pieces on the ground.

The two boys burst out in laughter. "Yeah!" says Larry pumping his fist.

"I want a rematch!" Ryan cries, his laughter fading.

He pulls his frames from his face, holding them up to the light. "Ugh, smudges!" he says. He growls, pulling his shirt up to clean them, clearly a little too dialed in.

Larry laughs. "It's just a game."

Amen glances at them from behind his computer in his workspace.

***

Ryan never liked wearing the helmet. Or the glasses. But he knew he had to if he wanted to be safe. His father grilled that into him from an early age. When he reached school, these two items made him a target. Some kids stared; others wouldn't play with him. Some would make him the butt of their jokes. One particular bully, a redhead named Matt, often singled him out, bumping into him on purpose and knocking his books off his desk when the teacher wasn't looking.

Fighting Blind

I wish I knew how to fight.

He asked his Dad if he could start wrestling. Amen coached the high school wrestling team and was a standout back in the day; Ryan thought this might be an in. No luck. He asked his dad about boxing. He asked his dad about kung fu. The answer was always, "No, it's not safe. We have to protect your head." His mother had no patience for the question whatsoever.

"You know better than to ask me that," she'd say, glasses at the end of her nose like an angry librarian.

But his desire never went away. He understood the risk fighting posed to him, as much as a grade schooler can understand risk. Larry would often intervene and keep the bullies at bay but he was a year older and in another class. Ryan worried what would happen if things escalated and Matt attacked him. If he knew how to fight, wouldn't he be able to protect himself? Wouldn't that be safer for his head?

He wanted to fight.

He watched his Dad coach wrestling. Larry attempted to show him some moves at recess.

And then his Dad finally offered the judo class.

He wasn't sure what changed his father's mind. His persistence? The fact that judo is a fighting style based on grappling and throwing not punching and kicking? Amen's own love of wrestling?

He wasn't sure. And he didn't know how his dad could have possibly sold the idea to his mom. He was just excited to be going.

***

Diane sips from a glass of cheap wine, leaning against the headboard. Her pill bottles sprawl across the bedside table. Her lids are heavy, and her head lolls to the side.

"You know you're not supposed to be drinking alcohol while taking your pills," Amen says, stepping into the bedroom. He closes the door behind him and sits on the edge of the bed, pulling off his loafers.

"You know you're supposed to be minding your own business," Diane slurs. "And besides, I'm not the one telling our injured son that he can fight. My head's on straight."

"Excuse me?" Amen says, turning to look at her.

"You heard me."

"We've talked about this," he says. "But you probably don't remember." He shakes his head. "We decided as long as he wears his helmet, and only does judo, he can compete. We went over and over it."

"I *don't* remember ever giving permission for our son, who has a brain injury, to fight, anyone or anywhere." She glares at him with glazed eyes.

"Well, you *did*, and there's no way we're going back on it now. We told him that judo was acceptable because there are no direct punches and kicks. And that he always has to wear his helmet." Amen stares at the wall and lets out a long breath. He shakes his head again. "Sometimes I can't believe you."

"*Me?*" Diane says, exaggeratedly touching her chest. "I have a condition."

"Yeah, you have a condition alright."

Amen puts his pajamas on and slides into his side of the bed, turning away from his wife.

"We are not going back on our word now," he says, reaching over and turning off the light. "You know how much this means to him."

Diane is silent.

Chapter 3

A couple of months into his judo lessons, Sensei Chan asks Ryan to step forward at the end of class. They'd just finished a morning session of *osoto-gari*, the large outside reap, a leg sweep used for taking down an opponent. Ryan was tired, but happy, as usual. He loved all of it – excited to try every new throw, position, and hold. This one seemed particularly easy and extremely effective. Both Ryan and his usual practice partner Nick got the hang of it quickly and were soon sending each other to the mat. Best executed when the opponent is stepping forward or backward, osoto-gari requires you to off-balance them onto one leg and get in close to make it work. Once you've done that, it's simply a matter of driving your reaping leg through uke's supporting one with force to complete the throw.

Ryan meets Sensei Chan in the center of the mats. He bows slightly and adjusts his gi. The other white belts in line look on curiously, the older kids have seen this before.

"I have something for you," Sensei Chan says. "You've been working hard, and I've been impressed with your dedication. Not many judoka come to this point as quickly as you have. I think you have a real future in judo."

The sensei reaches into his gi and draws out a yellow belt, still wrapped in plastic.

"I want you to wear this with pride," Sensei Chan says, bowing and wrapping the belt around Ryan's waist. The rest of class erupts into applause.

Ryan returns the bow, and accepts the belt, a wide smile never leaving his face.

"Thank you, Sensei," he says, bowing again.

"Don't thank me, Ryan. You have yourself to thank – it was you who earned it."

He looks at himself in the floor-to-ceiling mirror, an infectious grin lighting up his face again. Now, instead of an all-white "gi," a stripe of mustard yellow cuts him right in half, jumping out for all to see.

***

When Ryan gets home from school, he hears music coming from the living room. He puts his book bag down and walks toward it, peeking around the doorway to see his mother pounding on the keys of the piano. It sounds okay, but she looks like she's hammering rather than twinkling away, her fingers all straight out, coming down like pistons. Ryan stands in the doorway for a minute, watching. His mother hunches forward over the upright, her nightie all wrinkled up on her back. She pauses. Then slams down again. And again. The tune is unrecognizable.

What is that song?

Diane continues to play for several minutes. The old piano rocks and clangs like a beat-up jalopy. Ryan stands back and doesn't say anything, not sure what to do. He's tempted to put his hands over his ears.

Orange pill bottles sit on the piano bench next to his mother.

Wonder what those do?

After a few more minutes, Diane stops abruptly, rocking back away from the keys on the short bench. She sits with her hands on her knees, like an athlete catching her breath, quiet.

"Mom?"

She spins around and sees him, tries to pull herself together. Her eyes are wide. Wild.

"Oh, hey baby. Why didn't you tell me you were home?"

"I didn't want to disturb you. You seemed busy."

"Just playing."

"Yeah, I heard. That was intense."

"Maybe I got a little carried away."

She looks at him for a few seconds. Then smiles.

"You hungry?" she asks.

"Yeah."

"C'mon, I'll make you a snack."

***

"Fuck you, chosenjin."

Eiji Tanaka looks up from the chipped white sink, staring into the mirror. It's Ren, again.

"What'd you call me?" Eiji says, turning off the water.

A dozen other boys are in the bathroom, and they begin to gather around, sure a fight is coming.

"I *said*, fuck you, chosenjin."

Ren looks at Eiji with hard, oil-black eyes, almost as if he is looking through him. He's a head taller than Eiji, skinny, his white school shirt wrinkled and untucked. Eiji knows him from several of his classes at their Tokyo school. He's arrogant, thinks he's better than everyone, what one student called a "cry bully" – someone who liked to pick on others but was apoplectic if anyone ever spoke back to them.

"I believe you mean, *Zainichi*," Eiji says, looking back down into the wash basin, trying to remain cool as he dries his hands. Zainichi is the name for ethnic Koreans born and raised in Japan.

"I mean *chosenjin*, you Korean bastard. Why are you in a Japanese school?"

"I was born here. Just like you."

"You're as Japanese as a dog."

"You just compare me to a dog?" Eiji shakes the water from his hands and turns to face Ren. He can feel his chest tighten. Everything in the room goes out of focus except the taller boy.

"You might want to watch your mouth," Eiji says quietly.

"What are you going to do, *kimuchi yaro*?"

Eiji holds his hands in front of his chest, pretending to be waving them to dry them. He shifts his weight on to his right hip and then throws his right fist into the taller boy's nose. His knuckles crunch upward, catching the upper lip and both nostrils. Blood explodes into a mist all over the other kids. Ren's head rocks back, and a big pink stain spreads across his shirt. Eiji doesn't pause, hitting him again in the ear with a left hook.

The other boys begin to yell, jumping up and down in a blood frenzy. "Yeah, Eiji!" someone shouts. Others chant, "Ren! Ren! Ren!"

Ren shakes his head in an attempt to gather himself. He takes a deep breath and a step back. His eyes look dazed, unfocused. But angry.

The other kids chant, "Ren, Ren, Ren. . ."

Eiji takes a step forward, right fist raised again.

The door flies open behind him, slamming the wall.

"Hey, hey, hey!" Mr. Kaneko yells. He rushes up behind Eiji and puts his arms around him. Kaneko-sensei is so big he almost wraps all the way around Eiji. Kaneko restrains him there for a moment. Eiji keeps his eyes on his opponent. The room falls silent, the drip of water in the sink the only sound.

"When you least expect it," Ren says through bloodied teeth.

"All of you," Mr. Kaneko says pointing at the assembled mass, "into my classroom. Now!"

Several boys whine in protest, but they all shuffle out the door. Some grin at each other. Others whisper. A few glare at Eiji.

***

Fighting Blind

The judoka in the photo doesn't look any older than Ryan. He stares at the picture. He's looked at all of the images on the dojo wall before, but he never noticed the Olympic rings. On a flag in the corner is the colorful, unmistakable icon of the Olympic Games.

Olympics. . .

The guy might have a couple of years on him but not much more than that.

Looks barely out of high school.

A Caucasian male in a white gi, he's beaming like he's just won the lottery, standing beside Sensei Chan. It's clear from the backdrop that he's been at a tournament and has been proclaimed the winner.

Someone from my dojo, going to the Olympics. . .

Ryan looks at the scene, lost in thought, drying the back of his neck with a towel. He hears Sensei Chan hang up the phone in the office.

He walks over and rapped on the doorframe.

"Sensei, do you have a minute?"

His teacher points at the metal folding chair next to his desk.

"Sure, have a seat."

Ryan sits, leaning forward, elbows on knees.

"I was just noticing one of the pictures out in the dojo. It looks like one of your students, a white guy, won a bout. . ."

"Most of those photographs came from successful matches. . ."

"But at this one there's an Olympic flag in the background."

"I've had several students compete in the Olympics. At least at the trial levels." Sensei Chan puts down his pen. "I think I know the student you're referring to. He was a very good judoka. Really explosive and great on the ground. He was invited to the Youth Nationals. Won several of his bouts. From there, he went on to compete at the Junior Open, where he won again. I think that's where that photo was taken. Then he earned a spot on the US National Team. He competed internationally, but unfortunately was defeated and didn't qualify."

Ryan sits quiet.

Wow. From my own dojo.

Sensei Chan pauses. Then says, "Ryan, you could do the same if you put your mind to it. You have the dedication and the natural ability. I can train people to a certain level, but they have to have the inner drive – and the instincts – to reach that pinnacle."

"Really, Sensei?"

"Think of it like golf," the Sensei says. "I can help you improve your game, show you tips and tricks and better ways to hold the club, but you have to have the natural swing to become a great golfer."

"What would I have to do?"

"Keep working like you are. Maybe add a day or two a week to your training regimen."

"And you think I could get there?"

"Ryan, you're among the best students I've ever had. You could absolutely get there."

That was all he needed to hear.

***

"Ryan!"

"Yes, sir?"

"You seem to be daydreaming son." Mr. Peters looks at him, arms crossed on his chest. Everyone dreaded having the U.S. history teacher train his tortoise-shell glasses on them.

"Yes, sir."

Snickers come from all around. Ryan looks down at his desk. He's been doodling, stick figures doing judo throws in front of a flag with five rings.

A lean older man, Mr. Peters looks over his glasses: "You know if you don't keep your grades up, you won't be allowed to continue with the sports."

"Yes, sir."

More snickers.

Ryan does a quick survey of his classmates, and the giggles cease.

"All right, back to page 37 . . ."

He stares down at the hardback book open on his desk. The words make a puzzle in front of him, the ds looking like bs, and the ps like qs.

He looks up at the clock above Mr. Peters, who's now lecturing about George Washington at Jumonville Glen. The hands seem frozen.

Ryan lets out a long breath and puts his finger on the line he seems to be reading, moving it to follow along. Not a chance he's going to let judo get away from him. Took forever to get his mother to allow him to compete, he and his Dad working her for weeks. Months. Years, even, before she'd hear about him going head-to-head with another opponent. Finally, she relented, when his Dad pointed out that he'd be wearing a helmet and goggles, and that he, Amen, would be there overseeing everything.

Diane Bow almost never came to see his judo matches, even as he climbed up the rankings, putting his small dojo back on the map. On the one hand, he was kind of glad, because wherever she went, she had a pill bottle, seemed loopy and out of it. He understood that she had a problem – a condition, as his father put it – but that didn't make it any less difficult to deal with. It was always there, and he was always worried how she'd behave in front of the rest of the team. Course, nobody seemed to notice, and if they did, they would never say anything. Ryan may have been on the short side, but by now everyone knew he could take care of himself. He always said he wanted to fight, and boy could he. Number one in the region.

When Ryan competed in the Fall Classic, his mother told him she would attend. And she did. The local news covered the event, and he caught a glimpse of his Mom out of the corner of his eye as he was being interviewed by the lead reporter. His mother appeared to be smiling, but that might have been the pills. He couldn't tell.

"We're here with judo," the perky journalist looked down at her notes, "judo-ka Ryan Bow, the winner of the Against All Odds Award," she said to the camera, "which recognizes one disabled athlete from the state of Michigan. It's a tremendous honor for Ottawa Hills High School." She pulled her hair back behind her ear. What's it like for you, Ryan?"

"It's definitely an honor," he told her. "And I'd like to thank my parents, Amen and Diane Bow, for helping me get here.

His parents both beamed at the mention.

"And also my teacher, Sensei Chan, for believing in me."

"Tell us about your disability."

"Um, well, I have pretty severe problems with my vision," he explained. He pointed at the thick spectacles he wore, both lenses about an inch thick. "As you can probably tell from my glasses."

"Well, you're an incredible inspiration to other disabled athletes. What's next for you?"

"I'm hoping to get an invite to the Olympic trials. We'll know soon."

"Amazing, Ryan! We are so excited and proud of you. We'll be following you every step of the way."

"Ryan!"

***

He looks up. Mr. Peters is staring at him again with a tight-lipped frown.

"You are sixteen years old, son, stop daydreaming like a kindergartner."

***

"Bring me the cane."

Eiji's father barely moves his mouth when he says the words, his jaw rigid, his black eyes cold. Not a big man, he's still a head taller than his son and hard and ropey from days of work in construction. Eiji bows, turns on his heel, and walks to the shed. The cane is a walking stick, made of hard rattan; his father found it at work and brought it home solely for this purpose – to use on his son. Eiji starts combat breathing, just as his sensei taught him, preparing himself. He knows it will hurt – it always does – but he refuses to let his father know it does. He won't give him that satisfaction.

He hands the cane to his father and tries to keep his face blank while doing so. He turns and bends at the waist. His father raises his arm and brings the cane hard down on Eiji's thighs. He knows the behind has more padding and so swings lower. Eiji tightens his muscles with each blow. His father hits him ten times, each one more painful than the next, compounding on one another.

"Son, look at me!"

Eiji turns. A single tear slides down his cheek. He continues his breathing.

"No karate for two weeks."

Eiji nods and keeps his head down.

"Yes, Appa."

"I do not want to hear from your headmaster again."

"Yes, Appa."

Not being able to train would hurt more than any beating. Eiji is certain his father knows this. The dojo is his favorite place, the only place he feels he can be himself. The only place where he feels understood. Where he feels appreciated or successful or anything other than a disappointment. At the dojo, it doesn't matter that they aren't rich. Or that he doesn't like to read. Or that he is Zainichi.

All that matters is that he can fight.

***

Training for the Olympics. That was the reason why Ryan got out of bed every morning. Why he did his chores. Why he did his homework. It was all he could think about. He listened to books on tape about Olympic athletes like Jesse Owens and Jim Brown to find out how they got there. He listened to books on bushido and warrior philosophy. Sensei Chan made sure he understood all the rules, learned more than he ever wanted to know about USJF – the United States Judo Federation – Team USA, sanctioned events and Olympic trials. Whatever it would take, he'd do it.

His father was very supportive, reliving his own wrestling dreams through Ryan. His mother largely kept her counsel. She was both wrestling with her own problems and resigned to the fact that her baby was going to fight and there wasn't anything she could do about it.

***

Sensei Chan pulls him aside after class. "Ryan, a word?"

He bows. "Yes, sensei," and follows his teacher to his office.

Several of the other kids watch on with curiosity, as if one of their high school friends was just escorted to the principal's.

"Have a seat."

"What's up, Sensei?"

"You've earned a spot to compete in the U.S. Open Judo Championships. Olympic team scouts will be in attendance."

"Scouts!?"

"Yes, looking for talent. It's coming up next month and could get you some international exposure. It's an opportunity to test yourself against better judoka than we have around here."

"Count me in. I won't disappoint you."

"I'll get you the paperwork."

"Thank you, Sensei." Ryan bows.

And pumps his fist after stepping out of the office.

***

Ryan breaks from the line and grapples with his opponent, Duncan, a lean black belt who wears a mullet and has been competing for a couple years longer than he has. They circle, aggressively attempting to grip the other's lapel. Number one in his weight class, Duncan competes one division below Ryan, but they are on par height-wise, making him a valuable training partner. They hold on to each other and move in a circle, like two violent dancers, each attempting to position themself for a throw. Ryan attempts a *tani-otoshi*, a sacrifice throw, and Duncan counters with a *kosoto gari*, small outer reap, sliding his right leg behind Ryan, sweeping him off balance, and taking him to the mat.

"Come on, Ryan!" his father screams from the sideline. "We aren't going to the Olympics like that. C'mon, son!" Amen came to everything, and he was always the loudest voice in the crowd. He was always there with encouragement and advice. As a former wrestler and wrestling coach, he understood the nuances of judo better than most parents. While very different sports, they still had many similarities.

The combatants hop back onto their feet to go again.

This time, Ryan gets ahold of Duncan's right lapel. He feints by making two or three small tugs, then bursts into motion and leaps into a low *ippon seoi nage*, a one arm shoulder throw, surprising – and leveling – Duncan with his speed, audacity, and perfect form.

"Nice!" says Amen, clapping his hands together. "That's what I'm talking about."

Sensei Chan blows his whistle, bringing another bout to its end. Duncan climbs up and gives Ryan a pat on his shoulder before heading to the locker room. Ryan follows.

***

Eiji scrubs the floor of their first-floor apartment with a dust cloth. His father assigned him various tasks to complete each day since he was suspended. And Eiji knew if they weren't done to perfection, he'd get more acquainted with the cane. He'd already vacuumed and cleaned the bathroom. He worked quickly, but meticulously, so he'd have a little time for himself this afternoon. His father may have forbidden karate class, but that wouldn't stop Eiji from training.

He drags the cloth back and forth over the boards until they are as clean as he's going to get them. He rinses the rag, dumps the bucket in the toilet, and puts everything back in the closet. Then he goes to his room and changes into a T-shirt and shorts.

On the patio, he begins by doing sets of push-ups. He puts his knuckles on the ground, does 50, switches to sit ups, and does 50 of those before he rolls back over and does more push-ups. He ends at 100 of each. Then he works on his kata, throwing punches and kicks at the air, making his way through the positions of the Sanshin form. He does them fast and hard, tensing his muscles with each motion. Satisfied, he moves over to a *makiwara* striking post and begins to hit it with his fists, until the callouses on his knuckles start to bleed. After several minutes, he puts his hands on his knees and takes deep breaths.

He thinks about his father. And the assholes from school. And he raises his leg, cocks his knee, and slams his foot into the stiff board.

Chapter 4

The U.S. Open Judo Championships arrives in a blur. Set in a large convention center in Michigan's Upper Peninsula, the event consists of round after round of four-minute matches. Between participants, coaches, staff, their families, and fans of the sport, the complex overflows with spectators. They fill every seat and line every wall. Above them, Olympic flags. Ryan's head swirls at the excitement of it all.

Never fought in front of so many. Never knew so many people even knew what judo is.

Ryan stands on the sidelines, his father adjusting his stark white headgear. He pulls his clear plastic sports goggles away from his eyes and puts them back in place, both lenses thick, like his glasses. He looks down at his blue competition gi, which feels so unfamiliar. In judo tournaments, one participant wears white, the other blue to make it easier for the referee and judges to distinguish each participant.

"Remember what we talked about," Amen says. "Weather the early storm. He's going to come right at you. Outwork him. If it goes to the ground, make him carry your weight. He's young, but he's good. Undefeated."

Ryan nods, glancing at his opponent. He's baby-faced, but tall and has muscles on top of muscles. He's bouncing on the balls of his feet, first one foot then the other, like a boxer.

They are instructed to step to the edge of the yellow mat and bow to the referee, an older man wearing a suit and tie. At his nod, they walk out on to the mustard-colored mat, bow to one another, and then circle, hunched forward, each looking for an opening. The tall judoka feints several times, raising his right arm as if to go over the top to get a high collar grip behind Ryan's neck and then dropping back down to make a grab for the lapel of his gi at chest-level.

Ryan enters low, trying to get under his opponent's hips, but the kid recognizes it and shifts his weight backwards. Ryan protects his neck by crossing his arms and holding onto both sides of his collar to prevent his opponent from attacking. The referee steps between them and restarts the match with them both on their feet.

When they resume Ryan lunges forward with an *ouchi gari* leg attack; his adversary immediately counters with a clean leg attack of his own, sliding his left foot behind Ryan's and scissoring him to the mat. The fighter follows him down and lands atop him, pinning Ryan's shoulders.

Ippon. Defeat. Just like that.

The crowd starts to holler, stomping on the stands. Ryan slumps to the mat, his head between his knees. He knows that not only is the match over but with it his hopes of making the Olympic team – it's a single-elimination tournament. There are no second chances. His opponent extends a hand to help him up, but Ryan sits with his arms around his knees.

What's the point?

Thoughts swirl through his head. His mom and her struggles. His father's pride in him. Disappointing Sensei Chan. The reporter and everyone at school. The Olympics were what he had. Where he was going. His whole identity was woven into those five rings. What would he do now?

"Fuuuuuck!"

Ryan's shoulders shake as he begins to sob. Tears puddle on the mat between his legs. Everything blurs.

He feels a tap on his shoulder. Wipes his nose on his sleeve and looks up. It's the referee. Behind him are two other judoka waiting to begin their contest.

"Son, you'll have to please exit the mat," the ref says, leaning down, his tie swinging almost into Ryan's face. "I'm sorry. We have a schedule to keep." He gives Ryan a tap and stands back up, bobbing his head at the other competitors, who pretend to be busy straightening their gis.

Ryan rolls onto his knees and gets up, walking to the edge of the mat. He can see his parents standing up from their seats. His mom just looks sad, her eyes barely visible behind the sunglasses she always wears in public.

***

"Ryan, adversity is part of life," Sensei Chan says. Ryan studies the floor of the concourse. The sensei met

43

him outside the locker room, concerned how he would take his loss.

"Have a seat," Sensei Chan says, gesturing at the folding chairs near the concession stands. Ryan sits, still looking at his shoes, having a hard time meeting Sensei Chan's eyes.

"Did I ever tell you how I got here?" Chan asks.

"No."

"My parents brought me to Michigan when I was just a boy, a teenager. From Hong Kong. I know you've seen pictures of my father, the grandmaster of our dojo. Nothing I ever did was good enough for him. He wanted a better life for us than we had, living in a country on the tail end of British colonial rule. After the 1989 Tiananmen Square protests and massacre, we feared the Chinese government and the corruption that came with it.

"My years in Michigan were better but not by much. The kids called me 'China Boy,' if they ever even talked to me. But I was determined. Judo kept me focused on what little I had going for me. I became obsessed with opening my own dojo. To show them – and my father – that I could be successful. I had to live in my car for a time, because I couldn't afford to rent a home and a dojo."

By now Ryan is watching Sensei Chan, studying his face.

"I tell you this only to say that adversity makes us who we are. Remember the old judo adage: 'Our greatest glory consists not in never failing, but in rising every time we fall.' You have a bright future ahead of you, Ryan. So, you lost a match. It's only one. There will be many more in your future. You must continue to practice. I have ideas for you."

Sensei Chan pushes back his chair and stands. Ryan follows suit. "Go home. Put this out of your mind. Remember *why* you train judo. Come back to the dojo with a clear mind, and we'll build from there. A clean slate."

"Thank you, Sensei." Ryan bows his head. Sensei Chan claps him on the shoulder.

"Fall down seven times, get up eight."

***

After Ryan gets changed, he finds his parents in the concourse, his mother with a drink from the tumbler that she brings in her oversized bag, his dad pacing back and forth. They don't talk on the way to the car. Ryan keeps his head down as they exit the arena. A few people clap him on the back, but he just nods and keeps going.

On the way home, his mother sits silently in the back seat, lost in a medicated haze.

"Son, you did your best out there. There isn't much separating any of you at that level. More luck than anything else."

"Skill, dad. Judo is a skill. An art."

"Yes, it is. But at the level you're at, there's very fine line between winning and losing."

Ryan watches the landscape of Michigan's U.P. slide by. His father studies the road ahead.

"What do you think you're going to do next year?"

"Not sure. Thought I'd be training for the Olympics."

"What about college? Have you given it any more thought?"

"My grades aren't good enough."

"Son, there are a whole lot of schools your grades would get you in to."

"Not sure that's for me."

"There aren't too many options for kids with no degree these days. Convenience stores. Maybe one of the trades."

"I know, Dad."

"Maybe now's not the time to be talking about this," Amen says, gripping the steering wheel tighter.

Ryan looks at his mother, seated in the passenger seat. She stares out the window at the horizon.

"Yeah, probably not," Ryan says, leaning his head against the window, doing the same.

His father comes to a stop at a traffic light. He looks over at Ryan.

"It's not going to go away, though. Your future. You need to think about it, son."

The drive to Grand Rapids is long. Ryan spends most of it with his Walkman and headphones on, watching much of the state of Michigan pass by, or trying to sleep. He and Amen don't talk much.

***

For Eiji, school feels like a waste of time. He doesn't enjoy it. He doesn't feel he learns much or is a particularly good student. He makes it through on his wits alone, able to pass classes because of his raw intelligence. He keeps his head down, does what's asked, and bides his time until the end of the day. His grades would probably be much worse if his father hadn't insisted he make the honor roll if he wanted to continue karate.

For a guy who works heavy labor, he's awfully concerned about education.

He sits in history, learning about Japan's feudal history, the one class he doesn't hate. He's always admired the samurai – they were warriors like him – and enjoys reading Yamaga Soko, a Japanese military writer and philosopher under the Tokugawa shogunate.

"Hey," hisses a kid in the seat next to him.

Eiji glances his way.

"Heard about the fight in the bathroom."

Eiji nods.

"You can fight, they say."

Eiji just looks at him.

"My boss could use a guy like you. He's always looking for recruits who can handle themselves. There's good money in it."

"Who's your boss?"

The teacher raises his voice, a sure sign he can hear them talking.

"Korea town, tonight, behind the train tracks at Shin Okubo station."

Eiji faces the blackboard and nods again.

***

As soon as his father swings into their driveway, Ryan says, "Can I take the car, Dad? I need some time to think."

"We just drove six hours across the state, and you want to get back in the car?" His father takes the keys from his pocket and holds them out in his hand.

"You okay?" he asks.

"I'm fine, just need some time alone to process things." Ryan glances at his mother, who opens her door to get out of the vehicle.

"Don't be out too late, you've had a rough day."

Ryan nods and his father hands him the keys.

He pulls out of the driveway and down the street of their deprived neighborhood. He's not sure where he wants to go, just knows he doesn't want to sit at home staring at his judo posters, reminding him his days of competition are over. Doesn't want to listen to his father or worry about his mother.

He takes a left, heading toward downtown and the dojo, scanning the road ahead. Traffic is light, it being past midnight. When the minivan ahead of him switches lanes, cutting from directly in front of him to his left, he notices that it goes from bright red to pitch black, disappearing altogether. Although, he can sense it there, still ahead of him to his left. When he tilts his head enough that he can see it, it's exactly where he thought it would be.

I knew it was bad but never this bad.

He watches another car – a lowered Honda Civic – do the same, changing lanes ahead of him. This time he pivots his head to follow it. As long as it remains directly ahead, he can keep it in sight. Any variation, he loses it.

Ryan flips the blinker down with his right hand and exits onto a side street. He pauses at a light, tracking a yellow cab as it drives from his right to his left, trying to establish just when he loses it, exactly how much peripheral range he has. The light turns, and he pulls out in the same direction as the taxi, following it, moving his head from his left to right, concentrating on the limits of his vision, when his world explodes.

He comes to a minute later, roused by the sound of a car horn blaring, his head feeling like it has been slammed onto concrete. He lifts his neck and opens his eyes, looking at the world through a small dark tunnel. Gradually his vision improves, and he realizes he's driven full speed into the front of another vehicle. The car is crumpled, its hood accordioned up like a piece of paper, so he can't tell if anyone else is inside.

What the...?

He shakes his head and looks around. The sidewalks are empty. He panics, looks over his shoulder, pulling down the gear shift. He presses his foot down on the accelerator, unsure whether his car will even move. It does, and he backs away from the other vehicle. He switches into drive and swerves out into the street, pulling away from the scene. He looks in his rear view to see if anyone noticed him – and sees blue lights.

Shit.

He takes a side street, hoping to put some distance between himself and the cop. The blue lights stay right behind him. He noses down an alley and turns out onto his road. The strobes vanish for a moment.

Maybe. . .

He turns off his headlights and glides into his driveway, bolting from the car toward the front door, sirens caterwauling behind him. He yanks open the door and shuts it quickly behind him.

He rests his head on his chest a moment, catching his breath. When he picks it up, his mother is standing right in front of him, nightie on and drink in hand, as if she's been up all night waiting for him.

"What's the hurry boy?" she slurs.

"Just headed to bed, Mom. Goodnight."

"You wait just one minute, young man."

"Mom?"

"You didn't answer my question." She looks at him through her big, clear eyeglass frames, her eyes red. "Where have you been? What is your hurry?"

"Ah. . ." he tries to think of something. As he looks around the room, he notices the blue lights now flashing on the ceiling of the living room. Diane sees them, too, and she steps over to pull back the gauzy curtains and peer out at their driveway. Smoke pours from the front end of their car, and a pair of police officers, one tall and black, the other short and white, stride up their walkway.

"What the hell did you do?" Diane hisses under her breath.

Ryan drops onto the couch and puts his head in his hands.

The door pounds.

"Grand Rapids police, open up."

Diane looks at Ryan and then back at the door. She shakes her head and then steps over to it, her hand trembling as she grips the knob.

As soon as it cracks the officers are in, pushing past her. The lanky policeman stands in front of Ryan, while the stout cop holds back Diane.

"You are under arrest, anything you say can and will. . ."

"What is going on?" Diane says, trying to force her way between the cops and her son. The short officer attempts to restrain her without putting his hands on her bedroom clothes. Ryan gets to his feet, and the tall cop spins him around, locking handcuffs around his wrists.

"Hit and run, ma'am," the short officer says. "Please let us do our jobs."

Amen's feet appear on the stairs and then the rest of him. He holds the railing and surveys the scene.

"What the heck's all this?"

The tall cop holds an arm out in front of Amen. "Under control, sir. Please stand back."

"Officers there must be some sort of mistake. He's just a boy."

"No mistake, sir. We watched the incident ourselves. Please stand back while we test for alcohol."

"Alcohol?" Diane says, looking down at the glass in her own hand. "He doesn't drink alcohol."

***

Eiji scans all around him. Hoodlums often met here at the rear of the tracks where they were away from the public's prying eyes. It occurred to him earlier this might be a set-up, that the asshole who jumped him in the bathroom at school could very well be behind this meet. He'd only been back at school a day, and Ren was already asking about him. His father would put the cane right through him if he got in trouble again. But he'd be proud if Eiji had a job and could contribute financially to the household. So here he was.

He takes in his surroundings, signage from Korean mom-and-pop shops in the distance, light from the neon flickering in and out. Some written in Hanul, Korean characters.

At least in Shin Obubo, I don't have to deal with bullies and bullshit.

"Hey."

Eiji turns. The kid from class.

"Wasn't sure you'd show."

Eiji shrugs.

"Ok," the kid says. "My boss is looking for young people with skills. You can fight. I was in the bathroom, and the look in your eyes. . ."

Eiji stares at him.

I can definitely fight.

"Who is this boss? What would I be doing?"

"I'll take you to meet him."

"Yeah, well who is he? What's he *do*?"

"I'll take you to meet him."

"You don't want to tell me?"

The kid says nothing, just glances back over his shoulder. Eiji glares at him and then sighs. "Ok. When?"

"I'll tell him you're interested and set up a meet. May be a few days, he's a busy man."

"Ok. You gonna tell me *your* name? I know you know mine."

"Toshikazu. Call me Toshi"

"See you around Toshi."

Eiji keeps his guard up until he's back on the street.

***

Because he has no priors, Ryan is released into his parents' care almost immediately. His mother wouldn't even look at him, she was so angry. His father was almost as bad. He was grounded without the use of the car and allowed to go to 1. school, 2. judo, 3. his doctor's appointments. The crash concerned his parents for more than just his behavior – they worried about his condition. When he hit the other vehicle, his head whipped back from the impact, eleven pounds of cranium jerking forward, his brain slamming into the inside of his skull.

He didn't think anything of it at first. Then came the headaches. They were fierce, worse than anything he'd ever experienced. He didn't really mind being grounded – all he wanted was to lie on his bed with the shades pulled anyway. He ate a whole bottle of Tylenol, stayed home from school for several days; when he did return it was a slog. Too much noise and light, his migraines building all morning and exploding in the afternoon.

It was like this for about a week.

He made an appointment with Dr. Edleman, the family pediatrician, the same doctor he'd been seeing since he was in diapers.

***

When Dr. Edleman walks in, he's holding Ryan's chart.

"Not your head again?"

The doctor, a slender, aging, white man with glasses and salt-and-pepper hair, gives him a wry smile.

"Yeah," says Ryan. "Car accident."

"Hmmm." Dr. Edleman looks down at the file. "Headaches are bad, huh?"

"Yes, sir."

"I would think so. Sounds like a pretty substantial concussion."

"A concussion? I didn't even hit my head."

"You don't have to. Your brain hit the inside of your skull, causing it to bruise and swell. Happens all the time in automobile accidents. And. . ." he fixes Ryan with a serious gaze, "in sports."

"Whiplash?"

"Yes. It not only affects the neck but can also injure the brain. How is your neck, by the way?"

Dr. Edleman steps over and places his hand behind Ryan's head, walking his fingers up and down the spine, pressing in.

"Umm," says Ryan.

Dr. Edleman focuses his touch on the area that made his patient jump. He feels around it.

"Your x-ray showed no breaks, so it's just a strain, a sore spot where you asked too much of your spinal column."

He withdraws a flashlight from the pocket of his white jacket and shines it in each of Ryan's eyes.

"The good news is that your pupils look like they're getting back to normal, which means your brain is healing. Concussions are serious, Ryan, especially in someone like you, who experienced brain trauma in the womb. We need to keep an eye on this, and you have to let your brain rest. You might want to start looking for a hobby besides judo."

"That's not going to. . ."

". . . I'm serious, son. Your brain can't sustain knocks the way an average brain can."

"I'll be careful, doc."

"You had better."

Dr. Edleman looks at Ryan over the rim of his glasses. "Now, go home and get some rest."

***

He did five miles a day on the stationary bike. He liked riding. He could pedal and let his mind wander – or even rest. Since his loss at the U.S. Open Judo Championships, he's been spending hours and hours gripping the upright handrests of the bike, thrusting his legs down one after the other, like pistons, turning his frustration into corded muscle. He could almost feel the strength flowing into his thighs.

"Ryan."

Sensei Chan stands in front of him. Ryan pretends to swerve his bike, pulls his feet off the pedals, and they spin around and stop. He wipes his face with a towel and looks up.

"Sensei?"

Sensei Chan looks at him and then looks at the ground. Ryan can tell it's something serious.

"I just got off the phone with USA Judo. They won't sponsor us anymore. Not since. . ." Sensei Chan stares at the wall.

Ryan drops his head.

"How're we supposed to compete internationally without a sponsor?"

"We'll look for others."

"Yeah, like that's going to happen."

Ryan pounds the handlebar of the bike.

"Nobody fucking cares in this country. There's no future for the sport here."

"Ryan. . ."

Ryan sits up straight. Looks forward. Concentrates. Breathes deep and exhales.

"I'm sorry Sensei."

The TV catches Ryan's eye. Big block letters read: "UFC vs Shooto: America vs Japan."

He clocks reigning UFC heavyweight champion Randy Couture next to the pride of Shooto, Enson Inoue.

Ryan tilts his head at the screen.

"Sensei, how'd you get a hold of this fight so fast?"

"My brother is training at the Kodokan. He sent it to me."

"The Kodokan? In Tokyo?"

"Yes."

Ryan opens his mouth to say something, but the flurry of action on the screen distracts him. The two fighters slug it out in the middle of the ring. Enson fires a middle kick to Couture's midriff, and the American grabs his leg and takes Inoue to the mat. Enson slips a leg up and over Couture's shoulder to attempt a triangle choke. Couture knows how devastating that can be, and he hops to his feet, snaking his head out. Enson stands and rushes Couture with a barrage of punches. Couture pummels inside and secures a collar tie, his arm behind Enson's head as he dirty boxes. He thrusts uppercuts to the Japanese fighter's torso and head, then drags Enson back toward the ground.

From the bottom position, Enson controls Couture's wrist with one hand and grips his leg with the other, then shifts his hips out to the side. He brings his leg up over Couture's shoulder, hooking behind the head to secure the armbar. Couture tries to wrench his arm free, but Enson flips over, belly down, and leverages more pressure. Couture realizes he's beaten and taps out. The referee stops the fight. Enson throws his arms over his head in victory as the crowd erupts. His cornermen jump into the ring and run to him.

"Oh, my God," Ryan says. His eyes are wide. "Couture tapped out. To a jiu-jitsu fighter."

"You know, Ryan. I've been wanting to talk to you about this." Sensei Chan nods at the screen. "The Olympics aren't everything. You could give MMA a shot; it has less red tape and regulations, and it's on the verge of becoming a major sport. You win, you move up. Simple as that. Plus, you already have a solid foundation."

"But I don't know jiu-jitsu."

Sensei Chan chuckles.

"You didn't know judo either."

He gives Ryan a little smile and walks toward the door. Ryan sits back on the bike, deep in thought.

"See you tomorrow, Ryan. First thing."

***

The sixth hour bell rings, and students file into the hallway at Ottawa Hills High School. Ryan spins the combination to the lock on his locker, opens it, and throws his books inside.

Worry about my homework later.

He pads down the hall.

"Look at the bifocal-wearing, Bruce Lee wanna-be" shouts Tommy, a black adolescent wearing a Detroit Lion's cap and blue handkerchief around his wrist. "Bruce Lee wanna-be" he says again, liking the way it sounds. He shakes his head side to side and takes a few steps toward Ryan.

Larry places a hand on his chest.

"That's Mr. Bow's kid. He don't play," he says.

Larry jogs over to Ryan, his oversized pants sagging.

"Yo, how you been, man? It's been a minute. You still doing that sumo wrestling shit? You gotta show me some of that stuff. I bet I could take you." Larry does a wide-leg squat and grins playfully at Ryan.

"Naw, I messed that up when I lost," Ryan says, codeswitching. "I'm on some new shit now, MMA. . ."

My parents would kill me if they heard me talking like this. Or saw me talking to Larry.

"Gonna move to Japan and fight professionally. Just gotta figure out how I'm gonna pay for it."

"You know I can hook you up," Larry says. "Just say the word."

"You know I'm not about that life."

"I got you." Larry nods. He steps back and looks at Ryan, quiet for a second. Then says, "Fuck it. You know what. Don't sweat it. Flight is on me, for old times' sake." Larry reaches into his pocket and pulls out a fat wad.

He puts an arm around Ryan's shoulders as they step through the school foyer.

"Your mom and pops always been good to me, bro. Treated me like *family*. I will never forget that."

Ryan halts. Shocked at the kindness of his friend.

"I can't take your money."

"We good. Go to Japan. Put GR on the map!"

Larry shoves Ryan's shoulder and runs off towards his crew before Ryan can reply.

***

Ryan brushes past his parents and charges up the staircase.

"I didn't see any police, at least," Diane says, and she and Amen follow him, making their way slowly up the stairs. They find the door to his room closed. Diane pounds on the thin wood.

"Ryan, open up! We need to talk!"

She bangs her knuckles again, hitting harder this time.

"What do you want to talk about?" Ryan hollers from behind the door. "What *is* there to talk about? Didn't they just say it all?"

Amen gently moves his wife out of the way, giving her a bit of side eye. "Ryan, son. It's best if we can think this thing through. Discuss it together."

"Judo is over!" Diane screams from behind him.

Amen turns to her. "The doctors say his risks are the same as they've always been, Diane. This isn't about judo – and it's not what he needs." Amen stabs his finger at the door. "Calm down."

"I blame you, Amen," she says coldly. "Remember that. I do not want to hear it! Eighteen years too late!"

Amen opens his mouth to respond, and she holds up her hand and walks down the hallway.

After a minute, the knob on Ryan's door spins. Amen tries it and finds it unlocked. He nudges it open.

"Ry," Amen says, stepping into the room and closing the door behind him.

Ryan picks up his head and looks at his father.

"Listen. I'm sorry about your mother. She's not herself these days." Amen squats down next to the bed, his eyes on a level with his son's.

"I don't know what's going through your head right now, but maybe we should take a break from judo. At least until we understand a little more."

"What more is there to understand?" Ryan looks down at his mattress. "It doesn't matter anymore. I've made up my mind."

His father winces. "Made up your mind about what?"

"I'm going to keep competing. I have new goals."

"Ryan. . ."

"And I'm going to Japan."

"Japan!" Amen stands up and crosses his arms. "What in the Lord's name are you talking about?"

"Japan is where Judo originated and where the best coaches are. . ." Ryan says, still staring down. "I've already bought my ticket. I'll figure out the rest when I get there."

"Figure out when you. . ." Amen catches himself. Stops talking. His eyes go wide, almost as if he's doing a double take. Then he steps back, puts his hands on top of his skull, and shakes his head from side to side. He clearly hadn't expected this. He paces for a moment. Then wheels back to Ryan.

"Where'd you get the money from for this ticket?"

"A friend from school said he'd spot me the cash."

"Who?" Amen demands.

"Larry."

"Over my dead body," Amen says. "Larry? Larry. . . He's a good kid, always liked him. But he's been hanging around the wrong people lately. . ." Amen catches Ryan's eyes. "You know how he probably got that money, right?"

Ryan looks down at the floor.

He knows. . .

"Son, you are barely eighteen."

"Dad, the way things have been lately. Mom. Now, the doctors. College. I thought me moving abroad would be about the last thing you want to hear about."

"You're *right*, I don't like it. And I don't think it's a good idea. You have your whole future ahead. There are a lot of colleges that would be glad to have you, and you could start to build a life for yourself."

"That's the whole idea, Dad. I *am* building a life for myself. Doing what I need to do for *me*."

"What about your mother?" Amen says sharply. He steps toward the door.

Ryan's head drops. She seems worse than ever lately, so quick to anger, like lighting a match, one second, weirdly giddy the next. Often lost in a haze, her eyes far away, not even wanting to get out of bed. The doctors called it bipolar disorder, whatever that meant.

"Sorry, I shouldn't have said that," Amen says. "Your mother is not your responsibility."

"I know, but I worry about her," Ryan says. "I'll be back, Dad. And I'll call. It's not like I'm going away forever."

"I get that. And the healthy bird leaves the nest, as they say." Amen inhales slowly, deliberately, lets out another long breath, crosses his arms on his chest. He wasn't expecting this.

"I'm sorry, Dad. I know it's not what you wanted for me." Ryan looks at his father, studying his face. "But I feel like it's something I have to do. Judo's the only thing that I've ever been good at. If I *ever* want to make the Olympics, I need the best instruction, and the finest teachers are in Japan. Sensei Chan has some connections and said he would help me."

"I love you, son, and I want you to be happy. If this is what will make you happy, I guess I have to make peace with it. You had better call home often. And your mother, well. . ." He raps the frame of Ryan's door and pads off down the hall.

Ryan buries his head in his pillow.

That went well. How can I ever tell them about MMA?

***

Eiji stands in front of the station in Shin Okubo, glances at his wrist. Right on time. Commuters go about their day. An older man sits in his taxi, awaiting his next customer.

"Tsk." Eiji glances at his watch again.

Toshi is almost upon him before he even notices. Eiji nods coolly as his classmate walks up. "Shimoda-san will be here in a few minutes," Toshi says, pulling a pack of cigs out of his pocket.

"I thought you said to meet at 6?"

"Yes, Shimoda-san just got a little delayed. He's always running."

"So am I. I'm supposed to be home shortly. My father won't be happy."

"You want a job or not?" Toshi asks, cigarette waving up and down between his lips.

"Tell me again what kind of work it is?"

"Collections, mostly."

"Collections? Like a librarian?"

Toshi frowns and looks Eiji in the eyes. "A lot of people owe Shimoda-san money," he says, leaning in. "You go get it for him."

"Wait, like a loan shark?"

"You haven't figured it out yet?" Toshi folds his arms across his chest and stares at Eiji.

Eiji doesn't blink, staring back, his eyebrows raised. He wants to punch the smirk off Toshi's face.

"Really? You don't get it?"

Eiji looks down at his feet and shakes his head.

Toshi extends his right hand toward the Zainichi, his cigarette almost burning Eiji's knee. Ink peeks out from his sleeve, freshly done *kaze bori*, wind bars, still dark and healing on his wrist.

"You know what that means?" Toshi asks.

Eiji glances at the tattoo and shrugs, unimpressed.

Toshi gives him a tight smile. He is losing patience.

"It means I'm with the Shimoda family. You know what *that* means." He bobs his head for emphasis.

Eiji nods slowly.

"Shimoda-san is interested in you because you can fight. His family always needs new talent who can handle themselves."

"I can fight," says Eiji. "Been studying Kyokushin karate for years. My sensei says he's never seen anyone with my skills."

"You don't have to convince me. I've seen you in action."

Eiji spots a Toyota Century, the "Japanese Rolls Royce" rolling towards them. It stops in front of them, and the window slides down.

"Get in." Shimoda-san says from the back seat.

Black suit, white shirt, closely cropped grey hair. A cigarette hangs from his lips. He nods his head to Toshi, who bows, his eyes meeting Shimoda-san's as he steps into the car. Eiji follows suit.

"Eiji," the business tycoon says, turning in his seat and smiling. "Toshi has told me a lot about you." He extends his hand toward the fighter. Eiji bows and then takes it. A sleeve tattoo peeks out from his wrist, just below his cufflinks.

Hmm. Looks more like a CEO than a gangster.

"Toshi tells me you are Zainichi?" Shimoda-san says, settling back into his seat. He crosses his legs at the knee and looks at Eiji.

"Yes, sir, my grandparents are from Korea."

"Some of my best employees are, too," Shimoda-san says. "I think it makes you hungry. . . maybe even a little angry." He smiles again, turning to scan the people on the streets around him. "My grandfather used to bring me to this area as a boy." He gestures at the local family-run shops.

"He was the first of us to live and work in Tokyo." Shimoda-san stares at Eiji for an uncomfortably long time. Then says, "Toshi here says you can handle yourself. I need people like that in my organization."

"I studied karate with Master Oyama for ten years, before he passed. Fighting is about the only thing I'm good at," Eiji leans forward with his elbows on his knees and looks at the ground.

Shimoda-san nods. "I'm sure there are many things you're good at. I've heard of Master Oyama. He was

Zainichi too. As for fighting, it's a very good thing to be good at. Valuable."

"I don't know about that. . ."

"Oh, I do," Shimoda-san says. "If you would like a job with my organization, I would show you just how much your skills are worth."

"I'm listening," Eiji says.

"You have attitude, too, another useful trait. If you want to work for me, visit this address after school on Friday." Shimoda-san reaches into his pocket and pulls out a glossy black business card with Shimoda Enterprises embossed on it.

Shimoda-san reaches his hand out toward Eiji as the car pulls over to the side of the road. Eiji raises out of his seat. He takes Shimoda-san's hand and feels cash on his palm. The older man withdraws his hand, leaving a bill in Eiji's palm.

"For your trouble today."

Eiji bows, sliding the bill into his pocket without even looking at it.

"You'll find I can pay you handsomely," Shimoda-san says. He leans in and says quietly, "You might even enjoy the work." He claps Eiji on the shoulder.

Eiji bows again. Toshi bows. Shimoda-san smiles at both of them and signals his lieutenant. A big Japanese man dressed in all black, looking cool in Ray Bans, slides out from behind the wheel and opens the rear door for Toshi and Eiji to exit. Then the driver gets back in and the car speeds off.

Chapter 5

Diane and Amen drive Ryan to the airport, and Ryan notices his mother is unusually quiet. She hardly says a word as they glide through traffic, staring out the window and watching the highway speed limit signs flit past.

Amen picks up on this, too, and tries to fill the silence.

"You sure you got everything?"

"Yeah, Dad. Already told you."

"Just double checking. Never hurts to double check."

Ryan sits in the back. Excited but nervous. And sad to say goodbye to his folks.

"Gonna miss you, son," Amen says, looking in the rearview. "School will miss you, too. Won't be the same."

"I'll miss you, too, Dad. And Mom."

They arrive early and all walk to the concourse together. Ryan gives both of his parents a big hug.

Amen looks Ryan in the eyes and subtly nods. He slips a wad of cash into his son's pocket.

Ryan gives his parents one last look, then enters the air bridge.

***

He has a window seat in the last row. Unlike most of the other passengers, Ryan's fascinated by the goings on outside.

He watches the baggage men in their carts, racing toward the plane. Dressed in bulky suits – body armor against the Michigan winter – they disappear beneath him. He can hear the thump of bags being loaded into the cargo area. A crew works on the jumbo jet at the next gate, spraying the wings with a big hose. Ryan doesn't like the thought of deicing.

Flying through space is bad enough.

Before long, the plane lifts off, and Ryan studies the lights on the ground as the jet gains altitude. Detroit looks beautiful from the air, homes and businesses turning into constellations. People around him seem oblivious, flipping through the in-flight magazine.

People pay for sightseeing flights, but when they have a chance to look for free, they don't. . .

Within a minute or so, it's all gone as the plane climbs into a fog bank. Ryan can actually see the sleet pellets as they pelt the window. Then everything is white.

When they reach cruising altitude, the pilot dims the lights, and Ryan settles back in his seat as best he can. He feels squished in the seat.

And I'm only 5'5".

He doesn't want to sprawl into the little old white lady next to him, so he leans his head against the window, his hoodie over his head. He closes his eyes. The constant hum of the engines lull him to sleep.

He throws his hands up to protect his face. It takes a moment to remember where he is. The plane rocks with turbulence, like a fighter eating a blow to the body. He grips the arm rest. The little old lady next to him puts her gnarled hand on his knee. He looks down at her, and she smiles.

"Nothing to it, dear. Happens all the time."

The plane pitches again, this time the lights flash on and off.

Ryan glances out the window, but all is black.

***

On the drive over, Amen can barely contain his anger. He talks to himself. Slams the steering wheel. There isn't any parking in front of the dojo, so he's forced to cruise the streets, looking for a space. It doesn't help him calm down any. He ends up walking five blocks, practically stomping his way across the neighborhood. When he finally pushes the door open, he sees that Sensei Chan is teaching a Little Dragons class. A dozen first graders are lined up, listening.

This won't do.

Amen leaves before the sensei notices him. He walks down the street to Rosa Parks Circle and stands on the sideline of the makeshift ice rink, watching skaters glide over the ice. He pumps his right leg up and down. Checks his watch.

"Amen?"

He looks up. His colleague, Sonja.

"Hey, Sonja."

"How's it going? Haven't seen you around lately."

"Good, good," Amen says nodding. Sonja stands next to him, one hand on the guard rail to the ice rink where her children are skating, a steaming cup in the other.

"How's Ryan doing? I heard about the crash. . ."

"Ryan's doing good. Off to Japan to train judo."

"In Japan?" she says, shocked. "No kidding,"

"Yeah, he just left."

"It's bound to feel different without him around."

"Yeah, I miss him already."

"How about Diane?"

"She's good, you know. Getting better anyway, she's been sick."

"Yeah, I heard. Word travels fast in a small neighborhood. I'm so sorry, it must be difficult. Glad to hear she's on the mend."

Sonja keeps talking. . . "If there's anything I can do. . ."

Amen finds his mind wandering. His leg slows beneath him. He nods and smiles.

"Listen, Sonja, I gotta get going. Nice seeing you."

"You, too, Amen, take it easy."

Amen walks back across the park, glances up at the snowflakes begin to tumble from the sky.

He reaches the dojo, where the last Little Dragon, no taller than his belt, is shuffling out the door, struggling to carry all his things.

Sensei Chan sees Amen and holds the door open for him.

"Mr. Bow? What brings you here?"

"We need to talk," Amen says shortly.

"Please, come in."

Sensei Chan ushers Amen into his office and gestures for him to sit in the guest chair.

"I can't believe you told Ryan to move to Japan," Amen says, rubbing his hands down the thighs of his jeans. He fixes his eyes on the teacher.

Sensei Chan pulls back as if Amen swung at him.

"I didn't," he says. "I only learned he was going when he came in and said goodbye."

Amen looks at him, tilts his head, perplexed.

"I told him if he's going to take some time away from judo, maybe he should consider Mixed Martial Arts.

"What!?" Amen cries. "MMA?!"

Amen tries to gather himself before he explodes. He breathes out, staring straight ahead for a moment. Then has a thought.

"Did Ryan ever tell you about his condition?"

"Condition?"

"Yeah," Amen says, impatiently. "His eyes, his brain?"

"No."

"He had a stroke in the womb and has had vision problems since he was a child. Doctors say any head trauma could be devastating."

Sensei Chan reacts as if he's been punched.

"Why didn't you tell me this? He's been competing for years. . ."

"It's what he always wanted to do," Amen says, letting out a long sigh. "Ever since I can remember, he's wanted to fight. Used to watch kung fu shows whenever we'd let him. Since he was six years old. Makes those Little Dragons seem like college students. I don't know why or where it comes from. But he's always wanted to be a warrior."

Sensei Chan nods.

"I was a wrestler, so I probably encouraged him. I could never bear to say no, and I convinced my wife by telling her judo has no kicks and punches. That he'd wear a helmet."

"I see." The sensei drops his chin to his chest, his face dark.

"And now he's gone to Japan to train. Oh Lord. . ." Amen says.

Sensei Chan's head hits his chest again.

***

The plane touches down at Narita. All of the passengers step into the aisle, and Ryan waits for the long line in front of him to move. It seems to take forever. But eventually people right in front of him start opening the overhead compartments, gathering their bags, and shuffling toward the exit. Ryan half stands, squished beneath the baggage box, while the little old lady moves out of her seat. She steps into the aisle and tries to reach above her to get her bag down. Ryan slides out to help her, pulling her luggage out of the bin for her and setting it down on its wheels.

"Thank you, love." She pats him on the hand. "See, we got here safe."

Ryan nods and smiles.

They disembark, and Ryan walks through the crowded airport. He's never seen so many people, and the vast majority are Asian. For the first time in his life he feels average height, rather than short. A Japanese voice speaks loudly over the intercom, but he has no idea what they're saying.

Should have studied the language before I left. . .

He sees retractable belt barriers dividing the walkway up ahead into two lines and assumes it must be Customs, though he can't read the signage. Above one lane is a jumble of Japanese characters; above the other is a single word in multiple languages. He scans down until he hits English. "Aliens." He always knew he was in the minority in Grand Rapids, but this was another level altogether. He steps into that line and waits for the long queue ahead of him to subside. He finally steps up to a Customs officer who looks at him with a furrowed brow and blank, dark eyes. Ryan smiles.

The man puts his hand out and Ryan hands him his passport. His palms begin to sweat as the official pages through the little booklet, finding the pertinent information. He glances back up at Ryan, studying him against his passport picture. He makes a hard line with his mouth. Ryan wipes his hands on his pants. The clerk again stares at Ryan. Then he says something in Japanese and brings his stamp down hard on the page. He waves Ryan on. Ryan steps past him and breathes out a long sigh. He wrestles his bag over his shoulder – should've gotten one of those wheelers – and starts down the concourse. He's amazed at the size of the airport. It's like a little city all on its own, acres and acres of black steel and glass and recessed lights. He feels like an actual alien, all alone in a foreign world.

Ryan follows the human tide, scanning the signs on the walls, looking for anything that resembles a train. He hauls his bag for what seems like a mile before spying the unmistakable symbol of a locomotive on a glowing sign off to the right. He begins to wade through all the other people, crossing to the other side of the terminal. It's a series of pauses and acceleration, like trying to switch lanes on a highway, but he's finally across and the corridor opens up toward a set of doors. Above them is an even larger train sign.

Stepping through into the train station, Ryan finds himself again shoulder to shoulder with the hordes. A massive map on one wall shows the many routes into and around Tokyo. It's a winding, twisting maze with Japanese characters all over it. A turnstile blocks his way. He turns to see a ticket machine, covered with Japanese characters. He has no idea which train he needs or how much it will be and fumbles through his pockets for change.

"Excuse me," he says over everyone's head. Most people ignore him. "Excuse me?" People move away, many pulling on surgical masks. A tiny middle-aged woman steps over to him and says quietly in perfect English. "Can I help?"

"Yes, please," Ryan says, breathing out another long sigh. "I'm trying to get to Yokohama." The woman points to it on the map and looks back up at him. Ryan dips his head. The woman pushes a button on the ticket machine, picks the necessary bank notes out of Ryan's hand, and a moment later, hands him a slip of heavy paper. Ryan looks at the characters on the ticket, trying to commit them to memory. He bows his head and reaches out to shake her hand in thanks. Her grip is soft and clammy, and she purses her lips and takes a step backwards. Ryan pulls his suitcase and follows others toward the tracks.

Ryan matches the characters on the ticket with some he sees on a sign and walks toward that platform. When he arrives, he finds a train operator going through safety checks. The small man is pointing at buttons and mumbling to himself in Japanese. Ryan clears his throat, and the man looks over at him.

"Yokohama?" Ryan asks.

"*Hai*, Yokohama *he ikimasu*." He bobs his head toward the train. "*Go jōsha kudasai*."

Not understanding a word, the American nods. He takes a spot right behind the driver, placing his stuffed suitcase on the floor and gripping the strap above his head. The driver says something through the intercom, and Ryan relaxes slightly when he hears "Yokohama." Then there is a soft melodic chime, and the doors closed with a "shshshsh." Ryan has to catch his balance as the train begins to move.

The train pulls from the station, and Ryan gets his first glimpse at the Japanese countryside. Trees and greenery flash by the window. Every time something catches his eye – an Edo-style wooden house, rice paddies – they're gone before he can really get a look. The train rumbles on and on, shifting ever so slightly this way and that, causing him to shift his weight. He looks around at his fellow passengers. A lot of men in business suits. Women in skirts. They all sit or stand quietly, keeping to themselves, reading newspapers filled with short, horizontal and vertical lines. Ryan wonders if Japanese children get dyslexia, too, and what learning to read might be like for them.

The landscape outside begins to grow in stature – the buildings rising ever taller. Ryan notices a sign in English that reads: Tokyo. *But I'm not going to Tokyo. . .* He feels his palms sweat again. Then he notices a station map above his head that shows Yokohama on the other side of Tokyo, and he lets out his breath. The train clatters on into Tokyo, where skyscrapers, brilliant in the sun, soar up out of his view. A smile crosses Ryan's face when he sees a billboard with a picture of Enson Inoue, arms crossed to accentuate his biceps, hands wrapped for battle. Travelers hop off, others climb aboard, and the train pulls away from the station. He watches the countryside flit by.

The train begins to slow and cruises to a stop, the doors opening. Ryan peers out the window. The driver peeks around his big seat and looks at him. "Yokohama" he says, tilting his head sideways at the station.

"Thanks," Ryan says, "Um, Arigatou." He hauls his bag onto his shoulder, takes a deep breath, and steps out onto the platform. The station is crazy with activity, people and cabs and subways and bicycles moving in all directions, horns honking, bus brakes groaning. He exits to the street.

Never knew Yokohama was so big.

He thinks for a minute how we all think the world is limited to what we see through our own eyes, to our sphere of influence, but that massive cities filled with millions of people exist thousands of miles away completely independent of our existence. And also how U.S. schools and U.S. newspapers seem only to care about what goes on in the United States, otherwise maybe he'd have a clue what a major metropolitan area Yokohama was.

Looks even bigger than Detroit. . .

The bag weighs heavily as he stumbles with it down a busy sidewalk. He finds himself saying, "excuse me," "pardon me," over and over as he bumps into people on the crowded street. He has to focus on keeping his eyes forward, looking where he's going, because all he wants to do is check out the city. Other than travelling locally to compete, he hadn't ventured far as a kid, and now he was in one of the most unique cultures on the planet. What he sees, when he pauses to catch his breath, surprises him a little. He'd expected temples, shrines, and cherry blossoms, but what is in front of him is a vibrant seaside metropolis.

Pictures of apartments taped up onto a shop window catch his eye. He looks up. The sign is all Japanese characters, but among them is a line drawing showing the universal shape of a house. He knows he has to find a place to stay and steps inside. The building is stark, virtually empty, with a counter and a tall, thin man standing behind it. The clerk stares blankly at Ryan.

"I'd like to rent an apartment," Ryan says.

The man purses his lips and tilts his head slightly. He sighs. "I'm sorry," he says. "No English."

He hands Ryan a flyer filled with properties. It's printed in multiple languages, none of which does he speak. Ryan looks down at it, confused.

"Ah," Ryan starts.

"Gaijin okay," the man says, pointing at one particular building. The clerk nods to himself, repeating, "Gaijin okay."

Gaijin was one of the few Japanese words Ryan knew. It meant "foreigner," often with a negative connotation. It meant "Outsider." Or "Someone not like us."

I guess that's me.

Ryan nods to the man.

It takes him a while to find the place, which is in the Ishikawacho district, a historic neighborhood on a canal that runs to Yokohama port. As he nears the address, he sees signs in English for Yamashita Park, Motomachi, and Chinatown.

Chinatown? In Japan?

Ryan wanders the street looking for the address on the flyer. The Gaijin house in the picture is a grey, three-story dwelling, with long windows and a utilitarian design that felt more like a business than a home. He scans the buildings in front of him. Nope. These are all modern reinforced concrete, dual-purpose structures that could be in any city anywhere. He keeps at it until he spots a building very similar to the one in the flyer. He lets out a long breath, walks up the steps, and knocks at the entryway.

A man opens the door. Slender, in a bathrobe, cigarette hanging from the corner of his mouth. He looks to be in his early thirties and gives Ryan a small grin. "Shiomi" he says, pointing at himself with a subtle bow.

"Ryan." He points at himself and does the same.

Shiomi motions him inside. He says nothing, simply leads Ryan down a long, dimly lit hallway lined with doors. He makes it all the way to the end and stops in front of a door that's chipped and stained. He pushes it open and waves his arm inside.

The room is small and triangular, with just a futon on the floor. Some of the trim around the window is missing and several holes pock the walls. Ryan notices roaches scurrying back into them at their approach. Shiomi grins, raising his eyebrows, as if he's just shown a live one a penthouse. Ryan frowns. Shiomi shrugs.

"53,000 yen a month."

"That's how much. . .?"

"$475 U.S. dollars," Shiomi says, as if he does this all the time. "Won't find a better price."

Tired of carrying his bag, jet lagged after flying halfway across the globe, uncertain he will find anything better, Ryan just nods.

Shiomi stands there expectantly, eyebrows raised. Ryan puts down his bag, reaches into his pocket, and pulls out his wallet. He counts out 53,000 yen – leaving behind only a few bills – and hands the cash to Shiomi, who takes it, bows, and quietly slips out.

Ryan sits down heavily on the futon on the floor. He lies back, arm behind his head, and surveys the room. The carpets show the previous owners, stains everywhere. Even on the futon. A cockroach pops its head out of its home in the wall, checking to see if he's still there. It notices him and darts back. He nods his head.

It's a start. Everyone has to have a start.

***

Down the hall is a common area. Smaller than his living room back in Grand Rapids, it has peeling floral wallpaper and smells like decades of cigarettes. On one end is a beat-up TV. A couch and a few stuffed chairs sit against the walls. In them are a bunch of other guys, a random assortment of ages and ethnicities; because the room is so small everyone is practically on top of each other. Some look up as Ryan walks in, others continue to talk among themselves, ignoring him. Ryan has a Japanese MMA magazine tucked under his arm, and he sits down in a corner and opens it. At the centerfold is a photo of U.S. Senator, John McCain of Arizona speaking before Congress. Ryan can't understand a thing. Except for the English spanning the width of two pages with an image of the fuming senator calling MMA a barbaric form of human cockfighting, Japanese translation beneath. Ryan's head sinks, when he notices a pair of blue jeans in front of him. He looks up. They're attached to a tall, shaggy-haired guy wearing a retro, light-blue, short-sleeved shirt and holding a half-burned cigarette in his right hand.

"Hey, you're new," he waves his cigarette toward the American. "Where you from?" This with a British accent and a big, friendly smile.

"The U.S.," Ryan says.

"Another Yank! You guys are all over this place."

Ryan nods.

"I'm Jon," the fellow says, extending his hand. Ryan shakes.

"What brings you to the lovely seaside city of Yokohama?"

Ryan holds up the magazine for Jon to see.

"Mixed Martial Arts. I'm going to be a professional fighter."

"Whoa, that's not something you hear every day. Going to be tough to break in."

"No other future in fighting," Ryan says. "The sports as good as dead in the U.S." He points to the McCain article.

"*Nihongo wakaru ka*?" Jon says. Ryan looks at him quizzically.

"You speak Japanese?"

"Not yet," says Ryan.

"Everything will be much easier if you learn Japanese. I'm a translator. I can help you if you want."

The lanky Brit sits in the next chair, and they talk a while. In his twenties, Jon relocated from London to translate for a Japanese electronics corporation in the city, helping their upper management break into Western markets.

"Gaijin House?" Ryan asks. "Isn't gaijin something of a slur?"

"I wouldn't go that far. It can definitely be rude, though, for sure."

Jon's room is only a couple doors down from Ryan's on the second floor, and he reiterates his offer to help him with his Japanese. He gets up. At the doorway he glances back: "Any questions, you come knocking."

"Thanks," Ryan says and turns back to his magazine.

***

"Harder Eiji."

Oyama's successor, Sensei Matsui, stands with his arms behind his back, watching Eiji and his fellow karateka hit each other in the mid-section.

"I want you to explode upon impact. Loose until then."

"Hai, Sensei."

They trade blows. Eiji, the more powerful of the two, hits his dojo mate hard enough to rock him back onto his heels.

"Good, Eiji. Make sure your arms stay tight to your body. Again."

Eiji imagines Ren, the kid from the bathroom, sneering at him. And he pounds his training partner again. And again.

Short and stocky with closely cropped hair, Sensei Matsui smiles and walks over to the next student.

A smile. Not bad. Imagine if my father ever smiled at me.

Eiji keeps throwing punches, like pistons, one fist goes out, one fist comes back. It feels good to hit things.

Class is an hour and a half. After punches, they work on the final third of the Sanchin kata. Imported from

China, this slow kata was known as the "three battles or three conflicts" form, and it was shared with several other karate styles. Sanchin is intended to harden the body, to ready it for strikes from an opponent. Eiji used some of its techniques when his father brought out the cane. Like many other katas, it looks simple but takes years to master – some even said, when you master Sanchin, you master karate. He knew he'd have to have his form just right to pass the shime test, where instructors put pressure on various points to see if the student has proper structure and is stable. The kata is performed with the body tense, and involves a lot of deep, lower-abdominal breathing. Eiji is sweating and tired when he gathers his things and leaves for home. The dojo is about a mile from his house, and he decides to jog to give himself the maximum workout for the day.

***

"Good afternoon, my name is Ryan."
Konnichiwa, watashi no namae ha Raian desu.
Still doesn't sound right.
"Good afternoon, my name is Ryan."
He looks at the words in the book.
Konnichiwa, watashi no namae ha Raian desu.
He tries it again, still tripping all over the place.
So many syllables.

He closes his eyes. Exhales. He looks around the room. Exhales again.

He reaches for his left eye, gently pries back the eyelid, and removes a thick contact lens. He places it in its case.

83

He returns to the book, his left eye now drifting off to the side. He continues to practice common phrases with mixed success. Some of the short ones seem to come out okay. Anything multisyllabic causes him to stumble. He stares at the wall, speaking aloud. Over and over and over until he can't take anymore.

"*Oyasuminasai.*"
Good night.
"*Oyasuminasai.*"

***

On his way home, Eiji pulls the bill out of his front pocket. It's a crisp new 10,000 yen note. He looks at the business card again. Shimoda Enterprises sounds like some kind of front, but he knows enough about the yakuza to know they had an array of legit businesses that they hid behind.

I can always just ask Toshi more at school. If I'm interested. Am I interested?

He thought about the pros and cons. Money was the most obvious. If he worked for Shimoda-san, he would never have to be a wage slave like his father. He would have opportunities in a bunch of different directions.

His father, though. There was always his father. Number one in the con column. He would definitely have something to say about his son working for the yakuza. He always wanted Eiji to follow him into the trades, working on job sites like he did and his father did before him.

"We built Japan," he liked to say proudly. "We provide shelter for the nation."

He'll probably disown me.

Eiji could just imagine him: "I didn't raise a criminal. You know better. Your mother would be heartbroken. We are Zainichi, they already look down on us."

I don't want to be like him.

Work endless hours, left broken and stooped and angry. And for what? Barely enough to cover the basics. No time for anyone or anything. A rundown home in a dumpy *danchi*, government housing complex.

At least I could make some money. Serious money, if Toshi is to be believed. And I don't know how to do much besides fight anyway.

By the time he reaches his house, his mind is made up.

I'll go see Shimoda-san on Friday.

He pushes the front door open and sees his father sitting at the table, a bottle of sake in front of him. His eyes are red rimmed, blurry.

Here we go.

"You're late."

"I had a job interview," Eiji says, pulling out a chair.

"Hideo saw you get into that fancy ride."

"That's where my meeting was."

"With who?"

"Shimoda-san" Eiji stares across the table.

His father shakes his head from side to side then lets his chin drop to his chest.

"Yeah, he offered me a job with Shimoda Enterprises."

His father shoves back his chair and stands up. He steps around the table, looming over Eiji and looking down at him.

"Do you know what Shimoda-san does?" Eyes dark, drawn, hands clenched tight at his side.

"He said I could help him with public relations. Collections."

"Collections!" His father spits out the word. "Collections! Do you know what he means by collections? He loans money to desperate people – your neighbors – and then he makes them pay it back fivefold. If they can." By now his face is red. He pauses to take a breath. Opens his mouth and shuts it. "You will not work for Shimoda-san. I forbid it. No son of mine. . . A gangster!"

Eiji stares at him. Then shrugs his shoulders.

"I don't even want you talking to him."

Eiji keeps his eyes locked on his father's. He rises up from his seat, now tall enough to stand eye to eye.

"I'll talk to whoever I want to talk to."

The strike takes Eiji by surprise, an open hand hard across the cheek.

His father never sees his fist coming. Eiji hits him full force on the chin, staggering him back into a wall. The vibration shakes a picture of Eiji's mother off its hook, and it tumbles to the floor, glass shattering everywhere. His father puts his hand to his face and looks at Eiji, emotions swirling in his eyes. Shock. Hurt. Disappointment. Rage. The old man glances down at the broken frame and back up at Eiji. He points violently down at Eiji's mom staring up at them, wearing a shy smile and her nicest hanbok, a colorful traditional Korean dress. And then stumbles out of the kitchen.

Eiji quietly cleans up the glass and rehangs the picture, taking a long look at his mother as he does so, adjusting it so her face is level.

I'm sorry mother.

Chapter 6

H is futon is barely enough, and sleep is elusive. He sits up, rubs his eyes, and thinks of Sensei Chan.

Hardship makes warriors.

Cicadas buzz outside, and people are banging about in the hallway. Getting ready for work he assumes. Ryan grabs the table beside him to steady himself as he rises.

He slips into the hallway, covering the short distance to the bathroom and pushing the door open. He hangs his towel on a hook, and steps into the shower, bumping his knee on the faucet. He looks down. He has to think about it a moment before realizing, it's not the tub faucet but the showerhead.

Do I sit?

A peeling, laminated guide is stuck to the wall. Illustrated like a comic book, it's filled with step-by-step instructions on how to operate the shower.

I'm not the only one who finds this confusing.

The smiling stick figure reaches down and turns the handle. Ryan does the same. Water sputters and shoots out of the showerhead, and he adjusts the temp. It's warm but not hot. The stick figure sits on a stool. Ryan looks behind him and sees a plastic seat. He pushes it under the stream and lowers himself down. The water begins to cascade over him, though not in the volume he was used to in the States. He looks at the guide. The stick figure fills a bowl and uses it for his ablutions, apparently happy to do so. Ryan spies a plastic basin where the stool used to be, and he grabs it, filling it with water. This he dumps over his head repeatedly until he feels clean.

This will take some getting used to.

He pads back to his room, gets dressed in comfortable clothes, and slips on his shoes at the entrance as he leaves the Gaijin House, closing the door quietly behind him.

It's easy enough to find his way back to the train station. His destination doesn't look too difficult to get to – he's always had a decent sense of direction. He finds the signs indicating Yokosuka and buys a ticket at the machine.

He stands on the platform and looks around him. He realizes he's been holding his breath and lets out a sigh when he sees a map near a row of seats behind him. He's the only non-Japanese person that he can see.

He hears the train long before he sees it and steps toward the tracks. A long, glassed-in box, it comes to a stop with a groan in front of him. He finds a seat. Other passengers file in. A young woman stops at the seat next to his, then notices him, and moves on. An older man does the same. All the seats around him fill up. The last few people to enter the train grab overhead straps rather than sit in the open seats near him. Several of them stare openly at him.

A child sitting a few rows away looks at him with wide eyes. Ryan puffs out his cheeks and crosses his eyes. The kid quickly pulls back behind his mother, who reaches her arm around him protectively and glares at Ryan.

Excuse me. Ryan looks at his feet.

The countryside flashes by as they rattle along. Soon the intercom crackles. The operator says a bunch of stuff Ryan doesn't understand and finally something he does: "Yokosuka."

Ryan stands as the train sidles up to the station. The doors open, and he steps off onto the cement platform. He walks through the streets of Yokosuka, which look similar to Yokohama, except for all the American faces. The sidewalks are busy with people moving along the low-slung buildings of shop fronts. Unrecognizable signs in Japanese blend in with those in native level English and look down on him from all directions.

It's like a "Little America," right here in Japan.

He walks. And walks. Weaving through a wave of pedestrians on the narrow sidewalk. After about 20 minutes, he passes by the U.S. naval base. Cars flow in and out through its gates as two armed soldiers observe the traffic closely and check IDs. Ryan continues on. He spots a few people with oversized gym bags turning down a lane that seems popular with the locals. There, at the center of Dobuita Shopping Street, he finds the gym, Yokosuka Fight Factory. He can hear the sound of fists slamming into heavy bags through the cracked windows.

He pushes the door open and is hit with a wall of heat and the smell of sweat. Japanese men are jumping rope, pushing barbells up from benches, and riding stationary bikes. In the corner are the heavy bags.

A thirty-something Japanese man with broad shoulders steps over to him.

"Hey," Ryan says. "I'd like to join," he tilts his head sideways toward the gym.

The man looks at him, his eyes hooded. He makes no indication he's heard Ryan.

"How do I sign up?

The man raises his arm toward Ryan, as if he's going to shove him.

He loudly says something incomprehensible in Japanese.

"Sorry, I don't understand. English?"

The man crosses his arms in front of Ryan's face, forming a big "X."

He says in better-than-expected English: "No Foreigners. Military never pay on time. Always make trouble."

Ryan mutters, "I'm not. . ."

Before he can finish, the man is already headed back over to instruct his class. And he doesn't turn back.

Ryan can take a hint, making his way out of the building.

He decides to see the town instead and strolls along the shotengai, the local shopping street. A group of loud, obnoxious sailors flow out of a bar midday. Onlookers angle themselves away from them. The seamen catcall several female bystanders and shower them with unsolicited compliments.

I see why Americans get a bad rap around here.

Preoccupied with what he's just seen, Ryan finds himself walking the nearby boardwalk. He hops down on the beach and begins to jog along the city's famous strand. The sand churns under his feet, and he realizes he's running faster than expected, his anger propelling him along. He listens to the rhythm of the waves and looks as far out to the horizon as he can. He notices, far in the distance, Mt. Fuji looking like a cloud, all wrapped in snow. It's a majestic scene.

After a couple of miles, he turns and returns the way he came, the rage he felt earlier now spent. The sun makes a strawberry-orange parfait in the clouds as it slides into the sea.

***

On Friday, as soon as the bell rings, Eiji is out the door on his way to Shimoda Enterprises. He and his father had been avoiding each other as much as possible, which wasn't difficult, since the senior Tanaka usually left for work before Eiji had even gotten off his futon. But he knew there was no coming back from this. He'd have to find another place to live.

House was never the same after mom died anyway.

He hops a bus to get across town to the outskirts of Kabukicho, the district in Shinjuku where Shimoda Enterprises had its headquarters. Eiji has a general idea where he's going — Toshi had given him directions, standing at his locker — but the neighborhood he's walking through is far more residential than he was expecting. He glances again at the address on the card in his pocket, matching the characters on it with the ones on the street sign. He's on the right track. He follows the sidewalk, clocking the numbers until he's standing in front of a low-slung brown building — a fortified compound, really — that peeks up over a series of dense hedges and high walls.

Doesn't look very industrial.

The drive is cobbled, leading to a small gatehouse. Eiji notes the security cameras pointing down from trees all over. He saunters over to the gate, where he finds a guy reading a magazine. He taps on the window.

"Here to see Shimoda-san."

"Name?"

"Eiji Tanaka."

"Expecting you?"

"Yes."

"Wait," the guy says, holding up a finger. Eiji tries to get a look at his tats but no luck.

The sentry returns to his little booth, and Eiji can see him talking on the phone. While he waits, he surveys the complex, which consists of several low-slung buildings that look residential and another one that seems as big as a barn, but wears the same classy, dark cladding as the house.

A lot nicer than my father's.

He sees the same black Toyota Century parked in the circular driveway, next to a black Escalade, so new and shiny the fenders gleam. A couple of late model motorcycles lean nearby. The whole place reeks of money.

"Hey kid," the gatekeeper calls out, walking over to him. "Shimoda-san is waiting. Follow me."

As they walk, the guy turns to Eiji. "Seemed happy to hear you were here."

"Nice," says Eiji.

They follow some graceful brick walkways around to the left, past a couple of koi ponds and a garden lined with Bonzai trees, and the sounds of the street fade away. No one else seems to be around.

I could get used to this.

The guy leads Eiji to a door set off the rock garden. He opens it, and they step into a ritzy entryway, with marble floors and a grand staircase that sweeps down from the second floor. They climb and walk down a hallway until the guy stops and taps lightly on a doorway.

"Enter."

The guy gestures for Eiji to step in and he does so. Behind a big mahogany desk, writing in a small notebook, is Shimoda-san. He wears a dark suit, either a deep navy or black, Eiji can't tell. He looks up and says, "Welcome, Eiji, glad to see you. I wasn't sure if you would take me up on my offer." He extends his hand toward a cushy chair opposite the desk.

"Please. Sit."

Eiji bows and plops down.

"I had to think about it," he says.

"What were your concerns?"

"My father. He forbade me to even talk to you."

"Your father has heard of me?"

"Yes, sir. Says you're a loan shark."

Shimoda-san chuckles. "Well, I do loan money. I don't force it on people, they come to me. And if I'm going to pay out, I expect to make a return. I also expect people to pay it back. That's where you'll come in."

"Sir?"

"What I'd like to do is have you follow your friend Toshi for a few days. He works for one of my captains, and the pair of you will job shadow him, learning the ropes. Toshi has been with me for a while, but mostly just as a courier, delivering messages. I think he's ready for the next step. I know you are already." He smiles. "You'll need to finish school. I believe in education. So, you can work after school and on some weekends. How does that sound?'

"Sounds fine. But there's one other thing, sir."

"What's that?"

"I'm probably going to need someplace to live. When my father finds out I'm working for Shimoda Enterprises, I'm sure he'll throw me out."

"We have rooms. That is no problem whatsoever."

Eiji nods.

"We'll make Monday your first day."

***

The Gaijin House is all lit up when Ryan returns. He sees Jon sitting in the common area. The tall Englishman waves him over.

"How's it going?"

"Been better," Ryan says. "Got thrown out of a gym in Yokosuka, today."

Jon bobs his head knowingly. "They don't call us gaijin for nothing. For decades — centuries even — they forbade Westerners from even stepping onto the island."

"Well, you said it wouldn't be easy."

"The more Japanese you learn, the easier it'll get," Jon says. "They'll respect you for learning the language. Finding a job would be a good idea, too. It'll help you pick up words quicker and give you an opportunity to mix with the people."

"I could use the money."

"There's that, too. I know a club in Shibuya that's always looking for bouncers."

Ryan thinks a minute.

I could do that.

"I can handle myself," Ryan says.

"That's what I was thinking. . ."

***

The train pulls up to Shibuya station. Like everywhere else in Japan, the compartment is crowded, thronged with commuters and shoppers and families. The doors open onto a platform crawling with still more people coming and going. Ryan threads his way toward the stairs. He finds himself stuck behind an older woman who's shuffling along, bags in both hands. He moves to go around her to the left, but it's too thick with people. He tries the right. Same. He resigns himself to shambling along behind her. Nobody around him seems to mind the slow pace.

Ryan loosens up a bit and goes with the flow. He reaches the base of the stairs and follows the crowd out to the road, which is a massive square with soaring billboards and stores and restaurants and skyscrapers pushing up into the heavens. In the center rests a statue of Hachiko, the famed Akita dog who journeyed to Shibuya station every day to wait for his owner to arrive back from work, continuing a whole decade after the man's death. Unsure which way to go, Ryan pulls a wrinkled map from the back pocket of his jeans, makes his best guess, and takes the street that veers towards the left.

Seems to be more lights that way.

He treks up a hill and is surprised to see the place he's looking for, the bar wrapped in stainless steel called Womb, which Jon told him about. The heavy black door is closed. Clearly the club only opens in the evening. Ryan grabs the large handle and gives it a yank anyway. He's surprised – and pleased – to find the door opens, and he steps inside.

It's as bright as a cave, despite the daylight outside. Its interior is like a small arena with a long bar stretching along the right side of the place, neon yellow Sapporo and red Yamazaki signs glowing above mirrors that run the length of the counter. Bottles of every kind of liquor imaginable line the two shelves above the mirror. Because of the bustle outside and the sheer scale of the place, Ryan is surprised how quiet it is. He looks up at a massive speaker array.

Bet it isn't quiet when those are on.

Kamiya-san, a dapper middle-aged man, smokes at the end of the bar, four fingers in a glass in front of him. He looks up at Ryan and waves him over, and Ryan notices he's wearing tinted shades, even though he's in the dark indoors.

"You Jon friend," the man says, nodding his head up and down.

"Yes, sir."

"You have visa?"

Ryan shows him his passport.

"That tourist. Cannot work." He looks Ryan up and down and slowly sips from his drink. He thinks a minute.

"I pay you under table. Ok? No record."

Ryan grins.

"You start tonight," the man nods, returning to his drink as if Ryan were no longer there. He turns and looks over his shoulder. "Tonight? Tonight."

"Yes, sir. Yoroshiku onegaishimasu" Ryan says, attempting to use what little of the language he knows.

***

"Son, you are a disappointment." As Eiji suspected, his father evicts him.

Eiji glowers at him for a moment and then picks up his bags. He doesn't have much that he cares about, and Shimoda-san said he'd buy him a whole new wardrobe. He carries his belongings out the front door, and there, right on time, is Shimoda-san's Escalade, parked at the curb. Shimoda-san's lieutenant, Akio, gets out and opens the rear for Eiji to put his stuff.

His father stands on their small porch and glares at Akio.

"A disgrace," he calls to Eiji. "Your mother would weep."

Akio holds the rear passenger door open for Eiji, as if he's the boss.

He gets in without looking back.

***

Eiji settles in quickly. And the first few weeks seem easy enough. He travels with Akio when the lieutenant makes the rounds, collecting. Most people pay up quickly with no trouble. Akio seems to command respect – people bow, act deferential – something Eiji admires about him, especially when he learns that Akio, too, is Zainichi.

There's only one stop where Akio has to get rough. The owner of a curio shop fails to pay and gets mouthy when Akio tells him this is unacceptable.

"I will have the money when I have the money," the shopkeeper says.

"You incurred a debt. And debts must be paid," said Akio.

"I did no such thing. Your thugs told me they would burn my shop if I did not pay tribute to Shimoda-san."

"We are businessmen. Not thugs."

"Businessmen don't extort other businessmen."

"Has your shop prospered since you've been with us?" Akio asks. "Has anyone stolen from you or bothered you in any way?"

"Only you people."

Akio tilts his head to the side, as if he's thinking about what the man said, and he hits him fast and hard in the throat. The small shopkeeper staggers back, his hands clutching his neck. He gasps, chokes, struggling to breathe. Akio shoves him against a wall and holds him up by the lapels.

"You will have the money in a week," he says.

The man's eyes are wide, and he nods frantically.

Akio drops him, and he slumps to the floor, wheezing and clutching his neck.

On the way out, Akio says to Eiji over his shoulder, "next time it's your turn."

But weeks go by before anyone else fails to pay. Eiji begins to think that he won't have to – won't get to – do any collecting. By now, he's looking forward to it, pestering Akio. "When do I get to? Just say the word."

Akio just smiles at him. He never says much.

The missions continue this way for a few weeks. Eiji goes on collection runs with Akio. People seem to recognize them as they walk down the sidewalks and into businesses, and Eiji feels his chest swell a little. He remembers the old saying about warriors: "A samurai, even when he has not eaten, uses a toothpick like a lord."

Good to be known. Feared.

Shimoda-san calls him in to his office one afternoon.

"Eiji, I wanted to get a sense how it was going. Akio says you have caught on quickly, but I thought it would be good to hear from you."

"Thank you, sir. I've found the work enjoyable. Looking forward to being more useful to the organization."

"I'm glad to hear you say that," Shimoda-san says, folding his legs and leaning back in his chair. "We've been having some trouble with another family. They've been encroaching on our territory, and I'm going to have to have words. I'd like you to be there when I do."

"Yes, sir." Eiji says, bowing his head.

"Good," Shimoda-san says. "We'll go this evening. Meet in the courtyard at seven."

***

When Eiji arrives at the appointed time, a half dozen of Shimoda-san's crew are gathered in the courtyard. He's met all of them by now and steps over to stand beside Akio, who's still wearing his shades in the gathering dusk and tips his head ever so slightly in his direction.

"You been on one of these before?" Eiji asks him, leaning in.

"Yes." Akio says quietly.

"What's it like? Will we see any action?"

"Depends."

"On what?"

"Which outfit we're up against."

"Shimoda-san has multiple enemies?"

"All of the families tend to stay out of each other's way. But the Hsu have been intent on expanding into our neighborhoods."

Shimoda-san walks up and claps his hands. One of his big lieutenants opens the door of the Century for him and he slides in. The rest of the men hop into the Escalade, spreading themselves across its three rows. Eiji is in the back, and he watches the city flash by, his face reflected in the window, his hands in his lap. He's neither afraid nor excited, unsure what to expect.

It's just a meeting.

The ride passes quickly.

They must be getting very *close to our territory if we're already there.*

The luxury sedan pulls into the parking lot of a high-end hotel, all glass and chrome and greenery, and the Escalade parks nearby. Eiji piles out with everyone else. He follows Akio and they fall in behind Shimoda-san and several of his bodyguards, walking around back into a garden. Stone-lined paths wander past koi ponds, dotted with green-black bonzai and bright yellow Japanese magnolias, and beds filled with orange poppies and purple azaleas. It isn't hard to pick out who they're meeting, among the nattily clad hotel guests. In one corner sits a group of men in suits, looking much like those who surround Eiji. Big, tatted, impeccably dressed in dark blazers and pants. They all stand when Shimoda-san strides toward a middle-aged man among them.

Seems very confident.

Eiji steps forward to follow Shimoda-san, but Akio puts his hand on his shoulder, and he stops.

Akio says quietly from behind him. "We wait."

Eiji watches as Shimoda-san bows to the short, bald, middle-aged Hong Kong native, whose distinguishing feature is a jagged knife scar down the side of his face. The other man only nods his head, not showing Shimoda-san the same respect.

The two talk, the bald man hardly looking Shimoda-san in the eye. He looks this way, he looks that way, as Shimoda-san tries to converse with him. Eiji can see Shimoda-san beginning to tense up. His back straightens. His hands ball up. It's one of the first signs you look for in an opponent, how you know to be ready if they're going to come at you.

"Are you seeing this?" he says to Akio, whose eyes are hidden by the polarized lenses of his sunglasses and who seems to be taking in everything but the conversation, his head on a swivel.

"Mmm."

"Shimoda-san is not happy."

"No."

"Something going to happen here?"

"Probably."

"Should we be doing anything?"

"Patience."

Eiji lets out a long breath. He paces back and forth, never taking his eyes off the scene. The bald man's goons seem to be inching toward Shimoda-san.

"Don't you think we should. . .?" he says, turning to find himself looking at Akio's back. Members of the other crew have begun to flank them, two on each side.

"Easy," says Akio under his breath.

Their counterparts slowly move toward them from both sides, a coordinated pincer move.

"Not that I'm worried – I can take any three of them – but we're becoming outnumbered."

"Wait. Watch Shimoda-san."

Eiji spins around to see what's happening at the oyabun level. Shimoda-san and the bald Hongkonger are still talking. Shimoda-san gesturing, pointing with some emphasis. The bald man raises his eyebrows and looks off. His bodyguards have closed the distance to Shimoda-san, now standing just ten feet from him. Eiji purses his lip and nods. Shimoda-san seems absolutely unbothered.

"Wait, where's the rest of our. . .?" he says over his shoulder. As he does, he watches Shimoda-san tap his right front suit jacket pocket.

"Ah," he says.

Within a few seconds a black Escalade rolls up behind the bald man's men. He looks over Akio's shoulder to see a gray, late model Century come screaming to a halt. And then another, which looks almost identical. The other crew starts to get nervous. They stop moving toward Eiji and Akio and stop in their tracks, almost as if a policeman had hollered, "freeze."

The Hongkonger recognizes the situation, and his posture changes almost completely. He drops his head. Then picks it up and looks at Shimoda-san in the eyes for the first time. He raises his shoulders and extends his arms out palms up. Shimoda-san grins at him. He leans forward at the waist and gets right up into the guy's face.

"This is more like it," Eiji says.

"I told you, patience," Akio answers. "Shimoda-san has been in the game for a long time. He's not going to come to a meet with a new kid and a single warrior."

"I may be a new kid, but I can hold my own. That's why I'm here."

Akio smirks.

Eiji watches as Shimoda-san lays it on strong. He's now raising his index finger, almost to the other man's nose. He points all around him, making a big circle with his arms, as if to say, all of this is mine.

"Is this a territory thing?"

"Yes."

"Shimoda-san seems to be telling the bald guy this is our turf."

"Yes."

Eiji nods.

Moments later, Shimoda-san bows curtly to the other oyabun. Then he turns to Eiji and Akio, raising his eyebrows at them. He walks toward them and they spread apart, letting him pass. Then they all pile into the Escalade and fade back into the city.

***

The guy's nose breaks easily, snapping like a dead branch beneath Eiji's fist. His head rocks and his hands go right to his face. He staggers back, blood gushing from beneath his fingers.

I didn't think bones were so brittle.

Eiji cocks his arm back again and the man – a slight, middle-aged store clerk – raises his arms in front of him and retreats into the corner of his shop.

"Ok," he says, leaning against the wall, his voice thick because of his crushed nose. "Ok. I'll pay."

"You're right, you'll pay," Eiji says. "Shimoda-san has been very patient, and you are taking advantage of him."

"No, no, no," says the shopkeep, panicking. "I didn't understand. I understand now. I would never try to disrespect Shimoda-san."

"You'd better not. I'll be back for payment in full Friday."

"I'll have it, I'll have it," says the guy, his hands still held out in front of him. "I'll have it all."

Eiji nods. And turns for the door, where Akio waits, nonchalant, shoulder against the doorframe. He nods approvingly, lips pursed. Then claps Eiji on the shoulder as the younger man pushes past him.

That was easy. Fun even. Playing with fear. And power.

They pull open the doors of the Escalade and climb in. Toshi sits in the driver's seat and turns to look at Eiji.

"How'd it go?" he asks.

"Fine. Payment at the end of the week."

"Nice."

Toshi gestures at Eiji's hand. "How's the fist?"

Eiji holds it out. A few flecks of blood are the only evidence of what's taken place. His knuckles are hard and scarred from all the times he's hit the wall. No redness, no swelling.

"Nice," Toshi says, bobbing his head. "You really are a fighter."

I really am a fighter.

Chapter 7

That night, Ryan arrives twenty minutes before Womb opens. He meets another guy about his size out front and makes him immediately as a bouncer. All biceps and pecs, the guy looks Ryan up and down and nods.

"Hey" says Ryan. "I'm the new guy."

"Kiyomiya," says the man.

"Ryan."

They talk for a few minutes as a crowd starts to gather in front of the club, forming a line. Soon, it snakes down the street. The clubgoers are dressed for show. Women in loads of makeup, short skirts, and heels. Men in leather jackets and tight jeans. The relentless beat of house music begins to pound from inside the bar. It's so loud Ryan can feel the bass drum in his chest whenever the door opens.

Kiyomiya waves the first woman forward. He looks over at Ryan. "Check ID. Check customer. No outside drink," he says, stepping aside so the woman can pass.

"Also, check *mayaku*," Kiyomiya says over his shoulder.

Ryan thinks a moment. *Mayaku?* Then he gets it.

"Drugs?" he says.

Kiyomiya grins and punches him on the shoulder. "You do ok."

Kiyomiya gestures at the line. "You do."

Motioning for people to follow him, Kiyomiya walks down the queue and divides the crowd in two. He steps off to the left and starts checking IDs.

***

Eiji accompanies Akio for several weeks. They threaten people. Break noses. Snap fingers. Whatever it takes to get Shimoda-san's money. None of it bothers him in the slightest – if victims crossed Shimoda-san, stole from him, denied him his rightful remuneration, they had it coming – though sometimes he wonders what his father would think. It's a chance to use his skills in the real world, see what it feels like to follow through. Practicing in the dojo always meant holding back. You pull your punches, soften your elbows, restrain your kicks. Now, he's getting a taste for striking someone with full force. It felt powerful.

It felt good.

Eiji is relaxing in the common area at Shimoda-san's compound, a space set up for staff between meals and missions, with a TV, couches, and a bar, when Akio walks in. Always in black, he looks even sharper than usual today. Jacket, button down, slacks, everything pressed and just so. He steps over to the couch and looks down at Eiji.

"Get yourself ready. We're going out."

"Going out?"

"Yeah, clubbing. It's about time we celebrated."

"Celebrated?"

"Yeah, Shimoda-san is making you a full crewmember this week."

"What's that about?"

"Well, you've been *jun-kosei-in* long enough. Shimoda-san thinks you're ready for the next step – *kumi-in.*

"Soldier?"

"Yeah, that's what you are, right?"

"Yeah."

"Well, he's going to reward your loyalty. I'm pretty sure it's happening this week. So, we celebrate."

"*Okay. . .*"

"Wear that jacket we got you. Maybe bathe for once." Akio gives Eiji one of his rare half smiles. "I'll be back in an hour to pick you up."

***

Ryan waves at the guy at the head of the line in front of him.

Short, smirking, with slicked back hair, the clubgoer hands Ryan his ID. Ryan scans it but has no idea what the characters say. He looks at the picture. Glances up at the fellow.

That's him.

He has the guy open his jacket and spin around. The guy flips his smirk upside down but complies. Ryan sees no sign of booze or drugs or weapons and jerks his thumb toward the door. The next guy steps up.

Ryan begins to get the hang of things, but his line remains much longer than Kiyomiya's. Some of the clubgoers are getting restless, waiting.

He feels a tap on his left shoulder. Ryan turns to find Jon grinning at him. His white shirt is stuck to his chest and sweat drips down his face.

"How's it going?"

"Okay. Hard to read the IDs."

"Give it time. It'll come."

Ryan hears a commotion from Kiyomiya's line. A rugged guy is entering the building followed by a group of beautiful women and a few other big men. Ryan only gets a glimpse, but it's enough to recognize him. He's seen him hundreds of times before. Ryan grins and turns to Jon.

"Who's that chap?" the Englishman asks.

"One of the best, the heavyweight champ Enson Inoue. He's an MMA legend. I gotta say hello."

Ryan turns to follow the Japanese-American superstar but so has everyone else. Kiyomiya glares at him, as if to say, get back to your post. Ryan shrugs and resumes checking IDs. Jon smiles and pounds him on the shoulder.

The line seems endless. Kiyomiya continues to let people in, so Ryan does as well.

How many people does this place hold?

***

The club is called Womb. Akio's gathered together a bunch of other relatively new Shimoda family members, including Toshi, who sits next to Eiji in the third row of the Escalade.

"I thought you had been working for Shimoda-san for a lot longer," Eiji says.

"Nah, I started just before we met."

"You made it seem like you practically ran the organization. Like one of Shimoda-san's chief lieutenants."

Toshi shrugs.

"He told me to start recruiting, so I recruited. Would it have enticed you if I told you I was a nobody?"

"So, you're part of the family, like me?"

"You're not in just yet. . ."

"Akio says it's supposed to happen soon."

Toshi nods, looks out the window.

Two of the other new recruits, Haru and Daiki, sit in front of them, joking loudly.

Eiji looks at Toshi and rolls his eyes.

The pair of them are an embarrassment. . .

Before he knows it, they're pulling up to a club in the Shibuya district. The façade is dark and sleek and steel covered, fronting right up to the curb. Doesn't look huge.

They all thread out of the Escalade and follow Akio to the door. A couple of big bouncers look them up and down, and they push past them into the dimly interior. Bass thumps constantly, like a heartbeat. They stop at the bar and get drinks. Haru and Daiki both get Yamato Takeda for each hand.

"It's on Shimoda-san" Haru says elbowing Eiji playfully. Eiji leans low across the bar and says "ginger ale" to the barkeep, who looks at him, surprised.

113

"Ginger ale? What are you, a lightweight?"

Tall and gangly, his suit jacket too big for his slender frame, Haru pokes Eiji in the chest with his glass. Eiji shrugs.

"Somebody has to look after us."

"Aw, come on, little man," Haru says.

The Zainichi fixes him with a look. Haru recognizes power when he sees it and turns back to Daiki.

Eiji's father drank too much, and he never liked coming home to find him drunk and surly, smelling like sake. He didn't want to ever be like that, either. Eiji hated the idea of being out of control. If a fight came, he wanted to be fully functional. He knew that alcohol dulled senses and slowed response. People often said they drank to take the edge off. Eiji wanted that edge – honed so sharp it cut.

Ginger ale looked like alcohol in the glass, so most people wouldn't make an issue of it. Drinkers always had a compunction for not wanting to drink if other people weren't drinking, like they felt guilty about it. They wanted you complicit.

Eiji sips his drink and follows Akio and Toshi into the dark. Suddenly strobes begin to flash, like a lightning storm, and he can see how cavernous the club is. The ceilings soar for several stories above, and the dance floor never ends, packed with gyrating bodies. Eiji picks his way through them, behind Akio. For such a tight place, he's surprised how people part ways and make a path when they see Akio coming.

They know him.

Their entourage walks beyond the dance floor, past a glass half wall to the VIP lounge, where leather couches await beneath lightly glowing lamps. Haru and Daiki have finished both their drinks by the time they sit, and they flag down a waitress. She's lovely, Japanese, with a blond bob, a tight top, and stiletto heels.

Haru leers at her.

"Well, look at this. . ."

Both Eiji and Akio glare at him, and he squirms awkwardly into the booth.

Eiji scans the place. This isn't really his idea of celebrating. Too loud to talk. Not interested in getting drunk. Dancing's for the brain dead. He watches a few girls nearby who are grinding like mad to the deafening trance techno.

That's not bad, though.

Daiki and Haru pound back a couple more drinks. Daiki has no neck but still manages to bob his head to the hammering beat. After a minute he puts his face next to Eiji.

"Going dancing."

Eiji nods.

Better out there than here.

The music throbs, and the crowd is like a single organism, writhing and rocking.

Gives me a headache.

Daiki and Haru climb over Eiji on their way to the throng. Haru pushes Eiji's head down on his way out of the booth. It's meant to be affectionate, but Eiji grabs his hand and executes a *torite* joint lock, spinning his arm around and twisting his wrist up, pulling the taller man toward the floor, putting pressure on his hand. If he wanted, he could break the joint. Instead, he growls into Haru's ear: "Don't touch me."

Haru squirms, trying to pull his arm out.

"Okay, okay."

Eiji lets go, locking eyes. Haru's are red and heavy lidded from the booze, and Eiji sees fear there.

Daiki puts his arm around Haru, steering him toward the dance floor, attempting to lighten the mood.

Haru wrenches sideways and weaves his way out into the fray.

Eiji studies the pair of them, slithering up to women, bobbing their heads to the music. He leans over to Akio.

"What does Shimoda-san see in those two?"

"Youth, anger, willingness."

Eiji nods.

He watches as Haru runs his hands along the ass of a woman dancing with her back to him. She turns and tries to slap him, but he ducks. He smiles at her. She and her two girlfriends push their way through the crowd to get away from him.

Eiji shakes his head. Akio just smiles.

The waitress comes back. "Can I top off your drinks?"

Akio hands her his glass. Eiji put his hand over his. As this is happening, the music stops, and he can hear yelling from the dance floor. He turns to see the bodies parting and a scuffle happening. Who's at the center of it? Haru.

Fucking asshole.

***

After a half hour, the queue finally slows. As it does, Ryan hears a huge outcry from inside the building during a break in the music. He looks at Kiyomiya. Kiyomiya looks at him. They push open the door. The floor is thronged, a wall of bodies, and the place is electric with lights, techno, and body heat. Ryan can see a twenty-something drunk at the back waving his arms and pushing a commissionaire.

Ryan elbows his way across the throbbing dance floor until he reaches the troublemaker, and he slips his hands around the man, pinning his arms back. The guy struggles and tries to wrench himself away from Ryan, almost successfully as he's so slimy with perspiration. Ryan drags him across the dance floor. Enson watches the kerfuffle with interest from a raised table at the back.

"I see you found a dance partner," Jon says as Ryan passes by him.

Ryan smiles over his shoulder, grips the guy tighter, and hauls him toward the door.

Tall and slender, the man continues to wriggle, trying to free himself.

Ryan maintains his grip and makes it past the bar to the entryway. Kiyomiya opens the door for him, and Ryan gives the guy a shove down the ramp and onto the pavement. The offender hops to his feet and spins to face Ryan. His black silk button-down shirt is open, revealing an intricate tattoo. He screams, swinging his arms wildly. Ryan can't quite make out the dialect, but it doesn't sound like the Japanese he's heard so far. The man stumbles toward the parking area, and Ryan heads back inside.

Ryan sits on a stool just inside the door. The beat continues to hammer, lights bouncing off mirrors. The huge mass of people is jumping up and down, all in sync with the music, dancing with each other, dancing with themselves. Some are draped over each other at the bar. He notices some women looking at him and smiles.

Jon wanders up to him, his head bobbing with the beat. He leans into Ryan's right ear.

"You know that guy was yakuza, right?"

"Yawhat?"

"Ya-Ku-Za," Jon says slowly. "Japanese mafia."

Ryan looks at him.

"How can you tell?"

"His tats. Dead giveaway. You need to watch out. Be careful."

"Just doing my job."

"I know, but you don't want them to start just doing theirs. They're dangerous people."

"I'll keep that in mind."

Jon pats him on the shoulder and weaves his way back toward the bar.

***

Haru's was shoving a smaller guy, who was standing his ground. Eiji noticed the tats showing at the guy's wrists. Haru cocked his arm back to take a swing, when a rugged-looking gaijin bouncer grabbed it. He was short but stout and spun Haru around, yanking his arm up behind his back. Haru thrashed but the bouncer exerted pressure. A

Japanese bouncer waded into the sea of bodies and made an opening for his partner, who pushed Haru before him toward the door.

Eiji watched until Akio tapped him on the shoulder and nodded at the exit, and they slid out of their booth.

So much for celebrating.

In the parking lot they found Haru on the ground, laughing.

"You," Eiji says, stabbing him in the chest with his index finger, "are a fucking idiot."

Akio steps between them. Pushes Eiji backwards toward the Escalade.

"Enough. Let's go."

"We can't leave," Eiji says, straightening his jacket.

"What do you mean, we can't leave?" Akio asks.

"The gaijin put his hands on a member of our family." Eiji bobs his head with distaste at Haru. "That can't stand."

Akio looks at him for a minute. Then he nods.

"We'll wait."

***

As Ryan opens the door to leave, he notices Enson and his entourage at the edge of the parking lot. The MMA champ is chatting with some fans and stops to sign an autograph. Jogging down the ramp toward him, Ryan notices something flying out of the shadows to his left. A figure rushes at him, followed by a half dozen others. The American turns to face the one closest and recognizes the guy he threw out earlier, who steps toward him and launches a haymaker at his head. As he does so, the others swarm, throwing punches and kicks. Ryan blocks the first few and manages to send several of his attackers to the pavement, but he's overwhelmed. He keeps swinging until he can't anymore.

Everything is a blur, and he hears someone yelling. The men around him begin to back away. Enson and his entourage have come to Ryan's aid, punching, wrestling, and beating on the gang until the hoodlums scatter. When Ryan staggers to his feet, he sees a man in his mid-thirties leaning against a car, smoking. He's dressed in black and watching the whole scene, expressionless. The thugs run toward him, and the man flicks his cigarette away and gets into the back of a black, late-model Escalade.

Ryan feels something smash into his jaw, and he buckles to the curb, his head coming down hard on the tarmac. Enson yells something, and the final members of the gang retreat. They recognize him and want no part of a fight with the world champion.

"You okay, braddah?" Enson asks, kneeling down beside Ryan.

Ryan raises his head and attempts a smile. Then his eyes roll back in his head and everything recedes into black.

***

"Something to think about," Akio says. He and Eiji sit on a bench at a warehouse in Kabukicho. It's a big open space, with a small office off to one side, where

Shimoda-san is in a meeting with one of the other families. Akio keeps his head on the swivel, always watchful.

"You can fight better than anyone else in the crew."

Eiji nods.

"Think you'd do well."

"Fighting MMA?" Eiji looks around the warehouse. "What do I get out of it?"

"Fame and fortune." Akio pulls down his shades and raises his eyebrows. "And a cool nickname."

Eiji smirks.

Getting paid to fight. . .

"I like the sound of that."

"I think you'd be good at it. Another way to be an asset for Shimoda-san. He's putting some real money in, and you could help him get some out. And you could make a name for yourself. Money for you would be better than you're making now. You could really put your skills to the test."

Eiji gives him another wry, half smile.

"You ever go to these fights?"

"Of course," Akio says. "I told you, Shimoda-san is getting in on the action. So, I've been doing my homework."

"Mostly Muay Thai? Striking and clinch fighting?"

"A lot of that. But it's pretty brutal, no-holds barred stuff. A lot of jiu-jitsu and wrestling too. Even stomps on the ground. Most of the fighters have their preferred skillset, but everybody comes ready to throw down."

"I'm not the biggest."

"They have weight classes, just like in boxing and kickboxing."

"Hmmm."

"Look, if you're interested, I'll take you to a gym where several of our fighters train."

"You already have fighters?"

"Are you listening? Shimoda-san is getting into this. Several other families are already making a lot of money off MMA. Some serious yen. Crowds can be huge. People like to see other people beat the shit out of each other."

"Like gladiators," Eiji says.

"Just like gladiators," Akio agrees.

***

Ryan opens his eyes. He's surrounded by white curtains. He can feel the blood pounding in his head – every part of him throbs. He pulls himself up on his elbows to have a look around, and as soon as he puts weight on his left arm, his shoulder screams. He can hear people talking and a faint beeping far off. A hospital.

The club. Enson. Yakuza.

Voices get louder, footsteps shuffle toward his bed, the curtain draws back, and a doctor steps in. He looks just a little bit older than Ryan and has the tan of a surfer. He stops at the end of the bed and picks up a clipboard.

Old enough to have finished med school?

"Hello Ryan, Doctor Yuzawa. How you feel?"

"My left shoulder hurts. My head is pounding."

"You got beat good. Suffered severe damage. An orderly will take you for MRI, so we know if intra-cranial bleeding. I have nurse give you something more for the pain."

Ryan slumps back into his bed.

As promised, a young Japanese woman appears a little while later and unlocks the brakes on Ryan's bed, wheeling him out from behind the hanging curtains that create his little room. The hospital is massive, labyrinthine, and it seems like a half hour goes by before she pushes him through double doors into a bright white room with a towering, futuristic pod in the middle.

The MRI operator helps Ryan move onto a slimmer bed. As he slides off his and climbs onto it, he notices pain in areas he's never even felt before. He breathes through his nose the way Sensei Chan taught him. In and out, in and out. It helps. He shifts back and forth to find the most comfortable position.

The MRI operator explains the procedure.

"Are you claustrophobic? It will feel tight in there."

"Not that I know of."

"Good. Lie back. This will take a while."

She rolls him toward the massive round cylinder, with what looks like a long tongue in front.

Something out of a sci-fi movie.

He shifts on to a bed on the tongue, and places his head in a U-shaped pillow, as the operator straps him in. She puts ear plugs in his ears and then pulls a big ring into place around his cranium, before sliding him in. As his bed enters the machine, like a train heading into a tunnel, Ryan hears a head-splitting noise that sounds like a ship's horn as its docking. The curved white walls are extremely close on all sides, and he feels a twinge of panic, so he closes his eyes and resumes his breathing exercise. He's always been amazed how much it helps. The machine beeps and pings, echoing all around him.

A short while later, the same orderly arrives to take him back to his room, where he finds Jon sitting in a chair. Unshaven. Wrinkled. Bedraggled. His long legs crossed in front of him, one shoe untied. He looks almost as bad as Ryan feels. The young Japanese woman parks Ryan's bed, steps on the brake, and leaves. Jon gets up and stands by the bedside.

"Hey mate, how're you doing?"

"Waiting to hear. Just had an MRI. Doctor said I suffered 'severe damage.'"

"It didn't look good."

"You were still there? It was practically dawn when I got jumped."

"A bloody habit of mine, it seems."

"Did you see what happened?"

"Yeah, I was just coming out of the club. Kamiya-san told me I had to leave." He chuckles. Then turns serious. "It was pretty brutal. That's how it goes with those kind of guys. Not a crew to mess with."

"I guess I already messed up."

"Did you notice who was standing by the cars?"

"I saw a well-dressed guy over there observing."

"That's Akio. He's *shateigashira*."

"Which is. . .?"

"A mid-level lieutenant. Don't you know him?"

"Should I?"

"Well, he not only runs a yakuza crew, he runs much of MMA here. You're going to have to get used to dealing with them if you want to break into the business."

Ryan steadies his head with his hand.

"They're involved with MMA?"

"Quite. They've been in from pretty much the beginning here in Japan. When the first promotional company got started here, mob money was involved. Now, they're everywhere."

A nurse walks into the room carrying a cup with pills in it. She notices Jon.

"Sir, visiting hours are over."

"Ah, my cue to leave." He gives her a bow and does the same towards Ryan.

***

I could take all of these guys.

From the mat-covered wall where he leans, Eiji watches two sets of aspiring MMA fighters sparring. The gym is brightly lit, smells like new and old sweat, and is filled with a bunch of twenty-somethings lifting weights, jumping rope, shadow boxing, pummeling Thai pads, and exchanging blows. Eiji only recognizes one of them, a skinny Tokyo native who rode to a meeting with Shimoda-san. The kid has fast hands and feet but looks like he'd go over in a heap if any square blow connected.

Too much hair in his face, too. How's he see through all that?

Eiji watches for a few minutes before Akio comes back from the gym's office.

"And?" Akio says.

"I could level any two of them," Eiji says.

"Two, huh?"

"Give me three."

"I would pay to see that," Akio says with a grin. "But I guess that's the idea."

Eiji shrugs and watches the action. The kid he recognizes has his opponent reeling, hammering him with a barrage of fists. The guy finally falls to the canvas and holds his hands over his head in submission.

"That's our best guy so far," Akio says. "You meet him yet?"

"We rode in the Escalade together once."

"Hmmm. Well, he's got talent. Shimoda-san likes him. We're going to book him on the amateur circuit and see how he does."

"He's okay," says Eiji. "But he drops his hands a lot. When fighters have long reach – and are used to winning – they get a bit too comfortable, thinking they can't be hit. Any experienced fighter will notice that, get inside, and drop him."

Akio nods, listening.

"Unless he learns to keep his hands up."

Eiji watches as a couple of fighters touch gloves. Swapping in for one of them is another tall Japanese combatant.

"Wait, is that Haru?" he asks.

Akio shrugs. "Wanted to give it a go. Been a few times now."

"You got to be kidding. He couldn't even handle that Gaijin bouncer."

"He's really not bad. Watch."

Eiji sizes up Haru. When he takes off his shirt, he's more buff than Eiji expected. He bounces up and down on his feet and stretches his neck in a circular motion. Then he bangs his gloves together and steps out onto the bright red mat. He gives a polite bow to his opponent, another local fighter who's all arms and legs. They tap gloves and begin to circle.

Haru launches into an onslaught of punches the other fighter easily sidesteps. Eiji raises his eyebrows at Akio.

"Give him a chance. . ."

Haru's opponent responds with a couple of jabs and a teep, his long leg shooting out. Haru catches the kick and moves in, delivering a couple of hammering blows to the guy's mid-section. One lands clean on the liver. He buckles. Haru then pastes him on the chin with a downward right cross, which drops the guy to his back.

Nice combo.

Struggling to get back to his knees, the guy admits defeat. Haru helps him up and then steps to the side for a towel.

"Gotta say, I'm surprised," Eiji says. "Didn't think he had it in him. I wouldn't help him up, though."

"You've never worked with him," Akio says. "I've seen him level a few customers."

"Behind the goofy, asshole exterior lies. . ." Eiji jokes. Akio chuckles.

Haru notices the pair of them and bobs over, grinning.

"Fellas," he says, executing a stage bow.

"Nicely done," Akio says.

"Not bad," Eiji agrees.

"Well, we've all heard how tough *you* are," Haru says, pretending to jab Eiji in the belly.

Eiji looks at him coolly.

"You think you could take me?" Haru asks. He's bubbling with confidence.

"I know I can," Eiji responds.

"You want to give it a go?" Haru gestures toward the mat.

"Sometime. . ." Eiji says.

"Oh, I see. . ." Haru jests, smiling at him. "What are you afraid of?"

The look Eiji gives him stops him cold.

"Yeah, okay. Cool. Some other time."

"Some other time," Eiji says.

Chapter 8

Noise at the end of his bed rouses Ryan. He sees the doctor from the previous day, Doctor Yuzawa, who again reaches down and grabs his clipboard, this time flipping to the second page. Behind him is a fifty-something black woman in a lab coat.

Doctor Yuzawa glances at him and says in halting English, "Hello Ryan, feel better?"

"A little, thank you."

Dr. Yuzawa reaches behind him and puts his hand on the shoulder of the woman, stepping to the side to allow her to approach the bed.

"Ryan. This Doctor Canady."

"Hello Ryan," she says in perfect English. "I'm a neurosurgeon, and I've been asked to consult on your case."

"Your English is excellent doctor."

"I'm from the U.S."

"Me, too, whereabouts?"

"Lansing, Michigan."

"I grew up in Grand Rapids."

"The Winter Wonderland," she says with a smile.

Dr. Yuzawa looks confused.

"That's what people call Michigan," Ryan says.

Dr. Canady leans in to look at Ryan's eyes. He notices her perfume.

"I'm going to need to steady your face to get a good look at your pupils."

"Yes, ma'am," Ryan replies.

Doctor Canady puts her hands on Ryan's temples and looks intently into his eyes.

"Was it a typical TRPM7 situation?" she asks over her shoulder. "Cell-tissue atrophy, standard degeneration, cyst growth in replacement?"

"Intrauterine stroke, correct. Loss of blood flow and oxygen to 4.3 centimeters of parietal and 4.7 centimeters of temporal."

"Both parietal and temporal?"

Doctor Canady takes Ryan's file and removes MRI scans, placing them on a light wall at the side of the room. She looks at the images a moment with her arms crossed and then steps forward, sucking in her breath. She draws Yuzawa over to the glowing pictures, pointing. They murmur under their breath.

Ryan moves for a better angle, but he can't make out what they're seeing.

"Fascinating," says Dr. Canady. "It might be ten centimeters."

She turns to Ryan.

"How often do you feel dizzy?"

"Maybe once a day."

Both doctors looked surprised.

Canady: "Ryan, do you have any difficulty hearing? Smelling? Feeling? Trouble with any of the senses?"

"My hearing isn't the best in my left ear. And, I have issues with peripheral vision. Not much other than that."

Doctor Canady brings the scan over to Ryan's bed. On it is a baseball-size lump embedded in his brain. She points to it.

"This is a cyst. Most people with brain cysts this size suffer from cerebral palsy. They're in wheelchairs."

Ryan's mouth opens but nothing comes out.

"Growths like this exert a lot of pressure on the brain and typically cause equilibrium issues. They usually result in a host of problems – visual acuity, depth perception, all kinds of things. On a day-to-day basis."

Ryan takes a deep breath to steady himself.

"What are you saying doc?" he asks.

"What I'm saying is, I'm amazed you're upright and walking. Working as a bouncer. And I want you to know that another blow to the head like the one that sent you here could leave you blind. Or even dead."

Ryan is quiet. He holds his hands together in his lap then looks up. "Doc, I came here to fight Mixed Martial Arts."

"Woah, absolutely not," Doctor Canady says. "That's a death sentence. If you take another hard hit, it will lead to intracranial pressure. She looks down at him. "Swelling of the brain. Now imagine your brain swelling and pushing against that hard mass. Concussions are bad for anyone, but when you already have an unyielding mass in your skull. . ."

"Doc, I've been training my whole life for this."

"I'm sorry, Ryan," she says. "But yours is a very serious condition. I'm surprised you haven't suffered more ill effects."

"You'll be released later today, Mr. Bow," Doctor Yuzawa says. "Do take care."

The physicians leave Ryan. He turns and looks out the window. He puts his chin on his chest and lets out a long breath.

A nurse steps in a minute later.

"Mr. Bow," she says struggling with English. "Mr. Inoue come see you when you were sleeping. He want you have this."

She passes him a piece of paper with Enson Inoue's phone number on it.

***

Eiji's first fight lasts all of two minutes. It's a small, local, unofficial night in a tiny neighborhood auditorium. After jockeying side to side, he eats a roundhouse kick to the thigh from his opponent, a Filipino Muay Thai fighter. Eiji smirks and presses forward. The next kick comes to Eiji's body. This time, he catches it and thrusts a downward elbow to the guy's thigh. It's an illegal move, but the ref doesn't see it. Eiji hears the "oosh" as the Filipino backpedals, and he pounces. The fighter stumbles, lowering his head. Eiji steps forward and lays him out with a headshot.

That progresses him to the next round. This time his opponent is a tall, lanky Japanese guy with face tattoos.

His reach must be incredible.

It was indeed long, and the fighter tagged Eiji twice in the head before he even knew what happened.

Fast, too. First blood.

Eiji wipes red from his lip and pushes forward.

Not going to let that happen again.

The next time the guy throws a jab, Eiji slips his head off center. Spins and fires a spinning heel kick to the solar plexus. That staggers him back, gasping. Eiji keeps after him, on the offensive. The fighter retreats, trying to get away and regroup. Eiji never lets him get far, throwing punch after punch. Finally, he pummels the guy to the body again, which makes him bend forward. When he does, Eiji meets him with a knee to the chin that drops him. Eiji keeps on landing blows until the referee grabs him around the waist. He shakes the ref off and stands over the guy, the ref in between them. The whole fight takes about a minute.

"*Yaru ne!* Take no prisoners," Akio says on the drive back to the compound. Eiji has rarely seen Akio lose his cool, but tonight he seems genuinely excited.

"I thought you were all talk, just bragging, but you really did it. I like your kill or be killed style. Like a Kamikaze." Akio slaps the wheel and grins. "Nicely done."

"When can I fight again?"

"Takes a bit to set these things up," Akio says. "But I'll get on it." He stares at the road ahead, suddenly quiet, thinking. Then he looks over at Eiji.

133

"What about Eiji 'Kamikaze' Tanaka. Has a ring to it."

Eiji nods, looks out the window.

Akio worked tirelessly, and within a few weeks, Kamikaze was in the ring again. The crowd loved him, the way he nodded when he took a blow, as if to say, "Go ahead, show me what you got." They loved how he showed no mercy, viciously knocking out his opponents, and shoving the refs aside to hit them when they're down. And they went crazy when he'd jump on the top rope afterwards, fists raised high, and back flip off the ropes to the center of the ring. The fight money started to increase as well, providing Eiji with a level of comfort he'd never known before. Akio was ecstatic, and the boss seemed happy, too, paying him extra attention whenever he was in the compound.

Imagine if my father ever treated me like that.

Akio kept booking one fight after the next until, only ten months after he first entered the ring, Kamikaze had won his first championship, his face plastered on the sides of billboards, the newly crowned Impact World Champion. Now, whenever he went out in the evenings to collect for Shimoda-san, he was treated like a celebrity. Some shopkeepers would beg on their hands and knees for forgiveness to avoid upsetting Kamikaze Tanaka.

It happened fast.

***

Ryan's bag gets stuck in the doors of the train. His injured shoulder is in a sling, so he only has one arm to tug it out. He gives it a yank, and his water bottle slips out and rolls onto the platform. The train is about to pull away from the station, and he steps out to grab it.

A hand holds it up for him. Ryan looks up to find a Japanese woman smiling at him. Twenty-something, she's obviously a commuter, waiting for another train. She withdraws her arm and pulls her silky hair back behind her ear. Ryan smiles at her, captivated.

"Arigatou," he says, bowing his head.

"I hate it when that happens," she says in English, looking deeply into his eyes.

The doors close shut and the train begins to move.

She holds his gaze as the train pulls away from the station.

By now there are hardly any seats left. Ryan finds the last available one and sits down.

What just happened?

The middle-aged woman in the seat next to him pulls her bag tighter, stands up, and moves away.

What beauty.

Ryan looks out the glass, and he can't stop thinking about her. Yokohama melds into the great urban metropolis of Tokyo. Everywhere buildings and people. Rows and rows of apartments in little square towers flash by. The green landscape of the samurai has been gobbled up by pavement and steel, a city marching endlessly to the horizon. The colorful billboards, flashing neon, and street signs are unrelenting. And so are the hordes.

Never seen so many people in my life. I'd like to see her again. . .

Fighting Blind

The congestion never lets up all the way into the city. The train slows slightly as it enters an area packed with mom-and-pop shops hawking groceries, TVs, booze, CDs – everything under the sun. Interspersed between them are restaurants of all types. If it weren't for all the Japanese calligraphy on signs, it would look pretty much like every other city he'd been in. Ryan recognizes the characters for Meguro – he'd had Jon show him what to look for before he left. He transfers to the subway on his way to Shirogane-Takanawa station.

This is the place.

He disembarks at the next station, following a flood out onto the sidewalks. He and Jon also mapped the route, giving him a basic idea where he's going, and he walks six blocks north from the station, then takes a right and goes a couple more, beyond the fine dining and upscale shops Minato is known for. An area of warehouses, alleys, and non-descript low-slung buildings sits straight ahead. He crosses the road and heads for it.

Guess the rent must be cheap here.

He studies the signs until he finds the address he's looking for. It's a rundown old structure several stories tall, looking like nothing more than a beat-up box. Ryan enters, stepping around the wind-blown trash in the foyer. He pauses and looks over the building's directory in the dull fluorescent light, finding his destination on the fourth floor, then wanders down the hallway until he finds the cock-eyed doors of an elevator. He pushes the up button, and, when the door bings open, he climbs on, thumbing the number 4. Graffiti litters the walls and cigarette butts the floor. When he steps out, he sees the Japanese symbol for 5, giving him pause.

Pretty sure I pushed four.

He wanders down the hall and hears familiar sounds. He stops outside a clear door that says – in both Japanese and English – Purebred Tokyo. He takes a breath and pushes it.

The entryway is immaculate and brightly lit. The walls are whitewashed, accented with modern-looking black stripes. Ryan can hear fighters sparring over the pumping bass of P. Diddy's "Bad Boy for Life." No one is at the clean, spare desk, so he pokes his head around the corner.

Along one wall, about a dozen chiseled, shirtless guys in black-and-yellow shorts lift weights, do sit ups, and jump rope. In a corner, two grizzled, gloved warriors exchange blows in a ring, with trainers at the ropes urging them on. Ryan watches for a moment, impressed by their skills. They look much older than him and yet so dangerous. A handful of other fighters train in pairs on the mats at the base of the ring, sparring or working on Thai pads. Ryan recognizes one of them. In his early twenties, the guy is covered in tattoos, and Ryan remembers him from Enson's crew at the fight in the Womb parking lot. The guy clocks Ryan, his eyes fixed on the newcomer.

Ryan spots Enson walking among the students, a pit bull keeping pace with him.

That must be the purebred.

Enson pauses to talk to one short fighter, demonstrates how to control and punch from the S-mount position. He steadies himself by grabbing the far arm of the fighter on bottom, pinches his knees for control, and then thrusts a few hammer fists downwards, stopping just before the

137

bridge of the student's nose, in a lightning-quick motion. The student nods and tries to do the same. It's a close approximation but without any of the speed or power Enson generated. Inoue pats him on the back and then notices Ryan. He smiles and strides toward him, extending his hand, his pup at his heels

"Ryan!"

"Mr. Inoue. Thanks for the invite." Ryan gives him a wry grin. "And for saving my life."

"I figured you didn't plan on dying that night."

Enson puts his hand on his dog's head. "This is Shooto-kun."

The terrier looks up with happy eyes. Ryan notices his name is sheared into his fur in Japanese.

"Shooto?" Ryan laughs. "Just like the MMA promotion."

"You know it."

Ryan holds his hand out for the pitty to sniff, it does so and then offers a little lick.

"He likes you," Enson smiles. Then he's all serious. "You can scrap, braddah. Did well, considering how outnumbered you were."

"Thanks."

"I want to give you a chance to level up your skills."

Ryan can't believe it and just stares at him.

"We'll sponsor your training," Enson says, gesturing at the room behind him. "We can help you get a work visa if you need one, too."

Amazed, Ryan just stands there looking at him, the silence awkward.

"Let me know, if that's something you'd be interested in." Enson laughs.

"I'd love that. Thank you so much!" Ryan blurts out.

Enson bobs his head, pleased. He points to Ryan's shoulder sling.

"Take care of that. Let me know when you're ready."

And the champ and Shooto return to the action.

***

It's cold. Ryan's breath clouds up in front of him, like a cigarette smoker stepping outside for a break.

I didn't know it got like this in Japan.

Ryan's sling is tucked in a down jacket, the puffy sleeve floating uselessly, and he walks in place as he waits for Jon at Kamakura station, trying to keep warm before the pair board the Enoden train. A camera dangles from his neck, and he wonders what below-zero temps do to electronics. A train pulls up, pauses, and then clangs on down the tracks.

Ryan smells cigarette smoke, but that's omnipresent in Japan.

"Hey, mate."

He turns to see Jon striding up, butt in hand.

"Appreciate you playing tour guide."

Jon grins. "No worries. Beats a guidebook, for sure."

They make their way into the station. Jon reads the signage and buys two tickets from the automated machine, handing one to Ryan.

So much easier when you can read.

The pair take seats across from one another, Ryan sprawling, Jon folding his tall form as compactly as he can in seats designed for someone smaller. A Japanese man walks up, looks at the two of them, and plops next to Jon. Ryan takes the hint and sits up, with his knees together.

The train weaves through Kamakura's residential area, some distance from the scenic coastal views the Enoden is known for.

"This was one of the medieval capitals of Japan," Jon says as the train pulls into the station.

"These days it's more of a tourist destination, because of its historical significance, beaches, and the mountains." They exit and start walking down a major thoroughfare.

"Because it was a shogunate, there are several major temples and shrines here. The mountains wrap around on three sides, and the sea covers the other, making the place a strategic stronghold."

After walking about twenty minutes, they reach the Kotoku Buddhist Temple and stroll the grounds. A statue of the Buddha rises like a giant over the landscape, towering over the traditional single-story buildings.

"Oh, man," says Ryan, grabbing his camera and jogging up the long, wide flight of stairs that lead to the sculpture's base.

"That must be fifty-feet tall."

The Buddha is draped in robes and sits with his legs crossed, head slightly inclined with his eyes closed and a meditative look on his face. Serene. Green hills trundle away behind him.

"Actually 43 feet. Made of bronze," says Jon, wheezing from climbing. "Erected in the thirteenth century. They say there was a wooden Buddha here before that."

"Buddhist monks were among the original martial artists," Ryan says, nodding at the statue. "He looks so peaceful. Not a warrior. I thought Buddhists were not supposed to hurt a fly?"

"The Sohei – warrior monks – fought as protectors not aggressors," says Jon. "That's how they justified their fighting skills. They used to say they fought for justice with compassion as their primary weapon."

"What about the samurai who were Buddhists? Katanas were their primary weapons. . ."

"You're full of questions," Jon says smiling. "Good, grasshopper." He puts his hands together and mock bows.

Ryan grins.

"Buddhism and the samurai bushido code actually meshed pretty well. Buddhism is all about focus, self-discipline, personal development, and an acceptance that death is part of the program. As a trained fighter, you can see how that would all help a warrior." Ryan nods. He pulls out his camera and starts taking shots of the massive sculpture from all sides, transfixed. Deep, weathered green, a testament to centuries of the salty sea breeze and the relentless passage of time. Crowds wander around its base. Jon reads the plaque nearby. After a few minutes he walks over to Ryan.

"Let's see what the future holds for you."

He leads Ryan across the temple grounds, past a group of young Japanese students. As he passes the big pack,

Ryan's left shoulder slams into one of the kids. The boy staggers and his cellphone bounces on the pavers.

"I'm so sorry," Ryan says in Japanese.

The student bends over and picks up his phone.

"You okay?"

The student gives a quick assent and shows Ryan the face of the device, indicating that no damage was done.

"It was like he came out of nowhere," Ryan says after they left.

"You didn't see that big pack of kids?"

Ryan shakes his head. Jon purses his lips and nods.

"Gotta watch where you're going. Bob and weave, you know?"

He playfully shifts his hips and throws a couple of punches.

They reach the *O-mikuji* area.

"This is where they tell fortunes," Jon says. He pulls two 100-yen coins from his pocket and puts them in a narrow slot on the top of a small wooden box. Each of them receives a slip of paper with their fortune on it.

"Like a cookie," Jon jokes.

"O-mi-Ku-ji," Ryan says.

"Well done, mate. See, the studying is coming in handy already. Let's see what yours says."

Ryan hands Jon his fortune.

"*Dai-kichi.* A great blessing. It says, 'A chance meeting will open new doors to success and friendship.'"

Which chance meeting? Jon? Enson?

Chapter 9

"All healed and ready to go," Ryan says. He's back at Purebred, this time to train. The gym is packed with fighters – fists slam into heavy bags, jump ropes swish rhythmically on the floor, and everywhere men are grunting and breathing heavily. Japanese hip-hop pumps from the speakers overhead.

"Good, we gotta get you prepared for your first fight." Enson grins. "Locked in the date just the other day."

"Already!?"

"Sink or swim, that's how we do it here. It's at Tokyo Fight Night, an amateur MMA event."

Enson gets serious, fixing Ryan with a steady gaze.

"It's not going to be easy. The training will be grueling. You sure you're ready?"

Ryan looks him back in the eye and nods.

Then it's right into the ring. Enson wants to get an idea of where Ryan's at technically. He pits the American against Norifumi, the short, tattooed fighter who had come to his aid in the parking lot. Though not a big guy, he is powerful, arms and legs made out of braided muscle.

They touch gloves and take up fighting stances.

Hmm. Southpaw.

Enson referees.

"Alright," he says. "Protect yourself at all times."

The words have barely left the bosses' lips when Norifumi is on Ryan, flying across the ring and sending a lunging right hook at the American's face, flooring him.

"Didn't see that coming," Ryan jokes, trying to make light of it. He hops to his feet, embarrassed, determined to show Enson he has fight. He rushes in for a clinch, but Norifumi easily side steps, then savagely hits Ryan in the jaw, dropping him again to the canvas.

"That's enough," Enson says, clapping his hands. Norifumi's eyes meet Ryan's, and he dips his head.

They bump fists, and Norifumi backs off.

"I want another shot," Ryan says to Enson, nodding toward his opponent.

"Maybe another time." The champ turns to walk away.

Ryan walks after him. "Let me fight someone else."

Enson slowly turns and looks at him, his head tilted slightly to the side. He thinks a moment and begins to take his sweatshirt off revealing biceps like those of a cartoon superhero.

"Okay, fight me then."

They climb into the ring and take their places.

"Begin when you're ready," Enson says.

Ryan rushes him. Enson stands his ground, grabs him, and wrestles him to the ground, even faster and easier than Norifumi had. The champ drives his knee into Ryan's solar plexus from the knee-on belly position, and the American taps from the overwhelming pressure.

Ryan slams the mat repeatedly in frustration and lies on his back.

"You're strong, Ryan," Enson says, looking down at him.

"But that's just one of the many pieces of the puzzle. You gotta learn to fight to your strengths."

Ryan looks up at him.

"It's time to turn you into a real warrior – a *sougou kakutouka*, an all-around fighter. Think you can handle that?"

Ryan nods.

"Be here at seven a.m. tomorrow. Sharp."

Ryan sits with his arms around his knees, staring up at the ceiling.

That went about as well as the Olympics.

A hand extends down toward him. It's Norifumi. Ryan takes it, and the Japanese fighter hauls him to his feet.

"I'm Norifumi. Call me Nori."

"Thanks, Nori. I'm Ryan. Yoroshiku. Your power surprised me."

Nori waves off the compliment and pats the American on the back.

***

Training becomes all Ryan can think about – he doesn't have long until his first fight. He arrives at the

145

gym bright and early, and Enson puts the fight team through a ruthless regimen of cardio, strength training, and sparring. The champ pushes them hard, devoting a lot of time to each phase. Ryan spends his days covered in sweat, gasping for breath, eating punches. He works on footwork, clinch fighting, takedowns. He hammers away on a heavy bag lying on the ground, learning how to mix strikes in with his grappling skills. In the evening, he sprints up and down concrete steps near the Gaijin House that separate Ishikawacho and the hilly nearby neighborhood, Yamate.

And he spars, Enson constantly coaching him from the corner. Ryan's striking begins to come along. He sends two fighters to the canvas in one of his first returns to sparring, using a double-jab cross combo that causes one of the newbie's knees to buckle. Norifumi, skipping rope nearby, watches and nods in approval.

Sparring doesn't always go his way. Ryan is floored by a mid-level fighter and pummeled by another. He finds himself trying to clinch to avoid punishing strikes more often than he'd like, but it doesn't take long for his hard work to show. He feels stronger and better able to roll with the punches. His fists and feet – and more importantly, his head, his Fight IQ – get sharper. He breathes better. And his confidence grows.

After a few weeks in the gym, he goes several rounds with another up-and-comer, a Japanese brawler who'd been causing a lot of talk – Nori thinks he's the real deal – resulting in a draw. And he gets the upper hand against another rising fighter, launching him over his hip to the canvas and following it up with a barrage of head strikes. This gets people at Purebred talking about *him*.

One of the rare nights he's not bouncing at Womb, he's among the few remaining fighters at Purebred, sparring while the world sleeps. Ryan's partner is slightly taller and has a reach advantage, and the American struggles to get inside, especially when his opponent circles to his left. He eats a couple of blows that stagger him backwards, leaving him wobbly on his feet. He senses frustration emerging from Enson, who turns back into his office. Ryan takes a few breaths and gets his feet underneath him. He shifts his fighting stance, standing off-axis, giving him a better view of things coming from his left side.

He fakes a punch and charges at his partner, sending him flying with an *osoto gari*, a large outer reap throw, sweeping his leg and launching him to the mat. The Japanese fighter hits hard and is out cold. Ryan glances at Enson, who is talking with Nori. Their eyes are wide and their mouths hang open. Enson gathers himself and then nods. Nori grins.

Ryan checks on his partner, who's taking some time to come to.

"Aw, man, I'm sorry."

Nori leans in close to Enson. "Fight Night is coming up fast. Let's see what he can do."

***

A black man lugs a suitcase down a packed flight of stairs at Yokohama station and exits the ticket gate, a mixture of puzzlement and panic written on his face.

Fighting Blind

He stands out like a sore thumb. Wonder if that's how I look?

Ryan watches his father smile at the station attendant, who nods and gestures him forward. Amen wears a thick down parka, a camera around his neck, and he's a head taller than most of the Japanese who crowd the main concourse at Yokohama Station.

"Dad!" Ryan shouts and jogs toward him.

Amen grins broadly and makes his way to his son. They bear hug, with the eyes of hundreds of slightly disgruntled commuters on them.

"Ah ha, my boy!" Amen says, thumping him on the back of his puffy jacket.

"I can hardly believe you're here. When you called. . . If I'd known you were flying in, I would have met you at the airport."

Amen holds Ryan at arm's length and looks him up and down.

"You look good, son. Strong."

"Thanks. Been training hard." He pauses. "Wait, where's mom?"

Amen looks at his shoes a minute.

"Oh, she decided to stay home, son. She sends her love."

Ryan nods.

After getting Amen situated at his nearby hotel, the two return to the station. The train pulls up to the platform, and a horde flows out as lines of people wait on both sides of the train doors.

"This way," Ryan guides his father into the long car with the other passengers. The train is packed, and Amen looks around with wonder. Ryan gestures his old man further into the carriage. They latch onto the handrail in front of a row of seated passengers.

"You're a stranger in a strange land," Amen says, leaning into Ryan's shoulder.

"Dad. . ."

Amen smiles, watching the Tokyo metropolis grow outside his window. Turns back to his son.

"You're not wearing glasses? You get contacts?"

"Don't want to talk about it, Dad. No one here is going to know about my situation. Feel me?"

"Son, I'm not sure you want to hide this. . ."

"I need to do this, Dad. At least try."

"And if you get hurt?"

"I don't want to look back with regret. I understand the risks."

Amen pats his son's shoulder and looks out the window. He has a lot to say, but he decides now is not the time.

They fill the next several days exploring Tokyo and its surroundings. Ryan takes Amen to the Sensoji Temple in Asakusa, the Meiji Jingu Shinto shrine in Harajuku, Mount Takao in Hachioji, all kinds of places. They even ride the bullet train to Kyoto, where they walk the ancient samurai trail, Nakasendo, which once connected Edo, now Tokyo, with Kyoto during the Edo period.

They spend Amen's last night in Ryan's adopted hometown of Yokohama, taking the elevator up to the highest observation deck of Landmark Tower and looking out at the city from 895 feet above. For a time, they both marvel in the view, silent. The city gleams like a jewel on the edge of the sea with modern buildings and the Cosmo Clock Ferris wheel far below them, literally stretching to the horizon in every direction, with only far off Mount Fuji to stop it from consuming the entire landscape.

"Wow, son. I knew Japan was populous, but this really is something," Amen says. "So different, and so far outside my comfort zone."

"Sometimes it can be hard to find a little quiet," Ryan says, nodding. He points out nearby areas of Yokohama, where Gaijin House sits, Chinatown, Yamashita Park.

"But it's my home now."

Amen opens his mouth to respond but thinks better of it. He just gives his son a tight-lipped half smile.

They both keep their counsel for a moment, looking out at the waters of Tokyo Bay.

"Dad, about mom. . ." Ryan says.

"Yeah?"

"How's she really doing? Does she really stay in bed all day?"

"Some days she doesn't seem to want to get up. Just lies there."

"What's the doctor say?"

"Same things. Depressed. Bipolar. Taking a handful of pills."

"Why's she so unhappy?"

Amen puts his arm around his son's shoulders.

"Wish I knew. She says it's not me. And I know it's not you. The doctor says some people have chemical imbalances in their brains that lead to depression. Don't really know. It's a tricky science, diagnosing what goes on inside someone's skull."

"She's not angry about me moving?"

Amen turns to face Ryan, puts his hands on his son's shoulders.

"She doesn't love it, but that's not the cause of this. Don't ever think that."

He takes a deep breath.

"We're going to have to figure it out soon, though, because the medical bills are mounting. Every time she goes in for another test, it costs money. On a teacher's salary. . ." He looks off at the horizon and then surveys the vista beneath his shoes.

"I hadn't even thought of that," Ryan says.

"I don't want you to have to."

They stand, not talking, taking in the sweep of city below. People, cars, trucks, go everywhere, so small they look like grains of salt or particles of dust.

"How'd you afford this trip? Airfare to Tokyo is not cheap."

"Needed to see you, son. I'll figure out the rest."

Chapter 10

An older Japanese gentleman examines Ryan's eyes through a scope. The American does his best to sit calmly and keep his chin in the little cup designed for it. He stares straight ahead as the ophthalmologist shines a light into his pupil.

"Your eyes appear fine. The damage is within the brain, but. . ."

The doctor looks through the lens again and then slides it to the side. He gestures at Ryan.

"You may sit back. I will prescribe vision therapy. I don't know if it will help, but it most certainly won't hurt."

"What sort of vision therapy?"

"It is like physical therapy for the eyes. You can train them to work in ways that help offset the problems your brain has interpreting the data they send. Take this to the medical assistant. She will direct you to the vision therapy suite."

Ryan finds the vision therapy office at the end of a corridor in the same hospital and peers in through the open door. A young woman sits at a desk filling out paperwork, her back to him, her neck graceful. He knocks gently on the doorframe. She turns and smiles, running her hand through her hair.

She's radiant.

"Hi, I'm here for therapy?" Ryan says.

Don't stare.

"Hello," she says in English. "I'm Eriko. Your therapist."

She bows her head and extends her hand. He takes it, finding it warm and soft.

I know I've seen her somewhere. I would not forget that face.

Eriko gestures to a seat, and as Ryan crosses the room it comes to him:

"We've met before. . .," he says. "At Yokohama station. . . My bag was stuck in the train doors. . . You handed me my water bottle."

Eriko smiles. She fidgets with her rings.

She remembers me.

"Yes, I was happy to help," she says, all professional. "Tell me about your vision problems."

"I seem to be missing things in my peripheral vision. On my left side."

She smiles at him.

"Let's see if we can't figure out what's going on."

Eriko walks Ryan to a corner of the room, where a set of what look like baseballs dangle from thin wires affixed to the ceiling.

"Batting practice?" he jokes.

Eriko smiles.

154

"These are called Marsden Balls," she says, cradling one in her palm. "It's simple really. I let go of these balls, and as they swing back and forth, you walk forward, passing between them. It helps retrain and strengthen your peripheral vision." She puts her hand on his arm.

"Just don't let them hit you."

"I think I can handle that."

Eriko sets the therapy balls swinging and they pendulum back and forth. Ryan steps in between them. He has no trouble clocking the one on his right side, but whenever the one on his left passes by, he loses it. He's almost hit in the head several times, and he adjusts slightly. Noticing this, she catches the ball in her hand.

"I can see you're favoring your left side," Eriko says. "Don't turn toward it. Try to view it with your peripheral vision."

Ryan nods.

"Okay. Now walk back the other way. We'll do this for a while."

Eriko lets go of the balls, and Ryan starts from the other side. He slides between them, juking like a running back as they lazily swing back and forth. She smiles.

"You're from the United States?"

"Yeah, Grand Rapids. Michigan."

"What brings you to Japan?"

"Mixed Martial Arts. I'm training to be a professional fighter."

"Interesting," she says, drawing out the word.

"Ever been to the U.S.?"

"Never. Not yet anyways," she says.

"Nothing to see there anymore."

She tilts her head.

"Hmm?"

"All the available guys live here," Ryan says, grinning.

Eriko laughs.

Ryan continues trying to navigate between the Marsden Balls as their conversation unfolds. He's eager to learn more about her.

***

Ryan walks between the swinging Marsden Balls, still having trouble tracking the one on his left.

I should be better at this by now.

Eriko nods and offers encouragement. During the week, he found himself constantly thinking about his therapy session. He'd be sparring at the gym, and his mind would wander back to his therapist. He'd be checking IDs at Womb and imagining her face. When he lay in bed at night, repeating Japanese phrases over and over, she popped into his thoughts, beautiful, glowing, kind.

"I suppose you'll be going back soon?" Eriko asks.

"Why do you say that?"

"Your head injury. Surely, you're not thinking of fighting anymore? Wouldn't your brain injury make it impossible to continue?"

"Difficult. Not impossible."

She stops the therapy balls and looks at him.

"Everyone takes risks all the time," he says. "Life is about how we manage it. Every time we climb on a plane. Get in a car. Ride a bike."

"I never thought about it that way." She looks down, adjusts her white blouse. "Still, I'm not sure you should be taking *unnecessary* risks."

He opens and shuts his mouth.

She sets the balls in motion, and Ryan walks through a few more times before she stops them, the part of therapy sessions he always dreads.

"Okay. Finished for today," she says.

"Thanks for your help," Ryan says, standing up from his stool. "I appreciate you."

He grabs his jacket and walks to the door, pausing.

"Say. Uh," he hesitates. "I have a fight soon at Kitazawa Town Hall. You should come."

She blushes, looking down and smoothing her shirt again.

"I'll consider it. But I have to be honest. I don't think you should be. . ."

"Just think about it," he says. "Please."

She fixes him with her eyes.

"Well, if you get knocked out, I might have to be there to administer therapy."

Ryan laughs.

"See! You have to be there."

***

When Ryan arrives at the arena, Enson's talking to an attractive Japanese businesswoman. They're not whispering but speaking closely and quietly. Dressed in warmups from his own clothing brand, Yamato Damashii, the champ's leaning in and saying something very intently. She's dressed more formally, in a dark pant suit. Her brows are slightly furrowed, and she has her arms crossed, her back on the wall looking up at Enson.

They stop talking as Ryan walks up.

"Oh, sorry, didn't mean to interrupt," he says, spinning on his heel to walk away.

"No need. You're not interrupting," Enson says, waving him over. "I'd like to introduce you to Kobayashi-san. She's a fight manager."

The woman turns to Ryan, and they exchange polite bows before she looks back at Enson.

"Excuse us," Enson says, putting his arm around Ryan's shoulders. Kobayashi smiles. Enson leads Ryan down the hallway. People are beginning to arrive in droves, taking their seats.

"Who am I fighting?" Ryan asks when they're out of earshot.

"Wait'll you see," Enson laughs.

What's that supposed to mean?

Enson can see Ryan wants more.

"Name is Haru."

"Okaaay?"

Enson's eager to see how he reacts, but the name means nothing to Ryan. The American steps through the door to the locker room. A minute later, Nori arrives to help him wrap his hands.

"You ready?" Nori asks as he spins chairs around, aligning their backs. He gestures to one of the seats. Ryan sits, resting his hands on the chair back in front of him and extending his fingers. Nori gets to work, wrapping his fists, making sure they are nice and secure.

"I guess," says Ryan.

"Crazy, who you're fighting tonight, huh?"

"What do you mean?"

Nori looks down. Pauses. Then:

"Enson didn't tell you?"

"Tell me what?"

"I'll let Enson tell you."

Who the hell is this guy? Haru?

***

Ryan suits up, putting on his fight shorts and a Purebred t-shirt, then warms up with some shadowboxing to get a sweat going. He's third on the ticket, and he can hear the crowd outside roaring at fight two.

Sounds like a packed house.

He takes some deep breaths to focus himself.

The door squeaks open.

"You guys all set? It's almost time," Enson says.

"Ready," says Ryan, clapping his gloves together.

A staffer parts the curtains that lead into the arena. As Ryan and his team begin the long walk to the ring, he hears the announcer say his name. Kitazawa Town Hall is small as MMA goes, but it still seats almost 300, and it seems like there's that plus another 100 at least standing.

Fans liked the intimacy of the venue – it put them really close to the action – and many fighters on their way up had early bouts here. People turn in their seats to look at Ryan as he passes, like guests at a wedding.

Probably looking at Enson and Nori not me. . .

Ryan scans the crowd for Eriko, and he spots her just finding her seat. She looks up as he stares. He gives her a little wave, and she lights up, waving back. Jon's somewhere out there, too.

Ryan notices a fifty-something guy who could stand to lose a few pounds in a position of prominence in the front row. Dressed in a suit, the man has a hard time fitting into the narrow seats and wears a promoter's pass around his neck like a pendant. Kobayashi sits nearby, straight-backed, eyes forward, waiting for the fight.

"Here they come," Enson says clapping his hands together. "Let's do this, braddah."

Ryan uses the ropes to pull himself into the ring, and Enson and Nori take their places in his corner.

Looking out into the crowd, Ryan sees a posse moving down the rows, all sweatpants, T-shirts, gold chains, and tattoos. He can't quite make out the fighter among them, but he notices the stone-faced mob lieutenant from the Womb parking lot bringing up the rear, a stopwatch around his neck. Some fans get out of their seats to follow a member of Haru's crew, another fighter Ryan is pretty sure he's seen before. Other people scream as he walks by.

As the entourage nears the ring, Ryan gets his first look at Haru, and everything suddenly makes sense: Haru is the thug from Womb. The guy he ejected into the parking lot, who'd sent him to the hospital with a sucker punch.

The tall Japanese fighter steps through the ropes and into the other corner. He turns and fixes Ryan with a cold glare. Ryan glances back at Enson, who leans forward.

"Hey, I know what you're thinking. But there are no easy fights. This guy is good. And fast. He's also dirty, as you found out. Never take your eyes off him."

Ryan bites into his mouthguard. Breathes deeply in through his nose, exhaling long out his mouth. Then he pounds his gloves together and waits for the bell.

As soon as it rings, he's in Haru's face, and they exchange opening blows. Ryan lands a solid right, knocking Haru backwards, and launches a combo toward his jaw. Haru sidesteps and counters Ryan's punch with a cross right down the center, smashing into the side of the American's face. Ryan's head snaps backwards. He circles away, shakes his head to regroup, and reenters the fight with a lunging hook he learned from Nori. It catches Haru on the jaw and staggers him, sending him backward. Ryan moves in to clinch.

In a heavy accent, Haru says, "Gaijin, go home. This time I throw *you* out."

They wrestle a moment, each struggling to bring the other down, before Haru shoves Ryan away. They backpedal, and Haru circles around to Ryan's left – and simply vanishes. One moment he's there, stalking the American like a predator, the next the tall Japanese fighter is gone, as if he's stepped out of the ring.

What the. . .?

Ryan panics, jerking his head around.

Where the hell is he? How can I lose a guy that's 6'2"?

The American struggles to find his opponent, fully aware of what will happen if he can't – it'll be a repeat of the parking lot beating. He spins on his heel, doing a 360 in search of Haru. He starts breathing rapidly. He makes a full circuit and still can't locate him.

In the corner, Enson watches his fighter pirouette for no apparent reason. He flashes a confused look at Nori, a face that says, "Are you seeing this?" Nori shrugs.

Ryan continues to swivel his head, desperately looking for Haru, like a kid trying to find a bee that's buzzing him.

I can't see. . .

The Japanese fighter has vanished, like the Marsden Ball on his left. But there's no beautiful woman looking out for him this time, and Ryan has the sensation he's about to get hit.

Haru has no trouble locating the American, and he steps in close with an overhand right, immediately taking Ryan down with an outside leg trip. Haru climbs atop him, pinning him with his legs. He unleashes a series of savage blows at Ryan's head. The crowd screams, and Haru's entourage starts chanting and screaming "*Kurose ora*, a slurred 'Kill him, damn it!'"

"Better get used to losing," Haru hisses.

Found you. And that's exactly the wrong thing to say. . .

Ryan bridges hard and reverses Haru, sending the Japanese fighter to the bottom position. He follows with a flurry of punches. Some are wild, in his anger, but several land, and one chin blow stuns Haru, who kicks the

American away. As soon as Haru is back up Ryan rushes him. Haru leaps to Ryan's left, winding up with a haymaker.

Ryan is ready this time, rubbernecking, tracking him. Haru's fist is close, coming in at full speed. Ryan slips under it and spins to Haru's back. He hammers Haru with a crushing belly-to-back suplex that catapults the Japanese competitor into the air. He comes down hard on the canvas.

The crowd gasps.

Haru rolls to his knees, but Ryan has already gotten behind him and launches a barrage of blows to both sides of his head. Haru's body slumps, and he falls face down onto the canvas.

He doesn't get up. The referee stops the fight. The bell rings, and the referee raises Ryan's arm into the air. A Japanese ring girl steps over to him and places a medal around his neck. Ryan holds it out so he can read it. Tokyo Fight Night: Winner. Haru crawls back to his corner. Ryan and Enson watch him, and the other fighter glares back at the two of them.

"Not too bad," Enson says, patting him on the back. Nori does the same.

***

Kobayashi is ringside, right in Akio's face. Up on the balls of her feet, the petite Japanese woman is giving him what for. He's leaning down, looking at her, expressionless, cigarette in his hand. As if he couldn't care what a woman has to say.

"Do your family a favor," he eventually says. "Do *yourself* a favor. Get out of the fighting business," he blows smoke in her face and turns to walk off.

Kobayashi grabs him by the elbow, not finished yet. He wrenches his arm away.

"Maybe you should focus on your own fighters," she says. "Leave my business to me."

Akio fixes her with a smirk – he can see where this is going.

"Don't tell me you're thinking about taking on the gaijin?" He shakes his head. "What's the matter with you?"

Kobayashi waves her hand up like she's swatting a bug and walks away. She pauses and strides back. "So what if I did. What business is it of yours?" She steps away again. Stops and turns.

"He just beat *your* guy."

"One fight. Against a mediocre fighter."

"*Your* mediocre fighter."

"Let's see him do it against anyone else in my stable."

Akio drops his cigarette and crushes it with his foot. He glowers at her a moment and walks toward the exit.

***

Ryan and Enson head toward the locker room, the tired fighter slowly shuffling.

"Eh, you alright?" Enson asks.

"That guy was part of the same group that jumped me in the parking lot."

"And?"

"My buddy was telling me they're yakuza."

"And?"

Ryan looks at him, surprised.

"What?" says Enson. "MMA is a dangerous sport. You know that. You're here because it's been outlawed in the U.S. Never occur to you it might have underworld connections? Look at boxing in the U.S. *Raging Bull* and all that."

Ryan is quiet. For the first time he notices the tattoo protruding from Enson's sleeve. It reminds him of the ones he'd just seen in the ring. What Jon called "yak ink." Enson notices Ryan looking. He pulls up his sleeve.

"*Tebori dayo*," he says. "Done the traditional way, by hand."

Ryan remains silent.

"Hey," Enson says. "I'm not yakuza. But I have many connections. I float between the two worlds. Have to, to do what I do. Their money is in everything."

Ryan looks at him. He nods.

"Go on," Enson says lifting his chin towards the locker room.

***

Fresh from the shower, Ryan wanders back out into the arena. A crew breaks down the ring, hauling off the ropes and the posts, carrying the rolled-up canvas away. Ryan watches, lost in thought. He'd just dismantled Haru. . .

Is Eriko still here?

He scans the seats. A voice pipes up from behind him.

"Do you have a manager, Mr. Bow?"

Ryan turns to see Kobayashi. He gives her a respectful bow.

"Hello, Kobayashi-san."

"Representation?" she asks.

"Uh, no, not yet," Ryan says.

"Well, I would like to represent you."

She extends her business card to him, holding it between her two hands. Ryan takes the card with both of his hands. They bow slightly.

"Think about it," Kobayashi says. "Give me a call tomorrow."

She walks toward the exit. As he watches her go, a big smile crosses Ryan's face. Enson steps up behind him and reads the card over his shoulder.

"Nice," he says.

"Did you know about this?" Ryan asks.

Enson grins, claps him on the shoulder, and follows Kobayashi.

As soon as he's gone, Jon steps up.

"You did great, mate. Time to celebrate!" the Englishman says.

Ryan shows Jon Kobayashi's card, and his face lights up.

"You did *really* great, mate!"

Ryan's not quite ready to go. Jon follows his gaze. He's still searching the arena. Until he sees her, then he just stares.

"Ah," Jon says.

"Someone I need to talk to," Ryan tells him. "Let me catch up with you."

"Meet you outside."

Jon is barely gone before Eriko walks up.

"Thanks for coming," Ryan says, bowing slightly.

"My first MMA fight. You were. . . just," she looks down at the floor for a moment then brings her gaze up to his eyes ". . . amazing."

Ryan feels his cheeks get warm. His head hurt, but the feeling was unmistakable.

"Thanks." He looks over at what's left of the ring and then back at her.

"Listen, I'm going to grab a drink with a friend. Would you like to join us?"

"I wish I could, but I really need to get home. I'll see you at your next therapy session, though."

"Wouldn't miss it for the world."

They smile. She does a spin on her heel and makes for the parking lot.

"Eriko."

She turns.

"Would you have dinner with me sometime?"

"I would love to," she says over her shoulder, a skip in her step.

"I'll call you," Ryan says.

A fan rushes up to Ryan. A young Japanese kid, he can barely stand still.

"Can I have your autograph?"

Ryan's eyebrows go up. He steps over and scrawls his name on the kid's program. He spots Eriko by the door, watching. And then she's gone.

***

"I've wanted to be a professional MMA fighter for years."

Ryan and Eriko look out over Tokyo from the 38th floor of Chibo, an upscale restaurant in Ebisu famous for its *okonomiyaki*, a savory Japanese pancake. They have a table in a quiet corner with floor-to-ceiling views of the city, which looks miniature from this height, the high rises that roll to the horizon seeming like toys. Everything's so far removed and serene.

"Couldn't you do that in the United States?"

"No. The sport's banned and. . ."

"And?"

Eriko studies Ryan's face, and she notices something different about his left eye. She leans in closer to get a better look. Embarrassed, Ryan quickly looks away.

"How's your vision?" she asks, putting her hand over his. "I could tell you couldn't see that fighter on your left side. I'm really worried about you."

"No worries. You saw the fight. I'm feeling 100 percent."

Eriko frowns.

"You know what I mean. As your therapist, I don't think I could live with it if you get hurt."

Ryan takes her hand in his and looks her in the eyes.

"I was born for this. I'll be extra careful. And besides, with your help, my vision's improving."

Eriko smiles.

"Enough about me," Ryan says. "Tell me about you."

"You already know where I work. Other than that, I don't know what to say."

"Where'd you learn English?"

"My mother studied abroad in the U.S. I've wanted to travel since I was a child."

"She must be very proud of you."

Eriko's purses her lips and turns her attention to the scene out the window.

The server arrives with ingredients to cook on their tabletop grille.

***

His head feels like it's being driven over by a truck. Pressure. Pounding. An intense pain that doesn't ever let up. He rolls over, ducking under his blanket. At least the Gaijin House is quiet for once. He spends the whole day beneath his covers, his knees pulled up to his chest. The rare occasions when he does come up to feel the cool air on his face, the light coming through the window feels like a punch and everything is blurry. He thinks about the fight, from the opening bell to Haru on the deck.

How could I lose him like that?

All the bravado he felt with Eriko is gone and replaced with pain and worry. He groans and sinks into the blackness.

***

Ryan and Eriko sit on a blanket underneath a cherry blossom tree. Both wear traditional yukata, lightweight summer kimonos. The American takes her small hand

and she grabs his tightly. His head has been throbbing for days now, but he wasn't about to let that get in the way of a day out with Eriko. They'd started seeing each other a couple days a week, and it was the time Ryan most looked forward to.

Ryan picks up a fallen pink petal and rolls it between his fingers. The surrounding park is a small enclave of grass and ponds hemmed by the busy streets of Asakusa, but the 600 cherry trees that line the Sumida River make it feel like an oasis. They sit quietly, taking it all in. A mother zips by trying to catch her two toddlers. A teenage couple walk along holding hands. A schoolboy grasps his dog's leash as the eager wire-haired pup pulls him along the path.

Ryan turns to Eriko.

"Japan is starting to feel like home," he says. "Can't imagine being anywhere else."

He hadn't really thought about it much, but he realizes he doesn't miss Michigan. He misses his parents, sure, but his life in the U.S. is beginning to feel like a lifetime ago.

"How long do you think you'll stay?"

"Forever, I hope. It's like a dream I don't want to wake from."

He meets her eyes.

"In more ways than one."

Her cheeks take on a cherry blossom hue, and she gives him a coy smile.

As the sun sets later that night, fireworks shoot into the sky over the Sumida River, one of many Tokyoites' most beloved summer traditions. By now it seems there are more people than grass to sit on; everyone cranes their necks up, waiting for the show to begin.

And, with a boom, it does.

Ryan and Eriko watch as colorful explosions light up the river, streaks of red and orange and green above them fall like shooting stars. The crowd gasps as the pyrotechnics make smiley faces and hearts and palm trees – even the light-blue likeness of Doraemon, the hugely popular feline robot manga and anime character. The action is so fast and furious the sky looks like a garden at times with dozens of glowing orbs resplendent. Everyone stares upward, amazed.

Except Ryan. He tries to block out all the sound and is the only one not looking upward. All he can see is Eriko. The graceful lines of her neck as her head tilts to watch the show. The silkiness of her hair. The sparkle in her eyes. She notices him watching her and stares back at him. They kiss as the fireworks soar overhead.

Chapter 11

Ryan wipes the sweat from his brow as he jogs up to the Gaijin House. He's been putting in the miles at the park lately, Enson having impressed upon him the need for stamina. He spots Jon sitting on the step out front, a newspaper thoughtfully folded into a manageable size.

"Well, well, well," Jon says as he hears him approach. "If it isn't that famous MMA fighter Ryan Bow."

Ryan looks down and chuckles.

"Don't know about all that," he says. "Still just an amateur."

Jon puts the paper down on his knees.

"They're paying you, aren't they?"

Ryan shakes his head.

"Not until I turn pro."

Jon picks the paper back up, scanning an article. Even though Ryan's Japanese is improving, the dense spread of characters on the newsprint is daunting.

"I'll get there," Ryan says. "I'm signing with a manager this week."

"You know what you're doing?" Jon asks. "What do you know about the agency? Many of them here can be sketchy."

"Not much, really," Ryan admits.

"Be careful, organized crime is heavily involved in MMA. But you know that."

"Kobayashi-san seems different. I think she'll be good. She can open doors for me."

"Do you even have a hanko?" Jon asks.

"A what?"

"A hanko, a personal stamp used to sign documents. It dates back to the feudal days when samurai would cut their thumbs with their katanas and sign contracts in blood. The red ink of the hanko symbolizes the blood."

"What if I don't have one?"

Jon grins. "You have a sword?"

***

A few days later, Ryan finds himself sitting across the desk from Kobayashi in her office. He'd taken the train into Tokyo that morning and made his way to a sleek, glass building surrounded by designer shops in Aoyama, a sophisticated high-end Tokyo neighborhood.

Seems to be doing okay for herself. Can't fail yourself into a place like this.

"Do you have a hanko?" she asks. Dressed just so in another dark pants suit, she slides a piece of paper across the glass to him.

"No. Just heard what one was the other day. I brought my katana instead. . ."

She smiles.

"No matter. Look this over. I thought you'd appreciate it in English."

"Definitely helps" Ryan says in Japanese.

"*Good*," Kobayashi says. "Your grasp of the language seems to be coming along. Keep at it."

Ryan scans the document. He'd been reading about what to expect in an MMA contract, and it seems legit to him. Kobayashi agreed to represent him for three years or nine fights. She'd get 15% of each purse he won. He heard that some managers took as much as 30%, so he figures that's a deal. He looks it over for a moment and then signs in the places where she's put little sticky notes. When he reaches the last page, he places his thumb on the ink pad and stamps his print next to his name.

Kobayashi does the same and then stands up, extending her hand across her desk. Ryan takes it and shakes. Then he does a little bow.

"Thank you, Kobayashi-san. I appreciate your faith in me. I'm excited about the future."

"As am I, Ryan, as am I. I'll do what I can to get you booked right away."

"Great."

He turns to leave and pauses at the door.

"How about with the champ?"

She gives him another knowing grin.

"Let's not get ahead of ourselves. It's all right to dream big, Ryan, but we have to take the most appropriate steps."

175

***

Ryan's name starts to carry some weight on the regional MMA circuit, fight by fight, victory by victory. The venues are small – some barely holding 500 – but inside the ring, he's impossible to miss. While other fighters come and go, he leaves an impression, the kind that lingers in the minds of the fans.

He pummels a series of low-level fighters. He beats a mid-level brawler from Osaka. He takes a beating from another foreigner but manages to come back and get his hand raised – to the delight of the audience. Each win comes with a paycheck, pushes him up the ranks, and gets him a step closer to facing the toughest opponents. Bigger stakes. More money. Waiting on the horizon is one person whose defeat would earn him ultimate respect – and the Impact belt.

***

Enson hits him flush with a kick to the body. Ryan circles to catch his breath for a moment. He snaps out of it and counters Enson's next kick by catching it and sweeping his base leg out from under him. Enson goes down. He looks up, almost in disbelief.

"*Auwe*! Where'd that come from?" the champ says with a chuckle, clearly caught off guard.

Ryan extends a hand and helps him back to his feet.

"Good, Ryan!" Enson enthuses.

Purebred is quiet, all the lights off except the ones over the ring, giving it the feel of a lit-up arena. The only audience member, though, is Shooto, who licks his paw at ringside, no interest whatsoever in the goings on in the ring.

"Not much of a guard dog," Enson laughs. "He so used to this, he'd let anyone kill me."

"Listen," Enson says putting his arm around Ryan. "I'm not taken down easily." His face turns serious stabbing his fellow American with a glare, "Don't do it again."

"I'm sorry, I thought. . ."

"Just messin' with you," Enson grins. "You're getting the hang of it."

Ryan smiles.

Ryan's life has become a whirlwind – Eriko, therapy, nights at Womb, and every other waking second training to fight or fighting. He spends hours punching and kicking with his hands and feet tethered to resistance bands. He practices takedowns and groundwork with Nori. He lifts weights. Jumps rope. Pounds the pavement, putting in miles and mile every week. And he spars. Afterwards, he spars some more.

At night in his room at the Gaijin House, he watches MMA action aired live on a tiny TV. He lies on his futon, arm behind his head, and studies the new Japanese champion, Eiji "Kamikaze" Tanaka as he defends his belt versus Hiro "The Barbarian" Suzuki. Kamikaze is a karateka, and his fists and feet are electric. But that's not what stands out most. It's the sneer of confidence.

I know that mocking smile. Where have I seen him before?

Then it dawns on him. Ryan sits up on his futon.

*That's the guy from the gang who jumped me. . .*That's not all, though. Ryan stares at the wall, searching his mind. And the next puzzle piece snaps resoundingly into place.

He cornered my opponent in Tokyo Fight Night with their crew leader.

Kamikaze lands blow after blow, and somehow Suzuki manages to take them all. The two go toe-to-toe, trading punches in the center of the ring.

These guys are good. *They make my opposition look small and weak.*

He studies the pair as Kamikaze presses forward. The Barbarian flies into a clever spinning backfist that slams into Kamikaze's jaw. Rattled by the blow, Tanaka forces the Barbarian into a momentary clinch to collect his composure. They go round and round, one battering the other. Slowly, the Barbarian starts to fade. Kamikaze blitzes forward like a linebacker after a quarterback. He launches a series of punishing punches and kicks at the winded Suzuki. The bell rings to end the fight.

It's a split decision. The referee raises Eiji Tanaka's gloved hand.

Kamikaze is formidable. But Ryan sees a few areas of weakness. He trusts his power so much that he just goes all out in attack, like a berserker, ignoring the finer details. The importance of keeping his elbows in or his chin tucked. He doesn't seem to worry much about defense.

That's the fight I want.

***

Eriko hooks Ryan's right arm, and she rests her head on his shoulder as they leave the restaurant in Tokyo's Koreatown. This late at night, only a sparse crowd remains. They'd had *yakinuku*, a Korean BBQ inspired meal, and talked later than he'd expected. He'll take every minute he can have with her.

They round a corner and almost walk into two men heading the other direction. Ryan realizes immediately who they are – Haru and Kamikaze. It takes the pair a second, but soon recognition plays across the fighter's faces.

"*Hora, ano* Gaijin *yaro*," Haru says.

"*Kuso kurae*," Kamikaze sneers.

Eriko's eyes go wide. She pulls her arm from Ryan's and steps backward. Ryan takes her hand and tries to steer her around the pair as if they're not there. Haru blocks their path.

"Hey," Ryan says, putting his hands up. "Let's save it for the ring. I don't want any trouble."

"I don't care what you want," Haru responds. Without pausing he strides forward and swings at Ryan, who steps to the side, pulling Eriko with him. Ryan uses his arms to shield Eriko behind him and throws a kick at Haru, hitting him in the chest and sending him stumbling backward. Haru bounces back up, and the two fighters are on Ryan in an instant, launching a flurry of punches and kicks. Eriko screams and drops to her knees, crouching against a building, hands to her face.

Ryan does what he can, his fists a blur, trying to block and punch and counter, but they are two and he is one. He manages to land a few good blows – catches Haru square on his temple – but he ultimately falls to a hard strike to the head and crumbles in a heap on the sidewalk.

Haru and Kamikaze stand over him, not done, when a loud sound rings out. It's Kamikaze's phone. He steps aside to answer while Haru waits, staring down at Ryan like a guard over a cellmate. Haru has blood in his eyes, a predator ready to kill. Kamikaze hangs up and struts over. He leans in to Ryan's face:

"You just got lucky."

The pair stride off, quickly in conversation. Ryan watches them go, struggling to stand as pain courses through his body. Blood flows from a cut over his eye, his left cheek already swelling. Eriko walks over to help him as he staggers to his feet.

"Are you okay?"

"Fine," Ryan responds. "I'm fine."

"What was that all about?"

"I'll tell you about it later. Let's get going before they come looking for me."

***

By the time Kobayashi arrives, the conference-room table is surrounded by Japanese men in suits. There's a single chair left, and she takes it, gathering herself as she sits down. The older gentleman next to her shifts his chair away and clears his throat. Several of the others look at her coldly, watching. She gives it right back to them, glancing around the room as if to say:

"You got a problem with me being here?"

As a businesswoman in Tokyo, Kobayashi has seen it all before. She liked to joke to other women that it was the Land of the Rising Son, not the Land of the Rising Daughter. She adjusts her jacket and sets her poker face. Then she notices a teapot in the corner, pushes her chair back, walks over, and pours a cup.

The meeting drags on for more than two hours. She hardly has a chance to speak, and nobody takes her seriously when she does. She looks out the plate glass at Tokyo, all abustle below, her mind wandering.

"*Local* talent," she hears Mr. Ishihara say.

"No foreigners."

Kobayashi glances up. Akio, seated at the gray-haired gentleman's right arm, is staring at her and smiling.

"Ishihara-san," she says bowing her head. "My fighter has shown he deserves a chance to showcase his skills."

"Which is your fighter?" Ishihara asks in a growl, each word drawn out.

"Ryan B. . ."

He cuts her off before she can finish.

"He's out. Like I said, *Local* talent."

Kobayashi slumps back in her seat.

"Hai," she says.

What is she supposed to tell Ryan?

***

"Son, it's about your mother." Amen's voice sounds heavy on the line, as if he has a cold.

"What is it, Dad? Is she okay?"

"You know she's been struggling, Ryan. Fighting just like you. I guess she's starting to lose the battle."

"What do you mean, lose the. . ."

"Well, she's been hospitalized. For an overdose."

"An overdose!"

"Yeah, of the antidepressants her doctor prescribed."

"She just took too many?"

Amen lets out a big sigh. Pauses for a moment.

"Well, son, it looks that way. I came home and found her in bed, with an empty pill bottle next to her. Looked to me like she took pretty much the whole thing. I called 911 and the paramedics came and rushed her to the hospital, where her stomach was pumped, and she was given other medications. They took her in for observation for a few days. . ."

The line goes quiet.

"So, she's okay now?" Ryan asks. On a sidewalk pay phone down the street from the Gaijin House, he rocks back and forth on his feet in the booth, letting out a big sigh.

Amen slowly blows out his breath.

"Well, there's more."

"More?"

"Yeah"

"What do you mean more?"

"The Doc thinks it looks like she took too many on purpose."

"You're saying mom tried to kill herself?"

"I know it's hard to hear."

182

Ryan stops and leans against the glass panel. Then he slides down to the floor, his head between his knees.

He goes quiet.

"Ry, you there?"

"Yeah," he says, voice barely above a whisper.

"It's hard. I know. I've been trying to come to grips with it myself. . ."

"Why'd. . .?"

"Why'd she do it? Not sure. I guess it's a combination of things. She's been really unhappy. Again, not with you, or even with me. Just with life. The doctors insist it's a chemical thing, in her brain. An imbalance. So, there's that. And she's been drinking too much. Which she knows she shouldn't be doing with all her pills. She can't ever seem to rouse herself. Stays in bed. Takes her meds. Which only makes her mad at herself. And it's just become a downward spiral."

"Do you think it would help if I came home?"

"I do."

"All right. I'm on my way."

***

Kobayashi slams the door of her car as she gets in. The disrespect she faced galls her. First all the testosterone-laden bullshit from everyone. And then she had to grovel to another colleague to get him to lean on Ishihara and make him reconsider. And still, he wouldn't budge. Ishihara failed to recognize that a foreign fighter with raw talent and an outsider's mystique would make for the kind of headline-grabbing story they could sell.

What would my father think?

She wasn't sure most of the men there even knew she was from *that* Kobayashi family.

Probably wondered what I was doing there. Akio knows. . .

She pulls out and slices through traffic. It had been like this her whole life. When she was a girl, even her own father treated her like, well, a girl. He pampered her. Lavished luxuries on her in their Hokkaido hometown. Always assumed she had no ideas, had to be protected and coddled. So very different with her than he was with her brother, Kenji. He expected things from Kenji, set the pieces in place for him to take a leadership role in the work of the family.

"Kenji," he'd say, "Be good to your sister. One day you will be the provider."

When Kenji was killed in a clash over drug money with the Sakai family, her father was devastated, and he insulated Kobayashi even further from the family business.

Of course, the things that are forbidden have the most appeal. From a young age, Kobayashi was fascinated by her father's work, the ways of the yakuza. She remembered hearing stories of honor and respect from her grandfather when they would go for walks around his compound, she holding on to his hand, hardly taller than his knee. To her the life had a storybook feel – good vs evil, power, the bushido code – and she was very aware it provided all the fineries she enjoyed.

So, it was a big surprise to reach school and find out that others had a different idea of what her family was about, where their money came from.

"Hey crime lord," one of the girls on the playground said. "Hey Street Queen," said another. She had no idea what they were talking about. Her father went to work every day just like theirs.

"Why do they call me *onē-san*?" she'd ask her grandfather. "I'm the *little* sister."

"Don't listen to them. They're jealous. They want what you have."

But she couldn't help but hear them. And she began to look into what the life meant. Exactly where the money came from. She discovered that her family were mostly involved in gambling and loans.

"Like a bank," her grandfather told her. "We loan people money."

Both her father and grandfather were strictly against prostitution and drugs, wanting no part of either world.

"That just invites the attention of the cops" her grandfather would tell her. "It's dirty. Wrong."

If they leant money to shady characters? Her grandfather shrugged.

"Does the bank ask you what you do with *your* money?"

And if they don't pay it back?

Her grandfather gave her a wide smile and patted her on the shoulder.

"They know they must."

It was a loan to an early MMA promoter that got her family into the fight business. When the borrower couldn't repay, they simply took over his operation to clear the debt. Her father loved going to the fights, watching the young men he sponsored. When Kobayashi was old enough – a boy-crazy, teenaged girl – she begged her father to take her with him.

"This is no place for young women," he said. "No place at all."

She continued to harangue him. He continued to resist. She tried her grandfather, but he wouldn't go against the opinion of his son.

"Doesn't bother me, girls going," he said. "But I understand your father. And it's his house."

One night her father's attitude seemed to change.

"I saw a bunch of girls your age at the fight," he told her, upon returning from one of the big events in Tokyo. "So many girls."

He sat down on the couch next to her.

"They all seemed to be having a lot of fun. If they are allowed. . ."

His guard seemed down, like a fighter who's not paying attention. So, she asked him again.

This time, he relented. She could go as part of his entourage. But she was to sit in the stands only – no mixing with the fighters – and she was to stay with Daisuke, one of his lieutenants. She agreed. And so it began.

Probably because she had been denied it, she instantly fell in love with the drama and the spectacle. But there was more to it. She found herself drawn to the raw, animalistic masculinity. And, she hated to think, even the violence. She kept that to herself, going with her father whenever he'd allow it. Which, at first, wasn't all that often.

Chapter 12

Grand Rapids seems smaller. Simple. Sleepy. Dull and drab. Ryan leans his arm on the door of the cab and watches his hometown flash by.

Used to feel like such a big city.

The taxi driver swings into his driveway. He pays the fare and gets out.

"Thanks, man," the driver nods and holds up the bill. Confused for a second, it hits him. Ryan looks back and mutters an apology, "My bad. I almost forgot." Ryan says slides the driver a couple bills. In Japan, tipping isn't just unnecessary; in most cases, it is actively refused.

He drags his suitcase up the walkway, and it bounces over spots and gets hung up in divots. He looks down and notices grass growing through the stonework in places. The lawn looks like it hasn't been mowed in a while.

House could use a coat of paint.

He pauses on the steps. Hangs his head. Exhales. Then pushes the doorbell.

He waits. He can hear noise inside, but nobody's approaching the door. He opens the rattly storm door and raps on the wooden one behind. His father's footsteps. They get closer. Then the door groans open.

"You don't have to knock your own house, son," Amen says, giving him a big smile. Then pulls him into a hug. Ryan squeezes his father.

"Man, you are nothing but muscle," Amen says clapping him on the back. "So good to see you."

Amen lets go and steps aside to let Ryan in.

He looks old.

The house is a mess. Dirty glasses are strewn across the coffee table. A wrinkled-up pillow and a dangling blanket on the couch. Newspapers piled up in the dining room. An MMA mag draped over the armrest of his lounger.

Wonder where he gets those.

Amen notices his son looking at it.

"Got them from Sensei Chan. His brother sent them to the dojo," he explains with a smile, picking it up. A sticky note saves the page featuring Ryan in his win over Haru. "That's my boy," he says pointing at a photo of Ryan in action. "It took forever to get here, so I'm always months behind. But I've been following you."

"Thanks, Dad. Means a lot."

"Proud of you son."

They stand there for a second just looking at each other. Then Amen sweeps his arm at the disarray that surrounds them.

"Been real hard to keep on top of things. With work. . . taking your mother to her appointments. . .

had to take on a second job to help pay the medical bills. I'm teaching after school, now, and working at the hospital. . . There's hardly any time left in the day."

"Dad, you could have told me. I'd send you money."

Amen looks down a moment.

"I'm not asking my own son for money. . . besides, Tokyo's expensive."

"I'd be happy to help. I'm doing okay now."

"Yeah, well. . ." His father goes quiet a minute. Then, "Had to stop coaching."

"Really? That was your favorite thing."

"You were my favorite thing, actually, Ry. But yeah, I did enjoy it. There's just no time."

They stare at the floor. The clock ticks on the mantle.

"How you holding up?" Ryan asks.

"It's not easy, son. I feel like everything's getting away from me."

Ryan nods. They study the floor some more.

"Well," Amen says after an awkward minute, "we should go say hi to your mom." He claps Ryan on the shoulder and brushes past him down the hall.

As if it's just the most normal thing in the world. . .

***

The hospital is a fifteen-minute drive away. They don't talk much. Ryan's head feels heavy after the long flight. Amen pretends to concentrate on the traffic.

Ryan is struck again by how small-town suburban everything is. The roads are filled with cars and trucks and delivery vehicles, but it hardly seems like traffic after Tokyo. There are actually open sections of sidewalk, devoid of people. Acres of them.

When they arrive, Amen parks in the "Visitor" section and puts his arm around Ryan on the way to the entrance.

"I know this isn't easy. Hasn't been easy for me."

"I'll be fine."

"Well, you should prepare yourself. She's had a rough go."

Ryan nods.

The hospital is brightly lit. Nurses and orderlies flit this way and that. Amen steps over to the counter.

"Hello Mr. Bow, you can go on down," the young woman says. She looks up at Ryan and smiles.

"My son," Amen says, grinning. "He's in from Japan."

"Japan! You don't look Japanese," she jokes. "I've always wanted to see the cherry blossoms."

"They're beautiful," Ryan says.

Amen taps the counter with his knuckles, and they turn toward the ward. Ryan shuffles alongside his father, his feet dragging. Diane's room is only a few doors down.

Amen knocks on the door frame quietly and pushes open the white wood door.

Ryan can see around his father, who's standing just inside the room. It's dark, but he can make out his mother lying in bed, her hair an unruly pile on the pillow.

Looks like she's missing some hair.

She's asleep. Clothes are draped over the chair, pill bottles sit on the nightstand. A TV glows in the corner, a talk-show host making jokes to canned laughter.

Ryan lets out his breath.

His father turns and gently pushes him out of the room.

"Let's let her sleep." He closes the door behind him. "She'll be very excited to see you."

Ryan nods.

Doesn't look like she gets excited by much.

***

"I think you're taking too much interest in these young men," Kobayashi's father said one night over dinner. He'd allowed her to go to the fights for a whole year, and she'd taken in a dozen or so.

The family sat down for at least one meal together every day, traditional style, in their formal dining room. Her mother would prepare the food, they'd all sit around a horigotatsu with a recessed floor underneath, allowing everyone to sit comfortably with their legs extended. They'd express gratitude with an "*Itadakimasu*," and eat a leisurely dinner. Her father insisted they all participate.

"These traditions are what hold a family together," he'd say. "Otherwise, we'd all be gone, like a flock of birds, in different directions."

He held his bowl to his lips and looked at her over the rim.

"*Otōsan*," she said, "it's not about the boys."

"What is it about then?"

"I like the ceremony. The action. The suspense." She knew what would really grab him. "To me, it's like watching the samurai of old. Bushido."

He nodded slowly.

"I can understand that," he said, putting down his chopsticks. "It still feels inappropriate for a young woman to be in the company of so many young men."

"I'm sitting in the stands! With Daisuke!" She stared at him.

Her father set his jaw and sat for a moment. His eyes gave nothing away.

Did I speak too loudly?

"I will allow it," he said, extending his pointer finger. "But only if Daisuke is there to watch over you."

She grinned.

Perfect.

She knew not to push her luck.

After that, Kobayashi *made* Daisuke take her to the fights once a month, no matter how far they had to drive. More often than not, they would be in the smaller local shows on the northern island where they lived, but a few times a year they would take the 90-minute flight down to Tokyo to see the high-profile events at the country's biggest venues. She developed an even greater affinity for the sport, beginning to understand the different fighting styles – she especially appreciated judo – and recognizing raw talent in the competitors she liked. Fight day became the day of the month she looked forward to most.

Sometimes, she'd place small bets on her favorite fighters. She had an eye for picking winners, earning five or six times her bet. Daisuke knew, of course, but Kobayashi gave him money to wager, too, so he would never say anything to her father. He had a bit of a crush on her, despite the ten years' difference in age, and seemed to really enjoy their travels together. At a towering 6'3, he was a real presence in the crowds, and the pair of them became well known on the fan circuit. On a few occasions, she and Daisuke were invited back to meet fighters by friends of her father. Some of these men – connected, probably in the life – thought it was cute that she was so interested. She worried, sometimes, that they might report back to her father. About being a girl. About being backstage. About her gambling.

"Why do I keep seeing you at these fights, Kobayashi-chan?" asked one, an older oyabun from the west side of Tokyo. Shimoda-san was a man her father respected, and they often formed allegiances when the families gathered for important meetings to discuss business, territory, any factional disputes. This particular gentleman had been to the house on several occasions, and she always found him nice.

"I've become a fan," she said simply.

"A fan?"

"Yes, and I particularly like Mach, one of your fighters."

A grin spread across the face of the grey-haired man, and he clapped his hands.

"Mach is very good, indeed," he agreed.

"I think he's ready for a step up in competition," Kobayashi said. "I would book him in the event at Korakuen Hall next month. The purse is generous for a mid-tier fight, and with a win, he could move up the ranks. Maybe even toward a belt. I think he's that good."

"Do you, now? I will keep that in mind."

He studied her a moment.

"Do you offer your father advice like this?"

"He doesn't ask," she told him, looking down. "He doesn't think girls should have anything to do with MMA."

"I don't see why not," the old man said. "Especially when they have such a keen eye." He smiled and tapped her on the hand. "I will look into this fight for Mach."

***

When the MMA event came around, Kobayashi found herself willing Mach to win. She wanted to be right – and didn't want to let Shimoda-san down. The fight wasn't even close. Mach battered his competition, an up-and-coming fighter from Nagoya.

Yes.

On the way through the concourse, she and Daisuke found Shimoda-san waiting outside the locker room.

"Kobayashi-chan," he said with a slight dip of the head.

Her eyes lit up when she noticed him.

"You called it," he said. "I'm pleased I had the sense to follow your advice."

She smiled and bowed.

"Have any more tips for me?"

"I have been following Eiji Tanaka from your team," she said. "If you give him the opportunity, he could really make a name for himself."

"Ah, Eiji. He is a very good fighter. Headstrong, though. Maybe a little uncontrollable."

"He's confident and unpredictable. That will take you far in MMA."

"You are a bright one, Kobayashi-chan. But I think Eiji might need a bit more time to adjust."

"He will win," she said.

"Someday soon."

Shimoda-san patted her on the shoulder and padded toward the exit.

As if he were waiting for me.

***

"Daughter, I'd like to speak with you." Kobayashi's father met her as she came home from college one afternoon, directing her into his office, seemingly no nonsense, all business.

"Sit."

What did I do now?

"I have something we need to discuss."

"Okay. . ."

"You listen. I will speak."

She clenched her mouth shut and sat back in her chair.

"I had an interesting conversation this morning."

What is this about?

"Shimoda-san called me. He said he's been seeing you at the fights."

"Father, I've only gone as often as you said . . ."

"I will talk. You will listen."

She pulled her chin to her chest.

"Shimoda-san told me some things you said to him."

"Father, I. . ."

"Listen!" He rarely raised his voice, so when he did it scared her. He put his hands on the side of the desk and leaned forward.

"Shimoda-san said you offered him advice on a couple of his fighters." He walked around the desk and perched on the corner, standing right over her.

She just waited.

"He said this advice was exactly right. He made money. His fighter prospered. He said you had an exceptional understanding of MMA."

She looked at him, not daring to open her mouth.

"When I allowed you to go to the fights, I did not expect this," he said, bringing his hands together in front of his waist.

She opened her mouth as if to speak, and he stopped her with a glare.

"I will not tell you again to listen. I have an opportunity for you, but if you continue to interrupt, I will see that you are not ready to accept this opportunity."

Opportunity?

She sat back again and folded her hands in her lap.

"You," he jabbed a finger at her, "have to learn not to get in your own way."

196

He pushed himself off the desk and started to pace.

"Shimoda-san said you are an astute observer of MMA, even at your young age. As you know, our family is trying to extend our operations into the sport. I'd like you to continue to go to the fights and report back to *me* what you see. Fighters you think show potential. Who we could sponsor. Who we should drop. In other words, I'm offering you a chance to become involved in the family business. Keep your counsel to our family, however. Your brother had started working for me; this could be an opportunity for you to gain some experience."

"I thought you said MMA was not for girls."

"Perhaps not for girls with smart mouths," he said, crossing his arms. "I might have been too hasty. Shimoda-san is a very capable businessman. He and I think a lot alike. He tells me you have potential. I would not want to stand in the way of my own daughter. And I don't see why another family should benefit from your knowledge and not ours."

***

So here she was. Kobayashi realized that the road ahead won't be a walk in the park. She met with Ryan the day after the meeting, in the much more comfortable confines of her Tokyo office. Enson accompanies Ryan for the trip. She explains about the meeting, her voice quiet.

"I don't understand," Ryan says. "I won. I had the crowd on their feet. I had kids coming up to me for autographs afterward."

"I know. I get it. You don't have to convince me. It's the organization. They have other plans. They want to focus on. . ." she pauses, uncomfortable, ". . .they want to focus on local talent."

"I've worked so hard for this. I've earned the right." Ryan's voice rises. "I put my own health on the line."

Kobayashi and Enson exchange glances. She looks at Ryan, her brow furrowed, her lip in a tight line.

Ryan opens his mouth to say more. . .

Enson clears his throat. He gives Ryan a quick glance and stands. Ryan gets the message loud and clear. They thank Kobayashi-san for her time and head out.

Out of earshot, Enson says, "I know you're angry, Ryan, but she has it just as bad as you."

"What's that supposed to mean?"

"The nail that sticks out gets hammered down."

Ryan keeps his mouth shut, knowing better than to say anything.

***

Ryan runs through the park. In his hand he clutches the medal he won in his debut at Tokyo Fight Night. The small trophy has become a symbol for him, his most prized honor to date. When he pauses to catch his breath at the edge of the river, he finds that he's squeezing it so tight it's cut into his palm – the engraved coin is stained with blood. He looks at the waterline, which is covered in pink cherry blossom petals. In the light, the rosy hue of the blossoms makes it seem as if the river is bleeding, too.

I can't fucking catch a break. I can't fight in the U.S. And now I can't even fucking fight here.

Still breathing hard, he reaches for his ankles, stretching. When he stands up, he hurls the medal into the river, where it slides beneath the petals. Gone.

Chapter 13

"Ryan, that's too tight."

Eriko grimaces as Ryan lets go of her hand.

"I'm sorry, I didn't realize I was squeezing so hard."

They walk along a busy Yokohama street.

"Listen," she says, massaging one hand with the other. "You'll get another chance. I'm sure. Soon."

Ryan shakes his head and stares into a shop window. He's quiet a moment.

"I've been thinking. . ." He pauses for what seems a minute.

"Yes?" Eriko says softly, looking up at him.

"Maybe I should just go back to the States."

She looks like she's been struck. Then a look comes over her face. She pulls herself close to him and whispers in his ear.

"I've been thinking, too. Let's go back to your place."

"The Gaijin House is no place to take a woman."

She puts on a pout.

"Well, I live with my parents."

Ryan has another idea. He's gotten to know the district with his daily roadwork routine. They stroll down Motomachi, the stylish neighborhood nearby. Off the main drag, half way up the hill towards Yamate, stands a discreet love hotel. It's a modern, five-story hostelry with prices for short stays listed in the window.

An electronic panel displays illuminated photos of available rooms, each image offering a doorway into a different world. Ryan pushes cash under the glass in the lobby. Eriko takes his hand, and they walk up the steep stairway to their room.

***

The next day, Ryan all but skips into Purebred Tokyo, his gym bag slung over his shoulder. A repetitious groove – Ice Cube – echoes in the background. The famous rapper singing about a good day. The American fighter is feeling it, too. He has a big grin when he sees Enson checking something at the front desk.

"What's with you?" Enson asks. "Last time I saw you, you were pissed."

"Oh, you know," Ryan says, pointing up at the speakers. "Today was a good day."

"Ah," says Enson, chuckling. "You've got jokes."

He turns back to the desk calendar he's studying.

"Go get yourself ready. It's you and Nori today."

Ryan changes and begins skipping rope to get his body warm. After ten minutes, he puts a few rounds in on the heavy bag. He works around the bag as he punches.

"Slow feet don't eat," he says to himself over and over. "Slow feet don't eat."

He doesn't want to tire out before sparring with Nori, so he takes a swig of water and heads over to the ring. He stares at mural on the wall above the squared circle and remembers why he chose this life. It reads: "The only reason a warrior is alive is to fight, and the only reason a warrior fights is to win – Miyamoto Musashi."

Before long, Enson walks up with Nori.

"Ready?"

"As I'll ever be," Ryan says smiling at Nori, who gives him a grin and a nod.

They climb into the ring and tap gloves. Enson claps for them to begin. This time Ryan doesn't rush in, just circles Nori, who takes the center and tracks Ryan with his eyes. Then Nori fakes a step forward and launches a right hook at Ryan, who covers up with his guard high and uses the opportunity to tie up Nori's arms, move in, and grapple. The pair pummel in and out of position, each trying to get an underhook and gain an advantage. Nori executes a flawless duck under, slipping behind Ryan and pressing him against the ropes. Ryan twists to the side and attacks his teammate's arm with a Kimura arm lock and spins into it. Nori counters as they fall to the mat and scramble apart.

"Yes!" says Enson from ringside, clapping his hands. "Nicely done. Both of you!"

Ryan manages to land several convincing blows on Nori in the second half of the session and takes him down a couple of times. The more experienced fighter still has the upper hand, but the American is clearly gaining. They spar for several five-minute rounds before Enson yells, "Time! Good work today. Get something to drink. Ryan, meet me in my office."

Ryan takes off his gloves and grabs a towel, wondering what Enson wants. The last time they had a heart to heart it wasn't exactly roses. While he was still bitter about being shoved aside by the fight promoters, he knew it wasn't Enson's fault, and he was a little embarrassed about how upset he got.

Ryan taps the door frame with his knuckle.

"You wanted to see me, coach?"

"Have a seat," Enson says when Ryan steps in, still toweling himself off.

He slides into the armchair across from Enson's desk. Its upholstery is scratchy on his back, and he leans forward.

"I heard something I didn't like hearing, and I wanted to get your side."

Ryan raises his eyebrows and sits back.

"Okay. . ." he says.

"Ishihara-san says you started a fight in the street with Haru and Kamikaze Tanaka."

"*I* started it? They jumped *me*. I was walking home with my girlfriend, Eriko when they attacked me."

"I don't doubt you, at all, Ryan, I saw what happened the last time. They're *chinpira*, low-level foot soldiers, and that's how they operate. But that's what I heard, and it's why they're not letting you fight. Ishihara has a lot of clout with all the promoters. However it started, we can't afford to burn bridges with the gatekeepers of the industry.

Ryan raises his head to say something then thinks better of it. He puts his elbows on his knees and looks down at the floor.

"I hear you."

"Good."

"I ever tell you my story?" Enson asks.

"No, but I've heard a little."

"You know I grew up in Hawaii, yeah?"

"Yeah."

"Winning the belt didn't come easy." Enson points to it, shining on the wall behind him. "I was a small kid. A squirt. And Japanese. In America. So, I got bullied a lot. Classic push- me-down-take-my-lunch-money, put-my-head-in-a-locker type stuff. By high school, I was getting into fights in the street. I got tired of putting up with it. Which is why I pushed my folks to let me study martial arts and learn to defend myself. My brother did, too. We began learning jiu-jitsu from Relson, the only Gracie at the time teaching in Hawaii. My brother and I eventually had a falling out with the academy and decided to go our own way, the path less traveled and all. Eventually, we earned our black belt from John Lewis. Just want you to know, I feel you. Sometimes the journey is a lonely trek. Especially, when you feel like a koi out of water."

Ryan knows the legendary Brazilian jiu-jitsu fighter and sits transfixed.

"I've walked the path you're on. Between Kobayashi-san and I, we will give it to you straight. Help you weed out the bullshit and navigate the roads ahead."

The champ gets up walks around the desk and puts his hand on Ryan's shoulder.

"I hope you pasted those assholes."

Ryan gets up, breathes out slowly.

"I got in a few good ones."

"Good. Back tomorrow for another hard one."

Ryan looks at him.

"It's almost like, what's the point?"

"Your time will come," Enson says. "We're not going to manufacture it. But, believe me, you'll be ready for it."

The American heads for the door.

"Oh, and Ryan."

"Yeah, coach?"

"Put that smile back on your face." Enson plops back down at his desk and grins at him. Shooto looks up and smiles, too, his tail thumping the floor.

***

When they round the corner, Eriko stops short. Since the night they were attacked, she's been on edge walking anywhere with Ryan after dark. She clings to his arm, and her head constantly swivels, looking for threats. Standing in front of them is a middle-aged couple. A man and woman dressed for the office stop quickly when they notice Eriko. The woman's eyes are wide in recognition.

"Eriko?" she says.

"*Otō-san, Okā-san,*" Eriko bows her head.

Father, Mother. . .

She quickly slips her arm out of Ryan's.

Eriko's mother looks the American up and down, her arms crossed, her eyebrows bending down, her lips pursed.

Ryan bows. Gives them both a smile.

"Nice to meet you," he says in Japanese. "I'm a friend of Eriko's."

Her parents glare at him. Neither says a word.

Eriko's father breaks off his stare and looks at her, eyes dark, narrowed.

"We will discuss this later."

Her gaze falls to the ground, sadness clear in her posture.

Her parents walk briskly away, without another word. Soon, they're around the corner.

Eriko continues to stand there, eyes to the ground. Ryan notices she's shaking.

"Hey," he says, his voice quiet.

She looks up.

"Are you ashamed of me?"

"No, no," she says quickly. "But my parents are very traditional. They don't want me to date a foreigner."

"You haven't told them about me? About us?"

Eriko looks at him, her eyes soft.

"I haven't. I couldn't. . ."

He steps over and hugs her. She grabs him tightly.

"I'll talk to them," she says. "I promise."

Ryan walks her to within a block of her house, a traditional two-story Japanese home, with persimmon trees in the garden. She kisses him quickly and then turns away. When Eriko reaches the front walk, she slows and her head falls again, like a prisoner on her way to the gallows.

She opens the sliding *shoji* door, slips her shoes off, and tries to slink into her room, quiet on the tatami mats. The house is tidy and spare with a simple vase of flowers and a framed Edo-period painting, the only decoration. Her mother has been waiting.

"Eriko!" she says.

Eriko stops but doesn't look at her mother, who stands straight-backed with her arms crossed, her eyes fixed on her daughter.

"You will quit dating this man immediately."

Eriko nods and hurries to her room. It's a small space with just a low-set bed for one and a lamp on top of a bookshelf with a handful of titles. She pulls the door closed behind her, drops to her bed, and sobs into her pillow.

***

A new face at the gym pounds the heavy bag, a brash Japanese kid fresh from the street.

Ryan watches his younger teammate as he swings haymakers. The kid's been training for a whole two weeks and already thinks he's the real deal. Like a lot of newbies, he's spent too much time bulking up and not enough time learning the fundamentals.

This guy should be easy.

The American steps into the ring with the kid. Not enough work getting his footwork right either, he thinks as the young fighter rushes at him. Ryan sidesteps and hammers the newcomer in the side of the head with an overhand right. The kid's eyes swim in his skull. Ryan follows with another hard blow to the other side of his face. The kid's knees buckle, and he begins to wobble. Ryan notices Enson frowning at the side of the ring.

He hits the kid again. And again. And again. And again. He cocks his arm for another cross. . .

"Ryan!" Enson yells. "Stop!"

The kid wobbles to the other side of the ring and climbs out.

"What the hell's up with you?" the champ asks.

"Just getting some rounds in coach."

"You want to spar, spar with me."

Enson slips under the ropes and into the ring and begins to circle. Ryan watches his mentor carefully. Still, Enson cracks him with a punishing right to the left side of his face. He shakes it off. Enson hits him with another lightning-speed combination, causing Ryan to stumble backwards. The champ doesn't let up, on him right away. A left hook to the liver sends Ryan to the mat, and Enson climbs on him and keeps pounding, fists like hammers. Over and over. Ryan curls and covers.

Enson eventually lets up and stands. He extends a hand to Ryan.

"Doesn't feel so good, huh?"

Ryan hangs his head.

"My office," says Enson. "Now."

Ryan finds himself again seated across from Enson. This time feels different. He went to the principal's office once in grade school for fighting with a playground bully.

It's like I'm back in Grand Rapids.

Fighting Blind

They stare at each other across Enson's desk, a big gray steel thing with a phone, a laptop, and a handful of mail on it.

Enson studies him a minute.

"What's going on with you, braddah?"

"Nothing."

"Nothing? Seems like something." Enson crosses his arms and looks Ryan up and down. "This still about not getting a chance to fight?"

"No, I dunno. Some personal stuff."

"So, you take it out on your teammates? Especially rooks?"

Ryan looks down at the floor.

"Look Ryan. You're good. Really good. Good enough to hurt somebody."

Enson leans forward, his elbows resting on his desk.

"But you can't let your emotions get the better of you. You'll find yourself on the losing side real quick. Focus. . . Fighting is mental warfare, and it's this," he points at his head, "that separates the pros from the amateurs."

Enson pauses and watches Ryan.

Ryan nods.

"You're right. My bad."

Ryan looks Enson in the eyes.

"I'm sorry, coach."

Enson winks.

"We've all been there," he says, standing up.

He gives Ryan a grin and extends his hand. Ryan takes it and Enson pulls him into a bro hug.

"Sometimes it feels like we're invincible when we're in the ring. But we're only human."

As he leaves Enson's office, Ryan pulls out his phone and dials Eriko. Her voicemail picks up. Again. He's tried her a half dozen times already, and it's always the same.

"Hey Eriko," he says. "It's me again. I've left several messages. Please call me."

He heads for the showers.

***

Eriko's mother Mutsuko helps her into her traditional kimono, pulling on the sides to adjust the fit. She smooths the sleeves and kneels, making sure the hem hits the floor at the appropriate height. Mutsuko putters around, fussing with the silk robe, ensuring it's just right. Eriko's mouth is clenched, and her eyes stare straight ahead.

"He's waiting," says Mutsuko, smiling. "I think you're going to like him."

Eriko lets out a sigh, her head dropping.

"This is the third guy in the last couple of weeks."

"I felt the same at your age. Trust me. It's for the best."

Mutsuko walks around Eriko one last time.

"Come," she says.

In the living room, a Japanese gentleman is looking at one of her mother's paintings. In her spare time, Mutsuko is a water colorist, painting traditional scenes. This is a cherry tree, extending out over a stream.

"Lovely," the man says, when he hears them approach. He turns and takes in Eriko, grinning. He's at least ten years older than her and dressed smartly in a dark suit. He bows. She does the same, forcing a tight smile upon her rise.

"Thank you," says Mutsuko. "It's one of mine. I enjoy *ukiyo-e*." She's beaming, clearly impressed with this one, and she watches him all the way out the door.

***

Again with the headaches. They've plagued him since the beat down in the street, but he hasn't let on at the gym or with Eriko. Every so often, his cranium feels like it is going to crack from the pressure.

Like someone put the valve of a bicycle pump in my ear and started pumping.

He worries, reminded of the doctor's shock at the size of the cyst in his head. Today, he has to be out, supposed to meet Jon for dinner.

The Brit would understand if he had to cancel, wouldn't he?

I can't let it get to me, Ryan says, standing up and swaying. He puts a hand on the wall to steady himself while he pulls on his jeans. The room has a haze to it, as if a cloud has floated in through a window. The book on his bedside table has dull edges, and the door seems very far away. Ryan gets himself dressed and stumbles out into the night.

***

Jon tears into his sushi, like a shark. Ryan just pushes his around the plate. They sit in a dark bar, one of Jon's favorites, a short train ride from the Gaijin House.

"This is top-notch," the Englishman says, taking another bite.

"Mmm," says Ryan.

At least it's dark. . .

"Hey, the nail gets hammered down in all areas of life here," Jon says, wiping his mouth with a napkin. He takes a big swig of his beer.

"I dealt with it myself," Jon says, raising his glass. "Which is why I gave up trying to climb the corporate ladder. Being self-employed has its pitfalls, but it beats the 9-to-5 grind."

Ryan's friend continues to devour his sushi, as if he hasn't eaten in days. He pauses and looks intently for a minute. He starts to nod his head vigorously, pointing at Ryan with his chopsticks, but has to chew before he can get anything out.

"Maybe that's what you should do," he finally says. "How's your Japanese coming along?"

"Pretty good. I'm not sure I. . ."

Jon nods, cutting him off.

"Or, you could teach English," he says, chin up to avoid food falling out.

"I want to fight. That's why I'm here."

Jon nods and waves his chopsticks again.

"Then you might need to accept being the nail." He grins and raises his beer at Ryan. "You do seem pretty sharp."

Ryan stares at him and goes back to moving his food around. He rests his chopsticks across his bowl and holds the side of his head. The room looks a little less gauzy than his did at the Gaijin House earlier, but everything still wears a little fuzz. And the headache. . .

What is going on with my vision?

Jon continues to talk, gesturing, laughing, but Ryan can barely keep up. He nods and smiles where he thinks it seems appropriate but has lost the ability to follow along.

Jon puts his napkin on the table and takes a long look at Ryan.

"You okay, mate? You look a little woozy. Too much saki?" The lanky Brit glances at Ryan's glass, which has hardly been touched. "No, that can't be it."

"Na," says Ryan. "Just feeling a little off. Not myself. My head is pounding."

"You just depressed because of your girl? Or is your noggin' rocking from fighting?"

"I'm sure I'll be fine," Ryan says.

"MMA can be brutal on a brain . . . Our skulls were not designed to take a constant battering."

"Mmm," says Ryan.

"Let's get you back to your room."

Ryan weaves along next to Jon.

"You sure you didn't do any drinking before dinner?" Jon asks.

"What? No. I'm just not feeling well. Must be coming down with something."

"I'll say, mate. You really seem off your game."

When they reach the Gaijin House, Ryan heads right for his room and closes the door. Switching off the light, he puts his headphones on and turns on the Japanese language CD he was listening to before they left at a very low volume. He leans back on his futon and practices saying various words and phrases.

"*Shikata ga arimasen.*" "*Shikata ga arimasen.*"

He sits up and tears his headphones off, throwing them across the room.

Fuck this.

He pulls the covers over his head.

***

He knocks, politely at first. When this gets no answer, he bangs hard.

The door opens.

There she is. His heart jumps at the sight of her.

Eriko's eyes go wide. She looks over her shoulder into the house and quickly steps out, pulling the door behind her.

"What are you doing here?" she whispers. "You can't be here."

"Eriko?" her mother calls from inside. "Who is it?"

She turns and calls out, "No one, mother."

"No one, huh?" Ryan says.

She tilts her head to the side.

"I'm sorry, but. . ." She looks over his shoulder to the street. "You won't understand."

"You're a grown woman, Eriko. You can make your own decisions. In the United States. . ."

"This isn't the United States," she says curtly.

They look at each other.

"You're going to let your parents choose who you can be with? What is this, the fourteenth century?"

She frowns at him. "It's the way we do things here."

"You spent all that time with me, hiding it. . ."

"You should go."

"I love you, Eriko. This isn't right. . ."

"Eriko?" Mutsuko says from within the house. Her voice gets louder. "What is. . ."

"Go," Eriko says frantically. "Please."

Mutsuko opens the door and stands behind her daughter. She takes a step back when she sees Ryan.

"You," she says, placing a hand on her shoulder. Eriko hangs her head and disappears inside.

Mutsuko faces Ryan, all pretense of Japanese politeness gone. "You need to leave – now. I don't want to see you here again," she hisses.

And slams the door in his face.

Chapter 14

"I need something big," Ryan says. He sits across the desk from Kobayashi. She swivels her chair and looks out the window. She turns back, taps a pencil on the glass atop her desk.

"What do you have in mind?" she asks in Japanese.

Ryan shakes his head, leans forward to say something then sits back. He crosses his legs and sits there a moment, then leans in again, elbows on his knees. Finally he comes out with it.

"Kamikaze."

She shakes her head.

"Eiji Tanaka? You came here, taking up my time, for Kamikaze? You've had what, a couple fights? And now you want to take on the champ?"

She huffs. Then glares at him.

"C'mon, Ryan. We've been over this."

"What would it hurt to try?"

She puffs out her cheeks, pivots her chair again, and folds her arms, staring through the huge bay windows.

"We can't even get you a fight, and you want the champ. . ." Kobayashi says to herself, lost in thought.

Ryan squirms in his seat, waiting.

"The pro circuit is complicated," she finally says, turning to face him.

"You can't just challenge him for the belt. You'd have to beat someone who has given him a run for his money."

She stares at the wall above his head, lost in thought. Then, it comes to her. "The Barbarian," she ponders aloud. "And there might be an angle we could use. . . To get you the fight."

The American bobs his head up and down.

"Sometimes promoters will pit a strong Japanese fighter against weaker foreign opposition to build the local fighter's name."

Ryan tilts his head.

"But I'm local, from right here in Japan."

She smirks at him. Leans back and crosses her legs.

"And I'm definitely not weaker," he jokes.

"But. . ." she says.

"But what?"

"The Barbarian is good. Really good. You could be seriously injured."

"Appreciate the vote of confidence, boss," Ryan says. "First, I'm weak – now, I'm fragile too?

She smirks at him again.

"Let me fight him."

She nods her head slowly, her face blank. "This could work."

"Set it up," Ryan says.

Kobayashi picks up the phone on her desk and waves her hand at him in a shooing gesture.

"Wait outside."

Ryan gets up and leaves the office and starts pacing in the lobby. He can hear his manager in active conversation, a dull murmur. He watches her pace around the office through the small sidelights in the door, ankles rocking in her high heels. She nods. She shakes her head. She gestures with her free hand. He eventually takes a chair in the waiting area and pumps his leg up and down. He picks up an MMA magazine and pages through it. Both the Barbarian and Eiji "Kamikaze" Tanaka are featured.

Why not me? What do I have to do to catch a break?

He gets up and resumes pacing. Kobayashi's door opens and she steps out. She sits down in one of the chairs and motions for him to take the seat next to her.

"I just got off the phone with Maeda-san, the Impact promoter. He didn't even want to discuss it."

Ryan slumps back in his chair.

"Why? Seemed like you were on the phone long enough. . ."

She folds her arms, raises her eyebrows, tilts her head, and looks at him, like an impatient teacher.

He jumps to his feet.

"What's the address?" he says.

"Ryan, I don't think. . ."

"Tell me," he says.

She stands and straightens her skirt. . . She crosses her arms again, shakes her head, and then looks him in the eye.

"This is not a good idea."

"I have to do *something.* . ."

"This isn't how we do things in Japan. Maeda-san is very traditional."

"I don't care," Ryan says. "I'm tired of Japanese tradition. I'm done waiting."

"Ryan. . ."

"It's the fucking twenty-first century."

Kobayashi can see that she can't change his mind. She lets out a long sigh.

"Wait here. I'll go with you."

They don't talk much in the car on the way over, Kobayashi clearly uncomfortable with the position the American is putting her in. She simply stares forward. Ryan watches out the window, seeing high-rise hotels and flashing billboards before recognizing Shinjuku. Every square inch on either side of the street is covered in large, colorful advertising. Kobayashi pulls up in front of a four-story building that's showing its age, its cement façade glass-smooth and well cared for. Ryan gets out and makes for the front door, not even waiting for her.

He jogs up the stairs to the second floor and continues down the hall until he recognizes the Impact logo. He steps inside, where a dyed-blonde secretary sits typing at her desk in a very modern lobby. Ryan walks right past her toward a door that obviously leads to the main office.

"Excuse me, sir!" she says rising. "You can't go in there!"

Ryan enters without knocking. The office is large, with tall windows on to the street. Posters of Kamikaze Tanaka and the Barbarian adorn the walls. Maeda sits behind a large wooden desk, reviewing some paperwork, and he's startled as the door opens. Middle-aged, he fills out his dark, tailored business suit, though it looks more from Korean BBQ than from tae kwon do.

Ryan steps right up to his desk and bows, with Kobayashi trying to keep up, and the frantic secretary chasing them both.

"Maeda-san, my apologies for the intrusion," Ryan says.

"Shall I call the police, sir?" the secretary asks.

"My name is Ryan Bow, and I want to fight Hiro Suzuki, the Barbarian."

Maeda's brow wrinkles, and he begins to stand when Kobayashi elbows Ryan out of the way. She bows politely.

"I'm sorry, Maeda-san," Kobayashi says, "but there was no stopping him. He is ready. You were there when he fought Haru, and he's continued to win again and again."

The promoter puts both hands on his desk and leans forward, his face red. He stays this way for a long minute. Then he sighs and sits back down. He waves away his secretary, who bows, backs up, and closes the door behind her.

Maeda looks right past Kobayashi at Ryan.

"You have to go through proper channels, Mr. Bow," he says. "Have your manager call me. We can discuss this."

Kobayashi is indignant.

"I did call you," she says.

Maeda turns his attention to her.

"*You're* his manager?" His face hardens.

Ryan speaks in careful Japanese: "I have been an underdog my whole life, Maeda-san. Kobayashi-san and I both have. I'm prepared to die for this."

Maeda's gives Ryan a small nod. He thinks a moment. And then a little smile emerges as he realizes what he should have thought of all along.

***

The same conference room table is ringed with the same fight promoters, all dark suits, yak tats peeking out at the wrists. Attitude and male posturing dominate. Some talk in small groups, a couple check their phones. Akio leans against the corner of the table and his face twists into a sneer when Kobayashi enters. He's not the only one. Several of the businessmen regard her with at best, curiosity. Others point or openly stare. Hostile.

Kobayashi sees Maeda at one end of the long walnut table. He has his stout frame crammed into one of the narrow seats, and he bows his head ever so slightly at her. She walks over and pulls out a seat next to him. He leans in.

"Good luck. You'll need it."

Akio walks over and stands over the both of them. He says to Kobayashi: "Surprised to see you here. What's the occasion?"

"Same as you," Kobayashi responds. "Except I represent a true martial artist, not thugs."

"Not the gaijin?"

"Right," Kobayashi says. "The one who beat your guy."

Akio pauses a moment. Then he laughs.

The businessman at the head of the table, the stout, aging, Mr. Ishihara, claps his hands to get the meeting started.

"He ready for the big leagues?" Akio asks, moving away. "Are *you*? Ready for a seat at the big table?" He raps his knuckles on the tabletop and slides off to take his seat.

"Screw you."

Maeda watches this with a wry smile.

Kobayashi sits back in her chair and folds her arms tightly against her chest. She breathes out and looks around the room. Maeda notices her discomfort and leans in again: "don't worry about him."

Ishihara calls the meeting to order, and the men talk about upcoming fights and promotional opportunities. Akio pushes for a *vale tudo* event. These no-holds-barred fights are popular among audiences, but many venues want nothing to do with them. Several people point this out.

"We can find an arena," Akio says, sitting down in a huff.

No one bothers to ask Kobayashi for her thoughts or even look in her direction.

Anywhere but here, she thinks.

After an hour of talk, hashing out details, Mr. Ishihara says, "Ok. I believe that's it. The bout order for the event is set."

Kobayashi clears her throat and stands.

Several of the men snicker. Others roll their eyes. A couple walk out.

Ishihara holds up his hand for order.

"Kobayashi you may pitch your fighter."

"Saving the best for last," she says as she walks over to put a videotape into the huge conference room TV. All eyes turn toward it, curious if nothing else. What could she possibly know about fighting?

A lot, apparently.

Her fighter is good. They watch him stagger another fighter, a Japanese man whose back is to the camera. The gaijin stands toe to toe and slugs it out with a formidable Japanese opponent. The Japanese fighter eats a hard punch. He changes levels and shoots in for the takedown. The gaijin falls backward. On the way down, he snakes a leg over his opponent's shoulder and executes a perfectly timed triangle choke, rendering the Japanese fighter unconscious. When he comes to, they get a look at his face. They're stunned. All of them know him. The gaijin's opponent has become something of a legend in MMA despite his young age, and here he was bested by a virtually unknown fighter from America.

They begin to talk among themselves.

***

Nori taps out. There's no other way to escape the arm bar Ryan has him in. The American lets go immediately and springs to his feet. He gives Nori a hand up.

"Getting good," his teammate says. He pats Ryan on the shoulder and makes his way to the locker room.

Ryan hears his ringtone. He slides through the ropes and hops out of the ring, grabbing his mobile from his gym bag, hoping.

Please be Eriko. . .

"*Moshi moshi*," he says in Japanese.

"Ryan." He recognizes his manager's voice.

"Hey."

"We had another promotional meeting this afternoon. No one cared what I thought or wanted to hear what I had to say. . ." He can hear traffic behind her – she's obviously walking on the street. She's quiet for a minute, letting it sink in.

Ryan breathes out.

"Again? What the hell. . ." he says.

"But," she says, "I did manage to get them to watch a video of you fighting. . ."

Ryan starts to walk excitedly in little circles. Enson notices from his office and perks up. He watches his protégé through the door.

"And?"

"Hold on," Kobayashi says, and Ryan can hear her talking to another guy. She's buying dinner from a street vendor. "*Arigatō gozaimasu,*" she says, sounding muffled.

"Ryan, you there?"

"Waiting," Ryan says excitedly.

"Sorry. What was I saying?"

Ryan is rolling his right arm in circles in the air as if to say get on with it. Kobayashi is toying with him, like a veteran with a rookie in the ring.

"They watched the highlight reel" he says. "*And. . .*"

"And. . ." she says, pausing for another several seconds, "you have a fight with the Barbarian at Korakuen Hall in four weeks' time."

Ryan does a fast foot shuffle. Punches the air with his free hand.

"Oh, man. That is fantastic! Thank you, Kobayashi-san."

Enson glances up from his desk. He slams his palm down with a grin.

"Don't thank me, Ryan," she says. "You should have seen their faces when I put in the video of you throwing down, then choking out you know who with that triangle choke. Amazed. Astonished. *You* made this happen."

***

Eriko's eyes are fixed on the TV over the bar. Her date, the same Japanese gentleman, stands talking to another couple, dressed in their formal best. It's a black-tie fundraiser, with all of the fanciest people in Tokyo. Most women would dream of such a date – open bar, the finest sashimi, all of the country's most important people. Eriko only has eyes for the TV.

The volume is down, and she has trouble making out what the announcer is saying, but subtitles tell all. High-stakes MMA bouts are scheduled to go down at Korakuen Hall with two Purebred fighters on the bill. And there on the screen, standing beside the champ, Enson Inoue, is emerging star Norifumi "Kid" Yamamoto and rising American prospect, Ryan Bow.

My American.

She looks down at her black dress, which clings to her every curve, and sighs.

"Eriko?"

Her heart flutters. She can't believe he's getting back in the ring. She should be there for him.

"Eriko?"

She hasn't seen him in weeks. Her eyes well with tears.

Her date follows her gaze to the screen. He sets his jaw.

"Here's your drink," he says, putting a wine glass down on the bar and turning back to the other couple.

A Blessid Union of Soul's track hums in the background. A soulful anthem about the power of belief and love being the answer.

She looks back at her date and forces a smile.

***

Eriko reaches toward Ryan. They face each other in the therapy room, seated on stools. She has both arms extended, her index fingers pointing straight up. She looks at him all serious, totally professional.

"Look to the right."

Ryan keeps his head in place and follows her fingers with his eyes.

"Now, look to the left."

He does so.

"Very good," she says. "Are you doing your exercises at home? You can't slow down."

She writes on the clipboard in her lap. Trying to make as little eye contact as possible.

"How you been?" Ryan asks.

She keeps a straight face, looking over his shoulder.

"My parents have made arrangements for me to get married."

Ryan's head jerks back, as if he's just taken a jab.

"You don't want it, though. Right?"

She looks down at her lap. Her head nods slightly.

"Then don't."

"It's already arranged."

"Arranged. Is this the Middle Ages?"

She keeps her head bowed. Won't look at him.

"Unbelievable," he says.

She lifts her head, eyes welling up again. She finally looks him in the eye.

"How is your fighting coming along?" she asks, brushing her sleeve across her eyes. "I saw you on TV."

"Yeah, I have a big fight coming up."

"You should not be fighting, Ryan. Given your situation, you know it's too dangerous. But I hope you win."

"It's you I want to win, Eriko."

She drops her head and busies herself with his chart, the two sheets on the clipboard suddenly the most important things in the world. She studies them, folding back the first page to look at the second, and stays this way.

Ryan stands up and steps over to her. He puts his arms around her. She pushes against him and struggles, finally giving in and placing her arms around him.

"Introduce me to your parents," he says. "Properly. Trust me."

"I can't. Focus on your fight."

"Only if you'll be there."

228

"I can't. My parents." She pulls away. Looks at him. He stares at her, taking her all in. She can see that he's determined.

She's quiet for what seems a minute. Finally, she nods. Her face never brightens.

"Pinky swear?" he says.

Eriko extends her pinky toward him, and they lock hands.

"Cross my heart, hope to die, stick a thousand needles in my eye," they say at the same time.

"One thousand needles *dayo*," Ryan says, prompting a chuckle out of Eriko, for the first time breaking her all-business facade.

"No problem," she says.

***

Eiji can tell this one is different. When he, Haru, and Akio get to the meet, the tension in the room hits like a fist. Shimoda-san scheduled a second meeting with the Hsu family to discuss territory issues. The Hsu had been slowly moving into neighborhoods that Shimoda held on the west side of the city, despite their last interaction. Not only taking over Shimoda's protection rackets but also introducing prostitution and coke and meth. Eiji had never seen Shimoda-san so furious. A war of talk followed, occasionally spilling over into street violence, but did nothing to slow the Hsu advance. Shimoda-san met with the council and demanded one more meet in a neutral hotel conference room. A last-ditch effort before war between the families broke out.

The place was typically high end, all mahogany walls, floor-to-ceiling windows onto the garden and nearby koi pond. Even in the bustle of midday Tokyo, no sound penetrated the serenity of the lobby. The trio were to arrive first, scout the place, and send word back to Shimoda-san when it was safe for him. Akio was instructed to do all the talking; Eiji and Haru were muscle.

A hotel staff member shows them into a small meeting room, with a long, shiny black walnut conference table surrounded by a dozen red, fabric-covered chairs. The Hsu delegation is already seated on one side of the table, all wearing black suits. Each of the five seats on the left of the room are taken, and behind each chair stands another goon. Eiji recognizes the Hsu family patriarch, from the last sit-down between the two families. Short-statured and bald, with a grim blade scar, he sits at the far end, arms crossed, eyeing them as they enter.

"Gentlemen," Akio says. "If I'd known you were all wearing black, I'd have changed." He grins.

They all look back at him, impassive.

"Where is Shimoda-san?" the oyabun asks.

"Thank you for the kind welcome," Akio says bowing. "It is always good to show such respect in the modern era."

"Where is Shimoda-san?" the Hsu repeats.

"He'll be along shortly."

"Does he intend to waste my time?"

"He was held up," says Akio. "You know Tokyo."

The disgruntled mob boss rolls his eyes.

"I'll give him fifteen minutes."

While Akio is stalling, Eiji slips out to let Shimoda-san know the scene seems safe enough, that the Hsu family leader was there with ten of his men.

Ten minutes later, Shimoda-san arrives, surrounded by five more of his security detail.

While the two oyabun talk at the end of the table, Eiji keeps watch on the men.

Ten to eight, not bad, though Akio isn't much of a fighter. . .

They do the same, staring at Eiji, Akio, Haru, and the others, leaning against the wall.

Shimoda-san tells the Hsu in no uncertain terms to clear out of the west side. The Hsu leader flatly refuses.

"If you do not, there will be war," Shimoda-san says. "I don't think either of us want that."

"We are not afraid of you, Shimoda," his counterpart says. "Your organization faded long ago."

"My family remains the most prominent in Tokyo," Shimoda-san says. "Yours is a newborn barely crawling."

Hsu bangs on the table.

"You will not speak to me that way."

"Like an infant with wet pants." Shimoda-san grins, watching Hsu seethe. "I will speak to you however I want."

At this, Hsu's men all stand. Eiji pushes off the wall behind him, at the ready.

"This meeting is over," Hsu says. "I will not abide such disrespect."

"Then know this," Shimoda-san says, standing and leaning down into the opposing kingpin's face, "war is coming. When you least expect it."

Hsu grabs Shimoda-san's tie and pulls his face down toward the table. At this Haru, steps forward and smashes the mob boss' arm, causing him to release Shimoda-san's tie. A Hsu goon swings at Haru's face, connecting with his cheek. Chaos ensues.

Hsu men square off against Shimoda-san's cohort. An enforcer in a black suit punches Akio in the face, spraying pieces of his sunglasses across the table. Without thinking, Eiji elbows the guy next to him in the windpipe, grabs the temple of Akio's glasses, and stabs it into the eye of Akio's attacker. The man shrieks with such force that everyone in the room stops for a minute. Eiji uses the distraction to grasp a handful of hair from the next Hsu soldier he sees and bash his head into the tabletop. He does this repeatedly until the man's face is a pulpy mess.

"Oi!" Akio yells.

Eiji looks up. Akio points at Shimoda-san. Eiji hurries to his side and leads him out of the room, hustling him out to the Escalade. Akio, Haru, and the others get in, and the driver speeds away. Akio sits in the third row, next to Eiji, shoulder to shoulder. Akio leans into his ear.

"You might have killed that guy," he says.

"And?" Eiji looks at him, his face blank.

"And? We're already at war, and you may have just escalated things. . ."

"The point is, we're at war. People die in war. . ." Eiji says.

"Shimoda-san decides how far we go, Eiji, not a soldier. What you did. . ." Akio trails off and stares out the window.

Eiji clenches his mouth shut.

Chapter 15

The changing room at Korakuen Hall is compact with just a few wooden benches set between a couple dozen lockers. As Ryan gets ready, he watches a ceiling-mounted video monitor showing Nori's bout. He shadow boxes against a wall as Nori and his opponent, a larger Japanese fighter from the Impact stable, jockey for position from the clinch. Nori executes a nearly perfect outside leg trip and takes the guy down to the mat hard. Cheers from the crowd swell into the dressing room.

Ryan turns to see an official arrive to wrap his hands. They nod, and the guy, a seasoned Japanese man with spiky hair, takes out white, one-inch athletic tape and medical gauze. He makes three tight winds around Ryan's wrist before moving up to the palm with the gauze. He makes several passes around the back of the hand, then folds it multiple times over Ryan's knuckles to pad them. Next, he works tape between each of Ryan's extended fingers, compressing them slightly. He finishes by securing the wrap with the same tape, from the wrist all the way back up to the knuckles. He does the right hand the same way.

As he works, Ryan watches the monitor. Nori is getting the better of the lanky fighter. His opponent has a longer reach, but Kid knows how to slip the blows and get in close, taking away that advantage. Nori executes another takedown and then climbs aboard the grounded fighter, raining blows down one after another until his face is a bloody mess.

"Yeah!" says Ryan, clapping his hands. The official isn't done yet, and Ryan manages to unwind his right hand a bit in his exuberance.

"Sorry," he says. "My teammate just won." The guy nods, blank.

In the ring, the ref holds up Nori's hand while he beams. Enson pumps his fist in the corner.

Crowd looks huge. *I wonder where she is.*

The official wishes him good luck and heads out. As he opens the doors, the room once again floods with crowd noise. It fades a moment and then repeats with the arrival of Nori and Enson.

"You looked great out there," Ryan says to Nori, high-fiving him.

"I did it!" Kid says. His grin reveals bloodstained teeth and a swollen lip. More blood runs down his cheek from a cut above his eye.

"Now it's your turn."

"Let's get you warmed up," Enson says, picking up the boxing mitts. He puts them on his hands, slams his hands together, and holds them up for Ryan, who begins working his fists, throwing punches. He starts slowly and gradually speeds up, firing off combos.

"Good," says Enson, as Ryan continues to pound the pads, sweat beginning to drip down his forehead. "Now, get your feet moving."

After a few minutes, the coach says, "All right, we want you warm not tired." He pounds Ryan on the back.

The Grand Rapids native keeps bouncing in place, swinging his head back and forth to relax his neck. Enson drapes Ryan's robe across shoulders and again pats him affectionately on his shoulders.

"Let's go."

***

When they reach the hallway Kobayashi is there, waiting. Dressed in a dark navy pant suit, all Tokyo businesswoman, she leans against the wall with her legs crossed, the glow of her phone on her face. She glances up as they approach.

"How's my fighter?"

"Ready." Ryan says, bringing his mitts together.

She smiles.

"*Ganbare yo*," she says. "Good luck."

As the crowd cheers and music begins to pound, Ryan trots down the aisle toward the ring and is amazed to see American flags lining the way. A spotlight finds him, and the cameras pick him up, shooting his face onto a screen high overhead. The arena isn't as big as he thought, and the place gets louder as fans take notice – Korakuen Hall is an intimate venue, accommodating only 2,000, known for its seats right up close to the action and its status as one of Japan's most iconic venues for combat sports.

Looks like an oversized school gymnasium.

Ryan tries to scan the rows for Eriko — *she should be here with Jon* — without it appearing like he's looking for someone. He reaches ringside without seeing her and hauls himself up through the ropes. Time for business.

The Barbarian is sprawled in his corner, his arms up on the ropes, his trainer in his left ear.

"You got this," Enson says to Ryan, as he puts his mouthguard in. "You're every bit as good as he is." Ryan breathes out. He feels a tap on his ankle and looks down to see Kobayashi. He leans toward her.

"You see who that is next to Maeda-san?"

Ryan follows her gaze to the front row, where he spots Maeda. Sitting next to him is a very familiar fighter.

"My next fight," Ryan says, his mouthguard making it come out thick. "Kamikaze." He grins at her.

"First you have to get through *this*." Kobayashi tilts her head in the direction of the Barbarian. Her eyes are wide and she leans in even closer. "This is a big step up. Do not underestimate him."

"I won't let you down," Ryan slurs through his mouthguard.

"Win tonight and then call Kamikaze out," she says. "Make him acknowledge you."

Ryan nods, clapping his hands together.

A portly announcer in a suit jacket steps into the ring and pulls down the mic. The referee, a small Japanese man in his forties, climbs in behind him.

"Ladies and gentleman, welcome!" the announcer booms, a salesman at the mic. "And now, we present the main event. Introducing to you first, on my left, fighting out of Tokyo by way of Grand Rapids, Michigan. . . Ryan Bow!"

The crowd goes wild, and Ryan stands, raising his fists into the air.

"And his opponent. On my right, a formidable fighter from Toyama, Japan, Hiro 'The Barbarian,' Suzuki."

This too is greeted with excited cheers, and Suzuki clasps his hands over his head, as if already victorious.

The announcer climbs out of the ring, leaving the contestants separated by the referee. The music fades, and the fighters step to their corners to disrobe and get last-minute counsel from their coaches. Ryan glances across the mat at the Barbarian, who fixes his eyes on him, unblinking, and drags his thumb across his throat.

Bring it, Ryan thinks.

***

The referee signals for the fighters to approach. The Barbarian struts across the ring, his eyes still intent on Ryan.

"This is the main event. No biting. No eye gouging. No strikes to the back of the head. If you want to touch gloves, do it now."

The Barbarian slams his hands down on Ryan's and walks to his corner. Ryan backs up to his, never taking his eyes off his opponent.

The bell dings.

They meet in the center of the ring, and the Barbarian unleashes a barrage of punches, several of which Ryan eats. He steps back to gather himself.

"Circle, Ryan!" Enson yells.

Ryan begins moving counterclockwise. The Barbarian cuts him off and corners him, winding up and landing a roundhouse kick on the American's thigh. Ryan grabs him and forces the clinch against the ropes. He gets a collar tie on the Barbarian's head and pounds away at his gut. Suzuki side-steps and tries to knee Ryan, who parries it at the last moment. The Barbarian follows him and hammers his leg with another crushing kick. Ryan buckles and stumbles sideways. The Japanese fighter rushes in to finish him, and the bell sounds. The referee steps between the pair.

In the corner, Enson wipes sweat from his own brow, his face serious. Ryan winces as he sits on his stool. Squatting in front of him, Enson massages his leg to keep the blood flowing.

"Check those kicks," he says, looking Ryan in the eye. "And take the fight to the ground. Use your judo!"

The referee announces the start of Round Two. The Barbarian bounces off his seat and makes it to the center of the ring before Ryan gets there. The American stands off-axis, trying to protect his blind spot. This confuses Suzuki momentarily, giving Ryan time to slip inside and clinch. He lifts the Japanese fighter high into the air and drives him down on the mat. Ryan's shoulder comes crashing down on the Barbarian's diaphragm, knocking the wind out of him.

"Now, Ryan!" Enson shouts.

Ryan mounts his opponent and begins to brutally pound on him. The Barbarian scrambles and tries to force him off, but Ryan sticks to him. He follows him easily and continues the assault. He drives a knee to the body and feels ribs crack as the bell sounds. The Barbarian teeters to his corner, clutching his side.

The coaches cater to their warriors. Enson resumes his massage of Ryan's legs while Suzuki's applies an ice pack to his fighter's ribs. Ryan greedily drinks water, spitting out the excess. In the other corner, The Barbarian's coach whispers instruction while the fighter pours water over his own head.

***

The bell rings for the third and final round. The combatants circle then plunge in for the attack, aiming feet and fists at each other. Both are intensely focused, their eyes concentrated on their opponent.

The Barbarian feints forward and then leaps to Ryan's left, disappearing from the American's view. Ryan spins trying to find him and walks into a devastating right hook to the side of the head. He stumbles away but stays upright. He takes a moment to refocus, his eyes blurring. The Barbarian grins and jumps again to his left, lost in his blind spot. He pulls his arm back for the kill. Ryan jerks his head to the left, barely avoiding an incoming punch. He pivots to put the Barbarian on his good side.

The Japanese fighter keeps trying to attack his left and Ryan slides to compensate. He cuts off the ring and moves in to clinch. Again, he's able to sweep the Barbarian off his feet, throwing him to the mat. He lunges forward delivering a hammering Russian hook. The Barbarian's eyes circle back into his head and flutter back open. He leans forward to cling to Ryan, who throws a series of vicious punches to his body and head; Ryan continues to pound on the Barbarian, a seemingly excessive amount, until the bell rings. Suzuki's coach has to enter the ring to help his fighter back to his corner.

Ryan sits on his stool and watches the judges, who take a few minutes to confer.

"Why didn't the ref call it?" He says to Enson.

"Don't worry. It's all you."

In his corner, the Barbarian is barely able to hold his head up. His coach holds his shoulders, so he doesn't slide off his stool.

The judges gesture to the announcer and the referee. They all confer briefly, and the announcer steps back into the ring and pulls down the microphone. He no longer sounds like a salesman this time, hesitating.

"This bout is a draw."

The tension in the air is thick as the announcer's voice cuts through the crowd.

"There will be one five-minute overtime round."

Ryan whips his head back toward Enson, disbelief flashing across his face.

"What? Contract said there would be no overtime."

"Something feels off," Enson mutters, equally stunned.

Ringside, Kobayashi is practically foaming at the mouth, her face inches from Maeda's as she rages at him. Her words are sharp, but they're drowned out by the crowd.

"No time to argue about it. It's put up or shut up now, braddah. You're going to have to go again," Enson growls. "Lets do this."

"*Osu.*" *Ryan* shouts.

"Take him down and finish it. Don't leave it to the judges," Enson orders.

The referee motions both fighters to the center of the ring for the final round. The crowd falls into a heavy silence as the fight resumes. Ryan's pulse races as he measures the Barbarian's every move.

Without warning, Ryan throws a savage overhand right. Just before it lands, he shifts his weight, changes levels, and secures a single-leg takedown. The ring shudders as the fighters hit the canvas. The American quickly passes the Barbarian's guard to gain side control. His knee strikes with precision against his foe's already battered ribs, one after another as the Barbarian winces in pain.

But the Barbarian still has some fight left in him. He manages to scramble to his feet only to be swept back to the ground with a *kouchi gari*, a small inner reap. Ryan climbs into the mount position, locks his opponent's arms and smothers his face, mother's milking him. Ryan's weight bears down, crushing his opponent's airway, making it difficult for him to catch his breath.

Panic sets in. The Barbarian turns his head left and right, as he begins to run out of air. Ryan applies even more pressure downward, the Barbarian's nose completely flattened.

The Barbarian is out of options. He turns over and gives up his back. Ryan sinks in his hooks and a rear naked choke, draining what's left of his opponent's will to fight. Then, it happens. The Barbarian concedes and taps the canvas.

Gasping, Ryan rises to his feet and stumbles to his corner, waiting for the ref to make it official.

The fighters stand on either side of the referee, both exhausted. The announcer steps back into the ring and pulls down the microphone. There's no debating this time.

"And the winner, by rear naked choke, is Ryan Bow!"

The Barbarian's head falls to his chest. Ryan leaps on the corner ropes, his hands held high above his head. He looks toward Kamikaze and notices that Maeda has jumped to his feet, his face red.

The crowd howls with appreciation. Some chant Ryan's name. Enson waves his hands in the air, egging them on. They roar even louder.

Ryan walks over to the announcer and says something in his ear. The man grins and hands him the mic. Fans scream.

"*Arigatou gozaimasu,*" Ryan begins, thanking them.

They cheer and then quieten when Ryan bows toward Maeda.

"Maeda-san," he says, "I humbly request the opportunity to fight "Eiji 'Kamikaze' Tanaka."

The hall echoes with cheers.

"Ryan! Ryan! Ryan!" fans begin to chant.

Maeda turns red. He glances to his side at Kamikaze, who stares stone-faced at the presumptuous American.

The champion gets out of his seat and strides toward the ring.

The crowd goes crazy. People shout Ryan's name and scream excitedly.

***

Kamikaze pulls himself through the ropes and walks up to Ryan.

I didn't mean now. . .

Eiji gets to within an inch of Ryan's face, so close the sweaty fighter can smell his cologne. The Zainichi fighter stands there, not saying a word. His eyes bore through Ryan's head.

Then he raises his middle finger, putting it so close to the American it almost goes up his nose.

"Fuck. . . You. . ."

Kamikaze shoves Ryan with both hands. They square off. The referee tries to get between them. Kobayashi and Maeda watch on, stunned. Kamikaze throws a right hook that connects with Ryan's jaw. The tired fighter responds with one of his own that drives the promotion's champ back. He closes the space between them, and they crash into the ropes, fighting to get the upper hand. Kamikaze's eyes look stunned by Ryan's power.

Enson climbs into the ring. Nori follows, wearing only jeans. He saw the melee on the monitor and ran from the locker room. Ryan and Kamikaze trade blows, both connecting. The American clinches and drags Eiji to the canvas. Nori grabs Ryan, Enson snatches up Kamikaze.

The two Purebred fighters separate the pair, who glower at each other, both panting.

Kobayashi notices movement off to her right. She sees Akio, who nods his head in approval, liking what he's seeing. He raises a hand to her, his index and thumb forming a circle. His three remaining fingers extend horizontally. In America, this signals OK. In Japan it has an altogether different meaning: money.

Kobayashi responds with a small smile.

***

The next morning Ryan's eyes barely open. When the light hits them from underneath his door, pain radiates through his skull. He blinks, trying to make them work. Once again, everything is a blur, like he's trapped in a dream that refuses to come into focus. His head feels like it's been jackhammered, and his ears ring, like he's surrounded by singing cicadas.

"Ugh," he says, and lies back down, pulling the covers over his head. He doesn't move for much of the morning, just lies in bed. He has plenty of other throbs and pains – he took some intense blows to his legs and midsection – but nothing is as bad as his head, and he worries again about the cyst. His stomach eventually forces him up when he realizes the ache he feels there isn't from Barbarian's blows, but rather from hunger. He rolls off his futon and onto his knees and sits for a minute, placing his hand on his dresser. He uses one of the knobs as a grip to haul himself up to his feet and then slips out the door to the kitchen.

Jon is standing at the table, a newspaper spread out below him. He looks up when he hears Ryan.

"Hey mate." He surveys his friend. "Great fight last night. How you feeling?"

"Been better" Ryan says. He turns to his left so he can see Jon.

"No offense, but you've looked better."

"Yeah, Barbarian got in a few good ones. You don't really notice as much in the heat of the fight, but the next day is another story."

"Adrenalin is an amazing thing," Jon says. "I wish I could bottle and sell it."

Ryan puts his hand on the refrigerator handle and leans there for a moment. The overhead light in the kitchen is blinding, and he narrows his eyes to slits. Then he pulls open the fridge and withdraws a carton of eggs. He shuffles them over to the table and turns for a glass. The cicadas continue with their loud, high-pitched song, and he sits down for a moment to gather himself.

"Here, let me help you with that, my good man." Jon picks up the eggs. "How do you take them, scrambled, over easy, poached?"

"In a glass with protein powder."

"Of course," says Jon, snapping his fingers, "you're a fighter. Easy enough, then. You sit."

Ryan groans as he lowers himself into a hard wooden chair.

"Now is this usual post-fight pain or should we be concerned?" Jon asks, grabbing a tumbler from a cabinet.

"I think it's the usual," Ryan says. "But my head's just feeling it a bit more than before."

"Hmmm." Jon looks at him. "How many eggs and how many scoops?" He gestures at the huge round carton of protein powder.

"Two and three; milk for the rest. Arigatou." One elbow on the table, the other on the back of the chair, Ryan drops his head and closes his eyes.

"Nice," says Jon, who always appreciates it when the Yank uses Japanese. He mixes up the drink and hands it to Ryan, who downs it in three gulps.

"Well, your gullet seems to be working fine," Jon laughs. He folds up the newspaper and tucks it under his arm. "Got to get to work."

"I should get back to bed," Ryan says.

"Hope you feel better, mate."

"*Arigatou.*"

Jon heads down the hall. Ryan uses the table and the edge of the chair to push himself up to a standing position and begins hobbling back to his room. In the narrow corridor, he puts one hand on the wall to steady himself and the other on the side of his head.

Is this what being an MMA fighter feels like? Or do I have a problem?

***

"You wanted to see me?"

Eiji stands in the doorway of Shimoda-san's office. The boss is at his desk, Akio in the chair opposite him.

They stop talking at the fighter's voice. Shimoda-san looks up at Eiji, no emotion on his face.

"Eiji. Come in. Sit."

Eiji takes the second desk chair and looks over at Akio, who looks away.

Bored or too cool?

"I want to speak with you. About what happened the other day at the hotel." Shimoda-san leans forward, elbows on his desk.

"Ok. "

"Your reaction was out of line, Eiji. You overstepped your bounds. You cannot bring that kind of force without consulting me first."

Someone's been talking to Akio.

Eiji shoots side eye at the man in black.

"The man you slammed into the table has died."

Eiji shrugs.

"Soldiers die in war."

"Do not take that tone with me!" Shimoda-san pounds the table. "I will not tolerate such disrespect."

Eiji bows his head.

"The other man lost his eye."

Eiji looks away.

"None of this had to happen."

"I was only trying to defend you," Eiji says. "And him." He jerks a finger toward Akio. "If anyone else. . ."

"Enough!" Shimoda slams his palm on the desk.

Eiji hears commotion behind him. Shimoda-san's outburst has attracted a couple more of his men to the doorway.

"In this family, we fight. And we fight to win. But we do not kill; not when it isn't necessary. You have to learn to control your violent impulses." Shimoda-san waves away the onlookers.

"You are lucky," he continues. "The authorities have elected to not get involved – we have several detectives on our payroll. The Hsu have backed away from the territory in question."

"Backed away?"

"It seems they've come to their senses and decided those streets are not worth war."

"So, my use of force worked. . ."

"*Eiji*. . ." Akio says, his tone recommending caution.

"It is better to be a warrior in a garden than a gardener in a war. . ." Eiji says.

"No!" Shimoda-san says slamming his fist down on the desk. He takes a deep breath, head down. Then says quietly: "The best victory is won over *oneself*."

He looks at Eiji.

"We have just barely escaped consequences for your foolish actions. You need to have a moment with yourself, to examine where this violence comes from. You will not work for two weeks, to give you some time to reflect."

***

"Son, I hate to ask."

"Ok," Ryan says into the phone. "Let me think for a minute." He can't believe it's come to this – they could lose the house in Grand Rapids. His childhood home. The place most dear to his parents.

The Gaijin House is quiet for once. A few guys sit outside, smoking, but no one's around to hear.

Ryan takes a few steps in one direction and then heads back in the other, his sandals shuffling in the hall, like an oldster in a home.

"Ry, you still there?"

"Yeah, Dad. Just thinking."

"Ok. . ."

"I can send you some money right away. And I think I might have a way to get the rest."

"The rest? Ryan, we're talking tens of thousands."

"Yeah, I know."

Amen figures where this is going.

"Son, I don't want you fighting for us. . . I'd rather lose the house than lose you."

"Dad, we've been over and over this. I'm going to fight. Fighting is my life. It's what I do."

"But. . ."

"No buts. I've been to the doctors, seen all the studies, listened to all of the warnings. I understand the risks."

"Son, your vision. . . How can you fight if you can't see."

He doesn't know the half of it. . .

"I've been doing it. And I've been winning, Dad. Big prizes."

"You been doing it? How long? I thought it was just amateur stuff. And you can't even see. . ."

"I went to see a vision specialist a couple of years ago, I've been doing therapy."

"A couple of years! Ryan! Were you going to tell me?" Amen goes quiet on the line.

"You and Mom let me know you didn't approve before. . . I didn't think knowing about my eyesight would make things any better. . ."

"Ryan, you can talk to. . ."

"Not really, Dad. Not about this."

Amen is silent again. Ryan can hear him exhale slowly.

"I get that," he finally says. "Probably deserve it, but I could never forgive myself if I knew you were fighting to save us and something happened to you. . ."

"Dad, I'm going to fight. Full stop. It's just a matter of what I do with the prize money. And listen," Ryan says. "If I can get my manager to get me a fight with Eiji 'Kamikaze' Tanaka. . ."

"Kamikaze? You kidding me?" Amen bursts. "He's the champ. He's got fists like. . ."

"Dad. . ." Ryan chuckles. His father doesn't know how dangerous his own son is. How good his child has become. "You've been looking at those MMA mags again. . ."

Amen laughs.

"You got me."

"I have tangled with Eiji before. And I know I can beat him."

"How?"

"Well, he always. . ."

"Wait, that would be for the belt," Amen interrupts.

"It would be. That's why there'd be a big payday. Enough to cover everything."

"Son, I can't ask you. . . the risks are. . ."

"You're not asking. I'm offering. And *again* with the risks. . ."

"Sorry, Ryan. I love you. Worry comes baked in when you're a father. That's what it all comes down to. Someone once said being a parent is like watching your heart walk around outside your chest. I always liked that. . ."

"I love you, too, Dad. . ."

". . . And with you it's like watching your heart walk around and get pummeled. . ."

Ryan chuckles.

"I know what I'm getting into, Dad. Kamikaze's not all that."

"He's damn good son."

"I'm damn better."

***

Eriko tries to tiptoe into the house. Yuki, their Shiba Inu, gives her away, yipping in alarm. When he realizes it's Eriko, his tail starts wagging. But it's too late. As she slides open the door to her room, her mother appears.

"What's gotten into you, lately?"

Eriko can't read her mother's face, whether it's disapproval or concern. She ignores her question.

Mutsuko gathers herself and turns. She pads down the hallway.

"Remember, we have an appointment for you to try on wedding dresses tomorrow."

"I'm in love with someone else!" Eriko cries. She cowers and covers her mouth.

Mutsuko sighs. She studies her daughter and then extends her hand.

"Come, let's talk."

She leads Eriko to the kitchen and puts on tea.

"Your father will want to be a part of this."

Soon, Eriko is kneeling across from her parents. They look at each other, silent, as steam rises from their teacups. Finally, Mutsuko sighs and says,

"Life will not be easy dating a foreigner. Are you sure this is what you want for your future?"

"I love him," Eriko says. "You studied in America, I thought you of all people would understand."

"What I understand is that our customs and cultures are. . ." she pauses for effect. "Very different."

"The times are different. This isn't feudal Japan." She stares across the table. Her father is tight-lipped, uncomfortable.

"Please, just meet him. Properly this time."

Teruo gives his wife an expectant look, as if saying, you deal with this. But her resolve seems to weaken, and she nods. She reaches out and puts her hand on Eriko's arm. Their eyes meet.

"We will meet him."

***

When Ryan pushes open Womb's door, he can see the day's first rays of light. He ushers the last few patrons out and then checks the facility for any stragglers. When he's certain there's no one left, Ryan meets Kiyomiya and a new bouncer, Kubota, at a table. They all sit. Kiyomiya and Kubota both pour themselves a drink. Ryan knows better at this hour.

"In training," he says. "Got a big fight coming up."

"How big's big?" Kubota asks. He's several inches taller than Ryan and all muscle. Ryan watched as he threw out a hefty thug like it was nothing. He's native Japanese from Kawasaki, an industrial city wedged between Tokyo and Yokohama. Despite his size and power, he has immense respect for the American for what he's shown in the ring.

"The biggest," Ryan beams. "Versus the champ."

Kiyomiya grins. He tosses an MMA magazine onto the table in front of Kubota.

Ryan's mug is on the cover under the headline "*Beikoku-san Yamato Damashi.*"

"An American-born warrior with the heart of old Japan, huh?" Kubota laughs. "I guess you're going to need it if you're fighting Kamikaze."

He picks up the magazine and flips through it. Ryan, Enson, and Nori are in an ad for Purebred Tokyo on the back cover.

"Wow, you're everywhere."

Kiyomiya says, "you didn't notice all the people snapping selfies with him all night?" Ever since the Barbarian fight, fans have been stopping Ryan in the street for autographs and photos, and many have found their way to his workplace, too.

Kubota looks back at him defiantly: "No, I was *working*." Then he grins.

They all laugh.

"When is it?" Kubota asks.

"If all goes right, in a few months," Ryan says, pushing back his chair. "Gotta run. Lots of work to get done to make sure I'm ready."

***

"We both stand to make a lot of money," Akio says. He's sitting with Kobayashi in his office, a modern showplace with huge bay windows overlooking Tokyo harbor. A bottle of whiskey sits in the center of the table.

"I'm talking about the big leagues. An eight-man tournament. Taking it global. Creating superstars," he grins.

"Perhaps I was too quick to judge," he says, looking at her over the rim of his glass. He takes a pull and places it back on the table.

She tilts her head to the side and raises her snifter.

"As a woman, in this business?" He looks at her. "At least you have looks going for you. And, I heard your father is a man of considerable power in Hokkaido. I'd ride my father's coattails all the way to the bank, too."

"Not interested," she says. "And I'm not here to talk family history. . ."

"This life we chose, is built on family legacy. MMA and the families we represent are two sides of the same coin." He takes another drink and shrugs. "My money's on Kamikaze to win the entire thing. I don't see anyone beating him."

"I wouldn't count Ryan out. He's really come into his own. Did you see what he did to the Barbarian?"

Akio scoffs.

"But that was quite a stunt. The crowd ate it up. Which is money."

"Set it up," Kobayashi says. "And tell your goons to leave him alone. There won't be any money to be made if he's busted up in the hospital."

Akio clinks his glass with hers.

***

Ryan works with the new young fighter again. The kid has improved dramatically, following the same arc as Ryan: arrogant newbie, humbled by a pro, decides to better himself, and becomes a rising talent. He can now see why Enson took the Japanese fighter on.

He waits in the center of the ring while the guy circles. As the kid comes clockwise, Ryan feints high and goes low with a roundhouse kick that sweeps him off his feet.

Still has a lot to learn. . .

The American reaches down to help him up.

"Good work today." As Ryan offers the rookie some advice, his phone rings.

"Hold that thought," Ryan says, dropping and rolling under the ropes. He digs through his stuff until he finds his phone and answers. He's shocked to hear Eriko's voice and even more so when she tells him why she called.

Time can't go by fast enough.

Two nights later, he's seated at an upscale restaurant, reading the menu. Eriko has yet to arrive. Ryan grabs his phone to see if he missed any messages from her, and as he does so it bings as a text comes in.

"Held up at work. On my way now."

He glances up from his phone to see Teruo and Mutsuko enter. The hostess takes two of the big, hardbound menus and steers them to Ryan's table. He stands up, bowing as they arrive, introducing himself formally in Japanese.

They sit quietly, not saying much as they wait for Eriko.

"How long have you been in Japan?" Mutsuko asks, trying to fill the silence.

"Only a couple of years."

"What brought you here?"

"I wanted to be a professional fighter, mixed martial artist. I couldn't do so in the United States."

"Fighting for a living?"

"Yes, ma'am. Fighters can make a lot of money."

Ryan looks down at the napkin in his lap, remembering the Japanese prefer not to talk about money in polite conversation. He tries to change the subject.

"Ah. . . Eriko tells me you're a painter."

"I enjoy watercolors, yes."

"I'd like to see your work sometime."

Mutsuko nods and smiles. She adjusts the seat cushion underneath her and looks around for the waiter.

They sit quietly. Ryan looks at his watch.
This is going well. Come on, Eriko.

***

Eriko hurries out of work, skipping down the stairs and through the door. She jogs to the bicycle rack and pulls her keys from her purse, fumbling in her haste. They jingle onto the curb and tumble beneath a parked Mazda. She leans down to feel for them, trying not to drag her dress on the sidewalk. She extends her arm fully before she touches them. As she's doing so, she hears:

"Hey, what are you doing to my car?"

"I'm sorry," Eriko says, turning to face an older gentleman striding toward her. She does a quick bow. "I was trying to unlock my bike, and my keys fell underneath it."

His frown slowly dissipates.

"You find them?"

"Yes, thank you," she says, holding up her hand and swinging them. She bows. He nods, brow still furrowed, and gets into his black sedan, starting it, and nosing out into the line of cars threading through the city. Tokyo's streets are always busy, but at rush hour it's a parade that barely moves.

I'm lucky to be on my bike.

Eriko pulls her bicycle from the rack, swings her leg over the seat, and begins to pedal toward the restaurant. Sliding into traffic, she pumps the pedals furiously, flying past cars, which are hardly moving – she has been waiting for this meeting and is desperate for her parents to like Ryan, to at least give him a chance.

It has to go well. Please let it go well.

Eriko's so busy in her own thoughts she barely misses a car changing lanes right in front of her, swerving at the last minute, and almost careening into a small truck. The driver blasts his horn, and she peels away, her hands shaking on the handles. She bobs her head in apology, and pedals hard to get into place to make her next turn.

I'll be there soon. I'm coming, Ryan.

She uses a hand signal to take a left into an alley, weaving around a dumpster, and cutting through to the main road, which is in full flow. As she's merging onto the big boulevard, there's the screeching sound of tires locking up on pavement – a delivery truck sees her too late and slams on his brakes. The rig can't stop soon enough and plows through Eriko, sparks flying like fireworks as her bike is dragged along the pavement. Her belongings scatter everywhere, spraying out of the basket in front of her. She soars, too, over the top of a parked car, landing in a broken pile on the sidewalk. On her back, she's unable to move, her eyes wide skyward. Her chest rises up and down as she frantically gasps for breath, passersby milling around her. Then everything goes dark.

Chapter 16

Eriko lies still, unconscious. Her eyes are closed above an oxygen mask that's strapped over her mouth, its hose running to a machine in the corner that wheezes rhythmically, breathing for her. A handful of other wires and tubes crisscross her body, and monitors beep and whine. She's completely still. Peaceful.

In the waiting area down the hall, Teruo and Mutsuko sit side by side in stuffed chairs. Teruo blots tears from his eyes with a handkerchief. Mutsuko doesn't bother, openly weeping. Her arms are on her thighs, holding her upright as she sobs. Ryan sits across from them, fidgeting, unsure what to do with his hands. His right leg vibrates up and down with nerves. He doesn't know what to say or how to comfort them. Wanting to be there; wishing he was anywhere else.

A young doctor in a lab coat walks toward them, his eyes downcast. They all stand to meet him. Waiting, but fearful of what he has to say.

"I'm very sorry but. . ." He looks at his feet and pauses, hating this part of the job. The doctor has difficulty getting the words out. He doesn't want to say it. Mutsuko looks at Teruo, her eyes full of sadness.

"Eriko will not recover. Her brain is no longer functioning."

Mutsuko collapses. Teruo catches her before she hits the floor, and he awkwardly steers her into a nearby chair. Her head down, her torso heaves with sobs. Teruo puts his arm around her shoulders, hiding his face in her fine black hair.

"I'm so sorry," says the doctor again. He waits a moment and then excuses himself.

Ryan goes to Mutsuko's side, too, unsure of Japanese protocol. Her tears are endless.

***

After a difficult night at the Gaijin House, Ryan returns to the hospital to meet Mutsuko and Teruo. Tokyo bustles with the morning rush, and he can hear sirens wail as he steps through the automatic doors. The huge medical facility, too, seems full of motion, unlike the relative quiet of the previous evening.

A petite nurse ushers him into Eriko's room. His love looks just as she had the evening prior, at rest, eyes closed, arms at her side, as machines do the work of life, filling the sterile chamber with beeps and gasps. Her parents are already there, seated on the bed, and they nod at him as he enters. Ryan bows formally and then leans against the wall, again, uncertain of his place.

Perched at Eriko's side, Mutsuko strokes her daughter's cheek. She leans in close and whispers something Ryan can't make out. Teruo does the same. The couple remain next to her for several minutes, tears freely flowing down their faces. Again, part of him wishes he wasn't there, to allow them time to grieve without any awkwardness.

Ryan hears a quiet knock on the door and turns to see the physician from last night. Dressed in pale blue scrubs, he nods at Ryan and bows at Eriko's parents, clasping his hands before himself. A silent minute passes. Then the doctor looks at the pair of them over his spectacles. Teruo glances at Eriko, touches her face, and turns and gives him a curt nod. The doctor steps across the room to the large life-support machine, leans down, and switches it off. The ventilator instantly stops breathing, and the beeps of the heart monitor begin to slow and peter out. Wracked with sobs, Mutsuko puts her head down onto her daughter's bosom and hugs her. Ryan's eyes fill, his throat tightens, and he crosses his arms tightly across his chest, squeezing.

***

The household is a study in black. Family and friends enter wearing black suits, black dresses, black kimonos. Eriko's otsuya draws many who Ryan has never met. All of the traditions, too, are new to him. Jon talked him through what to expect at a Japanese wake, but everything was so different than it was in America.

"The wake is held as soon as possible after the death," Jon explained. "They call it *otsuya*, or 'passing of night.' Her

261

parents will close their shrine and place a paper cover over it to keep out unwanted spirits, and they'll place candles or incense and flowers beside her bed. Then they'll welcome friends and family to their home. At the funeral, you'll notice that once people pay their respects to her parents, they won't talk to them after that, allowing them space to grieve." This reminded Ryan how he felt at the hospital, as if he was in the way.

Jon went on to note that most people in Japan are cremated, an act which, according to Buddhist traditions, frees the spirit from its connection to the human world, allowing it to pass over.

Everything plays out as Jon predicted. The guests enter one by one, bowing formally as they arrive. Each brings with them a set of *juzu* prayer beads, in keeping with the Buddhist traditions Eriko's family adhered to, as well as a black-and-silver envelope – *kodenbukuro* – a monetary condolence. They take seats according to how well they knew Eriko, with family at the front, while a Buddhist priest chants a mantra. Wearing a dark kimono, Mutsuko sits closest to Eriko, with Teruo beside her, their hands clasped together.

Eriko's body lies covered with a sheet, ice packed around it. Flowers and photographs line the way to her. The priest continues with his chant, a nasal, sing-song incantation, long and drawn out; Ryan can only recognize a handful of words. Those in attendance walk up, bow, and offer incense at an urn placed near Eriko. Ryan is unsure whether he should follow and then notices Mutsuko motioning for him to join them. He walks over to her, falls to his knees, and weeps, the first time, at least in public, that he's let it all out. After a few moments, Teruo reaches down to help him up. Tears on his face.

He's exhausted by the time he returns to the Gaijin House, his chest heavy, like it was when he was little and broke down in tears in his room. Jon's in the hall and Ryan nods to him on his way into his room and then slumps onto his futon. The lanky Englishman wraps politely on the doorframe.

"Not now," Ryan says. "Sorry."

Jon nods and taps the door trim again.

"Here if you need me," he says as he walks down the hall.

***

Funeral day is almost unbearable. Eriko's parents, aunts and uncles, and friends gather at a nearby funeral hall the day after the wake. Ryan greets Mutsuko and Teruo in the reception area, joining a line of mourners. Those that didn't attend the wake step over to a table at the side to place their *okoden* – condolence money – into a tray.

"Please, sign the registry," a petite woman at the other end of the table says as he walks past. He does so, then steps into the main hall. There, an usher gives him flowers to place in the casket. The large room is brightly lit, with an altar at its apex, overflowing with white flowers. A framed photograph of Eriko, smiling, beautiful, is surrounded by chrysanthemums and lilies. The casket sits in front of this display, and on a dais below, is a table with urns, candles, incense, and rice. The setup is much like it was at Eriko's house, only on a much larger scale.

Ryan takes a seat near the front, leaving the closest chairs for Eriko's parents. He knows if he looks at the picture or the casket, he'll have a difficult time holding it together, so he puts his head down and waits. His brain feels like a cloud has settled over it, from the lack of sleep and the intense emotion, and his chest feels like a sponge. Other mourners make their way in, her aunts and uncles, couples, friends, young people she knew from work. The hall begins to fill. Everyone is dressed in black. Per tradition, the women have their hair pulled up and wear very little makeup.

When all are seated, a Buddhist priest begins to chant. It's a baleful, low, almost tuneless recitation, which repeats often. Again, Ryan can't really make out any of the words. After these sutras, everyone stands and takes a turn walking up to the table, where they bow to the family members, clasp *juzu* beads in their hands, and drop their heads, saying a short prayer to Eriko. Then they take a few pinches of incense, raise them toward the casket, and place them in a burner. They file past the casket and place flowers alongside Eriko. They then offer another prayer, turn and bow to the family, and move out of the room.

Ryan follows the couple ahead of him in the line and does what they do. When it's his turn beside the coffin, he almost breaks down. She looks so peaceful, so lovely, her arms crossed on her chest, eyes closed. He feels tears welling and chokes back sobs. He doesn't want to say goodbye to her, but he has to move on, both because the queue is backing up and because he knows if he stands there much longer, he won't be able to keep himself composed.

Most of those gathered exit after paying their respects, and Ryan follows the line toward the door. One of the officials takes Ryan's arm and whispers in his ear.

"The family would like you to stay for the cremation."

He nods and quietly walks back to stand behind Eriko's parents. After everyone has made their way through the procession, a handful of family members remain for the next phase. The priest picks up his sutra again, and the casket is prepared. Mutsuko and Teruo are the last at Eriko's side. Tears drip from Mutsuko's face as she places a cherished family memento next to her daughter and gazes upon her one last time. She steps back and Teruo places his hand on Eriko's arm and then silently closes the doors of the coffin. A staff member from the funeral home wheels the box toward a square door at the edge of the hall, where it's rolled into the cremation chamber.

An orange glow bathes Ryan's face as the flames light. Teruo touches him on the shoulder and sweeps his hand toward a side door, gesturing for him to leave. Ryan isn't sure how to take this. It feels abrupt, and out of keeping with the respect and inclusiveness Eriko's parents have shown him thus far.

"We will return in two hours," Teruo says, steering the American outside. "Come."

Ryan walks with the couple down the street to a nearby teahouse. He's surprised to find they select a modern take on the venerable Japanese tearoom, where they sit in chairs rather than kneel. They order bowls of *sencha* and talk little at first, all focused on their green beverage.

"It was clear to me how much Eriko cared for you, Ryan-san," Mutsuko says. "I have never seen her act that way with anyone else. I tried to get her interested in more, ah. . ." she looks down, "traditional, Japanese men, but she fought me all the way. Some of them were very handsome and very successful." She seemed at the same time disappointed in and understanding of her daughter. Teruo is quiet, stoic, staring off into the garden. He hasn't said much since Eriko passed.

"Where are you from in the United States, Ryan?" Mutsuko asks.

"Grand Rapids, Michigan."

"Ah. I spent time in the U.S. I sailed on the *Hikawa Maru* and went to school in Washington State."

Ryan nods.

Making small talk, Mutsuko tries to keep her mind off why they're here.

"I enjoyed your country. But it wasn't long after the war, and, well, the Americans didn't seem to enjoy me." She looks at the ground. "There was a lot of anti-Japanese sentiment, including violence and hate crimes. I returned to Japan shortly after that."

After close to an hour in the tearoom, they step out into the garden. All maple trees, small ponds, and gravel paths, it's a Zen oasis. They sit on a granite bench and watch koi fish circling. The wind ruffles the leaves of a ginko tree. Ryan looks up and sees a little yellow bird with a white ring around its eye hanging upside down on a cherry tree. After the dark dream of the past few days, it feels peaceful. Quiet. Serene. Tokyo seems a million miles away.

Why couldn't Eriko be here to enjoy this with me?

Teruo doesn't say a word, just keeps pulling up the sleeve of his black blazer to check his watch. Eventually, he looks, gets up, smooths his pants, and motions to Mutsuko and Ryan.

"It is time."

The trio push through a door in the tall bamboo gate and find themselves right back in the hurly burly of Tokyo. After the calm of the garden, it takes them aback. They return to the funeral hall and the director leads them to a large stainless-steel table. Next to it is a ceramic urn, decorated with a traditional Japanese scene and several sets of chopsticks. Faces downcast, Eriko's aunt and uncle wait there. Ryan bows in greeting and the couple give him brief nods.

Teruo gestures for Ryan to step aside. He gets the message: this is for family only, but he's allowed to watch. The two couples stand in pairs on either side of the table. Together they pick up bones with special, elongated chopsticks – working cooperatively, each person holding one end – and place Eriko's last remains into the urn.

Jon had told Ryan about *Kotsuage*, the bone collection ceremony, as well.

"It's a centuries-old tradition," he said. "And they say it's why it's bad etiquette for two people in a restaurant to pass things back and forth with chopsticks. Each participant uses a pair of chopsticks that are mismatched, symbolizing the separation of the world of the living from the world of the dead. Family members start at the feet, traveling up the body from there, so the deceased goes into the urn feet first. Some of the bones that remain are pretty big."

Ryan looks at Jon.

"I know, but it's very Japanese. When the ritual is over, the family takes the urn home for fifty days, putting it in a place of honor. And then it typically goes to a graveyard to be interred in some way."

Ryan stands back and watches Mutsuko and Teruo work. No one speaks as they slowly fill the ceramic vessel.

***

"What do you mean he won't fight?"

"Kamikaze's people have pulled out."

"Pulled out? I thought you said it was a go."

"It was."

Ryan looks at Kobayashi with disbelief. Then he lets his head drop.

"I know," she says. "I'm not happy, either. I've fought long and hard to get this."

Ryan stares at the floor.

"What changed?" he asks.

"Money. The major television networks are playing hard ball. They run the show," Kobayashi says. "They can do whatever they want."

"Always one fucking step forward, two fucking steps back. I don't know what I gotta do."

"Just be patient," Kobayashi says. "I'll work on getting them back on board."

***

Ryan stumbles along the sidewalk. He stops in front of a vending machine and puts his hands on the glass, looking at the three rows of beer cans in multitudes of varieties.

"Top shelf? Nah mate, I'll take whatever's closest," he says under his breath, affecting an English accent and bobbing his head. He puts his money in, retrieves the can, and downs the sixteen-ouncer in a matter of seconds. He buys several more, adding them to the plastic bag he carries in his hand and setting off down the street. People step aside as he makes his way by, shaky on his feet, mumbling to himself, eyes running over with tears.

He walks to Yamashita Park, a wide expanse of greenspace looking out over Yokohama Harbor and drops onto a bench facing the water. Across the way he spots the *Hikawa Maru*, the ship that took Mutsuko to Seattle, now a museum. The long cruise liner looks like a child's toy from where Ryan sits, antique and nostalgic with its central smokestack and masts, compared to the modern city behind it.

Not going to America anymore.

His ringtone jingles from his pocket. He lets it go to voicemail. He has some serious drinking to do. He pops another top, guzzles the contents of a can, and drops it on the ground next to his bench. Then he does it again.

By the time he makes it back to the Gaijin House, he's a mess, barely able to stay upright. He crawls into his room and passes out, not moving for hours.

He wakes to a knock. He can't tell if it's in his head or on his door. It happens again.

"Mate, you can't stay in there all day."

Jon.

Ryan can't make his mouth form any words.

"Anything I can do?"

He can hear the floorboards creak outside his door as Jon stands there waiting for an answer. After a while, the Englishman walks off.

***

"You really need to slurp your noodles, mate." Jon waves his chopsticks at Ryan's bowl of ramen. "You don't want to offend the chef."

Ryan cracks a smile.

"Now that's nice to see," Jon says, pointing at him. "A smile for once."

The American raises his eyebrows and looks down at his soup.

The pair perch on tall wooden stools in the front window of a ramen shop not far from Yokohama station. Ryan watches the steady parade of foot traffic pass by on the sidewalk. After a couple of years in Japan, he's still amazed at the number of people everywhere. An ambulance lays on its shrill siren, trying to make its way through the maze of cars, bicyclists, and pedestrians.

Wouldn't want that job. . .

"Finally got you out of your room," Jon says.

Ryan gives him the slightest of nods and then uses both hands to raise his bowl to his mouth, devouring the rest of his soup in a single slurp. Jon does the same. They look like little kids with their morning cereal bowls.

"*Gochisōsama deshita. Oishikatta desu,*" Ryan says a little louder than necessary in perfect Japanese.

"Look at you, sounding like a native."

Jon pulls his coat from the wings of his chair and claps him on the back.

They exit the shop and join the human mass on the sidewalk, making their way to the train station, which is strangely quiet, missing the usual hordes. When their train stops, and the pair climb aboard, it's half empty.

"Has there been a zombie apocalypse we don't know about?" Jon jokes.

"I'm glad you decided to come to the concert with me," the Englishman says, sliding his long form into the window seat; Ryan takes the aisle, and they settle in.

"Can't believe you haven't heard of Oasis. 'Wonderwall' topped the charts, mate. A bit of me back home."

Jon goes quiet, watching the world go by out the window, eternally fascinated by Japan. The gentle swaying of the locomotive rocks Ryan to the point of sleep. His eyes are almost closed when he feels a tap on his shoulder. He glances up to find a slight Japanese kid, dressed in jeans and a windbreaker, little taller than the seats themselves.

"Excuse me," the young guy says without looking Ryan in the eye. "You are American MMA fighter Ryan Bow?"

Ryan sits up in his seat and makes a fist, feinting a punch. The kid steps back, uncertain.

"Joking," says Ryan. "Yeah, that's me."

"Your last fight was *amazing*," the kid says. "Amazing!" he bobs his head up and down. "May I take a photo with you?"

"Of course."

Ryan turns to Jon.

"Would you do the honors?"

The passenger hands his phone to the Englishman. Ryan adopts a playful fighting stance again and the kid takes his cue, pretending to spar. Jon snaps a few pics and hands back the flip phone. The train comes to a halt and the doors open. People climb on and off.

Last to board is a rugged Japanese man, head down, shrouded in a hoodie. When he looks up, Jon recognizes Kamikaze. He looks back at Ryan eyes wide in warning.

"What a surprise," Kamikaze grunts in clipped Japanese.

Ryan nudges Jon out of the way and squares up to him. "This isn't the time."

Ryan turns and says to Jon, "Let's get out here."

As he does so, Kamikaze unleashes a left hook that catches Ryan behind the ear – completely by surprise. The American slams back into the seats. The champ is about to swing again when Jon reaches up and hauls down the emergency brake. The train screeches to a halt. Ryan uses the shock to burst out of his seat and clock his antagonist with an uppercut to the chin. Kamikaze staggers back into the train doors. Grabbing Ryan by the shirt, the Japanese fighter pulls him backwards out of the train and onto the cement platform. The American struggles to regain his balance and clinches Kamikaze. The two bump up against a large map of Tokyo. Kamikaze grabs the side of Ryan's head and drives it against the metal frame. Passengers scatter, terrified.

Ryan's knees wobble as the station, pedestrians, and passing trains begin to swim around him. He holds his head, trying to orient himself, his vision blurring. Kamikaze blitzes him like it's fourth and goal, tackling him to the ground. Jon tries to pull the Japanese fighter off his friend, but Kamikaze hits him with a backfist to the nose and climbs aboard Ryan, bashing his head against the concrete over and over. Self-preservation mode kicks in and Ryan does a bridge, heaving Kamikaze off balance.

The pair roll around on the ground, each trying to gain control. Ryan spins away and jumps to his feet, swaying as he does so. Kamikaze follows and they exchange blows, the American driving his knee into the champ's gut. This stuns him, and he doubles over. Ryan executes a leg sweep, taking Kamikaze down. Tanaka's head lands off the platform, sticking out over the train tracks, and Ryan grabs his throat, raising his fist back. . .

"Freeze, both of you!"

***

Feet in black tactical boots appear beside Ryan. He glances over his shoulder to see two police officers, one tall and thin, the other short and stocky, batons at the ready.

"Let go of him!" says one.

"Now, on your feet!" says the other.

Ryan releases Kamikaze and struggles to stand. The heavy-set cop grabs his right wrist and spins it behind his back, cuffing him. The second officer does the same to Kamikaze.

Jon walks over, wiping blood from the corner of his nose with his thumb. It reminds Ryan of the famous Bruce Lee scene, although the Englishman isn't trying to be intimidating. Leaning down to put his hands on his knees, Jon points at Kamikaze and says in perfect Japanese:

"He's the one you want."

The stout cop lets go of the American and cuffs Jon as well.

"What's this?" Jon yells, outraged. "We were jumped."

The officers put hands on Kamikaze's chest, gently walking him backward, and seem starstruck, dusting him off and smiling sympathetically as they go. When they turn their attention to Ryan and Jon, it's a different story.

"What are you two doing in Japan?" the lanky one asks in halting English, his eyes full of fire.

"What does that matter?" Ryan says in Japanese. "He attacked *us*."

"I ask question, you answer!" the cop says, jabbing Ryan's chest with his finger. "Let me see your Alien Registration Cards."

"Why?" Ryan asks. "We've done nothing wrong."

"No talking!" says the other officer. "Do as you're told."

"Please officer, we're telling the truth," Jon says in careful Japanese.

Kamikaze sneers and takes a step toward the Englishman.

"Liar! Bastard!" he hisses.

Jon retreats, his eyes big with surprise.

The tall officer sighs and puts his hand on Jon's back, steering him down the platform.

"We'll sort this out at the station."

Chapter 17

"What the hell," Jon says, still rubbing his nose. "Nothing like this ever happens to me. Can't remember the last time someone popped me in the face."

He grins and points at Ryan.

"You are an adventure, I'll say that."

The Englishman paces around the cramped jail cell. Ryan sits on a metal bench built into the wall. He nods, his head throbbing. He puts his hand to the back of his skull and comes away with a handful of blood. Shakes his cranium in an attempt to bring it back to life.

Kamikaze stands with his fists around the bars of the cell across the way, leering at them. Lucky for him – or perhaps for the other guy – he's alone. He lets go and starts doing pushups on the floor.

A corrections officer in a powder-blue uniform walks up and unlocks the door with a buzz. After freeing Jon and Ryan, he steps over to do the same to Kamikaze.

"You three must know people in high places. Out," he sweeps his hand in front of them. "You made bail."

Like a grizzly, Kamikaze bluff charges Jon in the hallway and grins when the Englishman backs up. Then he turns and makes his way to the front desk.

"Pleasant fellow," Jon says to Ryan. "Just lovely. I'd pay to watch you pummel him."

In the lobby, Kobayashi stands with Akio, she in workout clothes, he in a dark suit, as ever.

"Keep a tight leash on your guy," she says loudly to him. "He obviously doesn't play well with others."

Akio chuckles.

Several cops approach the Japanese champion, asking for selfies. Kamikaze obliges, posing with his brows furrowed, his teeth clenched, his muscular arm cocked for a punch.

Kobayashi shakes her head and puts her arm on Ryan's. They exit down a set of stairs to the street. She can tell something is off with her client – he's slow and unsteady on his feet – and then notices the blood all over his hand.

"Yours or his?" she motions at all the red.

"Mine," says Ryan, pointing to the back of his head.

"Nice," she says with a curt bob.

They walk a few blocks to her car.

"Let's get you home."

Traffic is thick, and it takes the better part of an hour for Kobayashi to maneuver her late model Lexus sedan to the Gaijin House. Ryan slumps in the back, leaning his head against the cool of the window, oblivious to the bustle of Tokyo. Jon rides up front with Kobayashi.

"Tell me what happened," she says to the Englishman with a sigh. "I'm guessing it was you who started it." She gives Jon a sly smile.

"Me?" he laughs in mock shock. "Well, you know me. I always gotta *go*. You know. Up against the baddest fighter there is."

"Maybe I ought to sign *you*." She studies the road ahead, brake lights reflecting in her eyes. Then she shakes her silky black hair. "I told Akio to keep his animals on leashes."

"He literally stepped onto the train and sucker punched Ryan," Jon said. "Boom! Right in the back of the head, out of nowhere."

"Seems he has a habit of that."

"Yeah, he might want to seek counseling, I'm thinking." Jon tells Kobayashi the whole story, from first seeing Kamikaze to the champ's antics in jail.

"Fighters gonna fight, I guess."

Jon nods, sitting back in his seat.

They pull up to the Gaijin House and get out. As Ryan walks to the door, his legs like cooked spaghetti, Kobayashi powers down her window, leans across the passenger seat and says, "You going to be okay?"

Ryan turns.

"I'll be fine."

"Do you think you should see a doctor?"

"I'll be fine. Taken worse in the ring."

"Hope so." She smiles at him. "But I haven't seen a lot of concrete in the ring. Go get some rest. There's a lot riding on this fight."

***

Ryan wakes up with his guts in turmoil. He slept fitfully, if at all, finding slumber difficult with his head ringing constantly. He bolts upright and makes a run for the bathroom, barely reaching the toilet before he vomits uncontrollably. He kneels and grips the porcelain, heaving again and again. He sits back on his knees and takes a deep breath, steadying himself on the filthy bowl.

"You okay, mate?"

Ryan can feel Jon's presence behind him.

"I'll be fine."

"You don't seem fine. Vomit like that indicates a serious head injury. Methinks you need to see a doctor."

"I can't."

"What do you mean, you can't? A professional fighter without insurance?"

"It's not that," Ryan says, wiping his mouth with the back of his hand. "No one can know. They won't let me fight."

"There has to be someone you can trust. Someone not connected to the fight world."

Ryan shakes his head. But it gives him an idea.

Later in the day, he stands in front of Eriko's house. He knocks on the front door. Mutsuko answers. Seeing his condition, she puts her hand to her mouth and lets out a little gasp. Then she sets her face with typical Japanese resolve and steps out to take Ryan by the arm. She helps him in, holding onto his side while he slips out of his shoes.

Such a different reception than the first time I was here.

She takes him to Eriko's room, and he lies on her bed. Mutsuko dims the light and pads off down the hall. She returns with a cold compress and applies it to Ryan's head.

"You rest," she says, patting him on the arm. She gets up and closes the door behind her. Ryan sits and looks around the room, taking in everything. He's never been here. He scans the bookshelf. He knew Eriko loved literary romances but wasn't aware of her fondness for Korean novels – stories she cherished that he'd never hear her tell. He relaxes back into her futon, removing the cold compress, and placing his head on her pillow. The smell of Eriko brings everything back, and his chest tightens, the hurt in his heart distracting him from the pain in his head. He weeps into her sheets and falls asleep.

***

Mutsuko sits on the bed beside him, dabs his mouth with a handkerchief, and checks his temperature with the back of her hand, placing her fingers behind his neck.

"You're so hot. I will bring you aspirin."

He nods his thanks, and again she's off down the hall.

"Take this," Mutsuko holds her hands out to Ryan, giving him two tablets and a glass of water. He leans forward and takes the pills, Mutsuko's hand on his back. Then he lowers himself slowly down onto the bed. The room seems to flow around him, like waves, his equilibrium lost. His cranium aches, like something is compressing around it. Mutsuko puts a cool towel over his eyes and forehead.

Everything fades away.

***

The smell of cooking rouses him. He gets up and makes the bed, noticing crusty blood on the pillow. He shakes it out, but it leaves behind stains. He puts it back in place and tells himself he'll mention it to Mutsuko. Then he walks down the hall in search of the source of the aroma.

Mutsuko sees Ryan and extends her arms toward him.

"You've been out for a whole day," she says. "I was beginning to worry." She gestures at the table. "Come, join us."

"Thank you," he says. "Something smells good."

Ryan bows formally at Teruo, who sits at the head of the low, dining room table. Eriko's father gives him a curt nod. Ryan kneels and waits quietly with Teruo, who says not a word. Mutsuko walks to the kitchen and works while Ryan and Teruo wait quietly at the table. She returns and places a bowl of *okayu* (rice porridge) in front of her guest. She serves her husband next and then sits down herself. They all eat, the only sound their chopsticks tapping the edge of the ceramic bowls.

Mutsuko puts her chopsticks down.

"Ryan?"

"Yes, ma'am?"

"I have called our family doctor. I think someone should take a look at you after the trauma you suffered. I noticed that you're bleeding even as you're sleeping. From your nose. It worries me."

Mutsuko reaches out and puts her hand on Ryan's arm.

"I appreciate your concerns," he says. "But I'm feeling much better. I think it was just a little nosebleed. . ."

"Ryan, you were *attacked*. I think the damage is far greater than you realize. . ."

"I'm happy to see your doctor," Ryan says, bowing. "I appreciate your concern."

Later that same afternoon, Ryan hears a knock on the door to Eriko's room. He opens it to find a familiar face.

"Dr. Yuzawa. . ."

"Hello Ryan."

"I wasn't expecting you."

"I thought Mutsuko told you. . ."

"Well, I was expecting a doctor. I just didn't know it was going to be you."

"I've been their family physician since Eriko was in high school." Dr. Yuzawa gestures at the bed. "Please have a seat. Let me take a look at you."

Ryan drops to the edge of Eriko's bed, and Dr. Yuzawa leans over him.

"Tell me, how you are feeling."

"Much better than before," Ryan says.

Dr. Yuzawa nods and kneels, taking Ryan's wrist and feeling his pulse. He shines a light into each of Ryan's pupils and then scopes each ear. He holds Ryan's skull on either side and feels all around, almost as if he's giving the young man a scalp massage. He uses his light to look up the fighter's nose.

"Lie back, I'd like to check your abdomen."

Ryan reclines, and Dr. Yuzawa uses his palms to press on his torso, especially the soft tissue below his rib cage.

Ryan winces, which only causes the doctor to focus his exploration, using his fingers to probe for sensitive spots.

After a few more minutes of tests, he stands up.

"Ryan, have you been having headaches?"

"Yes, sir, they were bad for a while but seem to be going away."

"Your eyes are dilated, son. The pupils are large and fixed. This is usually an indication of brain trauma. We see eyes like this when people have a concussion."

"I think I definitely was concussed."

"That's what Mutsuko suggested. Have you thought any more about our previous conversations? The danger to you if you keep fighting?"

"Sir, this didn't have anything to do with my fighting career. I mean it did, but I wasn't in the ring. I was jumped on the train."

Dr. Yuzowa looks Ryan straight in the eyes.

"Your brain doesn't really care how or when it happened. Only that it did. If you continue to fight, you could lose the use of your eyes. Perhaps other neurological functions. Dementia. Those are the best case."

"The best case? What's the worst?"

"Simply put, you could die. If your brain isn't allowed to heal before it's injured again, it could lead to internal swelling the brain can't recover from. Remember, you have a big hard mass in there."

"How long will it take to heal?"

"Depends, but almost certainly weeks."

I don't know if I have weeks.

***

The security guy at the gate isn't sure what to do. It's Enson "freaking" Inoue. How do you say no to the champ? What will he do if you tell him to get lost?

"Wait here, Mr. Inoue" he says. "Shimoda-san's guests typically make appointments."

Enson puts his hands in his pockets and paces around the entrance to the compound. The walls are eight-feet tall and two-feet thick, and he can't see the main building, so it must be set a ways back. A lot of ground to cover. The front yard is dotted with a dozen Japanese maples and long spreads of cypress that would provide some cover. He clocks at least five guys providing perimeter security. No matter. He's sure he can take them all. Even if they come at him in multiples. He knows most yak families don't use firearms, and without guns, who's going to stop him? So, he waits, his head on a swivel. Checking their positions and the exits.

After a few minutes, the guard comes back. "Shimoda-san would like you to state your business."

"Just here to talk," Enson says, placing his hand on his chest. "Respect."

"About what, Mr. Inoue?"

"About that's my business and Shimoda-san's."

The security guard sighs.

"Wait here."

The process repeats itself. Enson pretends to be patient while surveying the scene, taking in as much as he can. He doesn't expect trouble but knows it's always best to be ready for it. Now, he counts a total of eight yard dogs. None appear to be armed. That's one area where he hopes Shimoda-san adheres to tradition.

After another ten minutes, the guard reappears.

"Mr. Inoue, if you'll please follow me."

Enson follows him to a black Escalade.

The guy holds open a door.

"Please."

Enson hops in, and he's transported around a long circular drive, a ride that takes several minutes.

Quite a place, he thinks to himself.

The SUV stops at a dark, low-slung building covered in Shou Shugi Ban with a drive-up entrance. The driver gets out and opens Enson's door. The champ gives him a nod and steps out. He notices the CCTV cameras flanking the front door and follows the driver down a long hallway. They climb a sweeping set of stairs, and he takes note of a few interior guards. At the next floor, the driver turns right and leads him to an office, sweeping his arm to indicate Enson should enter.

"Mr. Inoue," says a gray-haired gentleman seated behind a desk. "Have a seat." Another guy, who Enson recognizes from the fights, sits in an armchair off to one side, knee over knee, all clad in black.

Enson drops himself into a leather guest chair opposite the desk. He keeps his arms on his lap, ready to move if need arises.

"Usually, people make appointments to see me, Mr. Inoue."

"Not a social call," Enson says.

"I see." Shimoda-san purses his lips. He glances over his shoulder at Akio.

"I'm not used to being spoken to in such a way."

"Not here to make friends."

"Excuse me?"

"I think you probably know why I'm here."

"I'm not sure that I do. And please show me the proper respect."

"Yeah, well, respect is a two-way street. One of your fighters jumped one of mine, Ryan Bow, in the street. He almost killed him, slamming his head against the pavement. I won't stand for this kind of treatment."

"Oh, really?"

"Yeah, really."

"What do you suppose you can do about it?"

"I can tear apart everyone in this compound, for starters. Burn it to the ground."

Shimoda-san looks at him calmly, brushes some lint off his knee. Then he glances again at Akio, who tilts his head to the side.

"Mr. Inoue, there's no need for threats. I understand you are upset. I don't doubt you could disable a few of my men – you were a fine fighter – but there are far too many here for you to do as you suggest."

Enson stands.

"I'm not worried."

"Neither am I. Please. Sit."

They stare across the desk at one another.

"I understand your anger," Shimoda-san says, finally. "If another fighter did that to one of mine, I'd be in the same position as you. What can we do to make things right?"

"I don't care how you do it but, get the TV networks back on board. Make the fight happen. Don't go back on your word. Have your fighters show respect. I can think of plenty of things you can do."

"Mr. Inoue, I don't like your tone."

"I don't care."

Shimoda-san sighs.

"You're lucky, I'm a patient, forgiving man. I don't appreciate you charging in here, threatening me, and giving me this kind of attitude. Most men wouldn't make it back to the gate." Shimoda-san stands up behind his desk.

"But I'm going to give you what you seek. And I'm even going to send Mr. Bow some money for his medical bills. Because I agree with you that Eiji was out of line. I don't mind a little street action to raise interest in a bout. But there was no bout scheduled and, even if there was, Eiji was a bit extreme, and his violence was unnecessary."

Enson stands, meets Shimoda-san's gaze.

"But, Mr. Inoue, if you ever disrespect me in this way again, you will regret it."

Enson nods.

"My driver will see you out."

***

For the next couple of days, Ryan stays at Eriko's, Mutsuko taking care of him. She cleans the wounds on his scalp and brow, gives him pain medication, and checks for signs of internal bleeding, just as Dr. Yuzawa instructed. She keeps the curtains drawn and the lights dimmed during this time too, to allow his brain time to heal.

After years at the Gaijin House, it's comforting to have home cooking and someone to fuss over him. Ryan and Mutsuko develop a rapport, and Ryan even gets her to smile a few times. Teruo is more stoic, and the American can't tell where he stands with him.

The fighter helps out around the house, to show his appreciation. He takes out the garbage. Vacuums. And he plays with Yuki, the family dog, a Shiba Inu, who lavishes love on him. Ryan throws the ball for what seems hours, playing fetch in the small backyard. The most popular breed in Japan, the Shiba Inu was used as a hunting dog by the samurai and was famous for its ear-piercing bark. Yuki's no exception, wagging his coiled reddish tail, and yowling as he goes. Ryan is amused by the pup's ability to smile. There's no question when Yuki is pleased, from the way his dark lips curled upwards and his eyes brightened.

Always had a soft spot for dogs.

Ryan accompanies Mutsuko and Teruo on their first visit to Eriko's grave. He stares at the simple gray tombstone for what seems ages, unable to believe this is all that's left of the love of his life. Eriko's father and mother exchange a shared glance as they stand silently shoulder to shoulder. The tears come without any warning, and they begin to freely roll down Ryan's face. He drops to his knees in front of Eriko's memorial.

"How could this happen?" he sobs, quietly. "I can't believe you're gone. How can I live without you?" He sits back on his calves and puts his hands over his face, his torso heaving with grief. After a few minutes, he feels a hand on his arm and turns.

"Ryan-san," Mutsuko says, on her knees beside him.

"I want you to know. . ." she begins, pausing. She looks into his eyes. "She loved you. I'd never seen her so happy."

"I should have. . ." Ryan says, "If only we. . ."

"There's nothing else you could have done. You brought her great joy, and I thank you for that."

Ryan nods and inhales deeply through his nose, trying to regain control of himself. He closes his eyes and breathes in and out, rhythmically.

"When Eriko told me you moved to Japan to become a professional fighter, I was shocked," Mutsuko says after he's calmed.

"Un." Ryan says as he nods.

"We would like to honor her last wish by attending one of your fights." She takes Ryan's hand. He squeezes.

"Pray with me," she says.

They both put their heads down and silently pay their respects.

As they get up to leave, Ryan turns to face both parents. He instinctively begins to bow and then pulls them both into a bear hug. He holds them for a moment, despite their discomfort, and then lets them go.

Chapter 18

Enson and Ryan sit on opposite sides of the Purebred boss' desk.

"You sure you want to do this? There's not a lot of time for prep."

Ryan sighs. He looks at the champ and then away, unable to hold Enson's gaze. He pats Shooto-kun on the head briefly and then releases a slow heavy sigh. Enson cocks his head, wondering.

"Coach, I haven't been completely honest with you."

Enson's brows gather, and their eyes lock.

"What do you mean?" he asks, hackles raised. He just risked his life confronting Shimoda.

As he looks at Ryan, the boss notices the American fighter's left eye, wandering ever so slightly.

"I'd like to show you something."

Ryan stands and walks out of the small office. Enson follows him to the matted area. It's about lunchtime, and the place is relatively quiet. A few fighters lift weights, another runs on a treadmill. In a corner, a newcomer that Ryan doesn't recognize works the pendulous heavy bag.

Ryan steps out onto the mats and says to Enson, "Stand in front of me."

Enson raises his eyebrows, but he squares up in a relaxed fighting stance.

"*Okay. . .*" he says, drawing out the word.

"Take a big step to your right."

Enson does so, tilting his head to the side and keeping an eye on Ryan as he does.

Ryan breathes out. He's quiet for a second. Then lets out a big breath and says, "I can't see you."

"What do you mean you can't see me?" Enson says. "I'm right in front of you."

"When you are standing there, at that angle, it's like you've completely disappeared."

Enson blinks, and his head bobs back.

"Ryan, that makes no sense. I've watched you fight. A lot."

"I've been fighting blind."

"Fighting blind? What do you mean, fighting blind?"

Enson throws a mock right hook at the left side of Ryan's face. The younger man doesn't flinch, staring straight ahead.

Inoue steps back and shakes his head.

"What the. . .?"

"I had a stroke in the womb," Ryan says. "It left me with a brain cyst and no peripheral vision." He explains that he's been going to visual therapy, that that's how he met Eriko.

"I've noticed that eye wandering before," Enson nods. "That makes sense. Jesus, you've hidden it well. I can't believe you beat the Barbarian with one eye."

He shakes his head again.

"What are you, a Jedi? Luke Skywalker with the helmet on fighting that flying droid?"

Ryan chuckles.

"I did wear a helmet as a kid. . ."

And then he drops his head.

"Coach, I. . . I. . . I'm worried about this fight. Really worried."

Enson says nothing, pacing back and forth, his bare feet shuffling on the battle-worn mat. Ryan stands there, arms crossed, not knowing what to say or do. He watches the new fighter's fists make the heavy bag heave and sway. Then Enson looks up, snaps his fingers, and a wide smile breaks out across his face.

"I think I can help you," he says.

"Yeah?" says Ryan, surprised.

How can you possibly help me with a vision problem?

"Yeah," says Enson, still grinning. He shakes his hand loosely in front of him and then pats Ryan on his shoulder.

"You can fight on the inside."

***

For the next twelve weeks, Ryan works out at Purebred even more than usual. Pounding on opponents, slamming the teardrop bag with knees, jumping rope, and doing crunches until he can barely get up off the mat. While he's at it, he's distracted from his thoughts of Eriko. He has nowhere else to go, no one else he wants to see, so he trains. And trains. And trains. Jon tries to get him to go out, eat, drink, and party, but all Ryan wants to do is prepare for the upcoming bout.

Tonight, he's wrestling with Nori, working takedowns. The gym is empty except for the two fighters and Enson, who is clapping his hands and shouting commands at Ryan. The only lights in the place shine down on the ring, like a spotlight.

"When you're in the clinch, you don't need to rely on your eyesight, Skywalker. Close your eyes. Feel your way. Use the Force. Your body knows what to do."

Ryan and Nori each struggle to get the upper hand, trying to gain the inside position, their feet sliding and gripping on the mat below. The Japanese fighter gets there first. Ryan overhooks Nori's arm and turns his hips into him. He thrusts his right leg upwards, catching Kid on the inside of the thigh. Simultaneously, he leans forward, pivoting on his base leg and hurling Nori over his hip to the mat, like a farmer heaving a big sack of grain. It's a perfectly timed *uchi mata*, inner thigh reaping throw.

"See, there you go." Enson claps his hands together. "Nice!"

Ryan helps Nori up. They exchange fist bumps as Nori slips between the ropes.

Enson replaces him, holding up Thai pads for Ryan to work. Ryan hammers away at them, forcing Enson back. He chains punches and kicks together seamlessly and connects solidly with his knees on the inside. He bounces around in front of Enson, up on the balls of his feet, moving back and forth. Without warning, the coach catches Ryan's kick and sweeps his base leg out from underneath him, and he tumbles to the mat. Ryan looks up with a frown, rubbing his forehead with his gloved hands.

Enson glances down at him.

"Expect the unexpected," he says. "You think your opponent is always going to do what you think he's going to do? Telegraph every move?"

The champ waves his arms at Ryan.

"Come on, get up."

He makes a circle in the air with his hand.

"Show me what you got, braddah."

Ryan rolls back up onto his shoulders, places his hands behind his head, and he rocks himself up onto his feet, like a gymnast. Enson tosses aside the Thai pads. Ryan watches as the coach moves counterclockwise around him. But Enson is quick and crafty and ends up behind Ryan, takes his back and slams him onto the deck.

The younger fighter pounds the mat. Then he shakes it off, rises to his feet, and squares up against Inoue. Enson tries to flank him again, moving into his blind spot. This time, Ryan pivots, and takes a step in, coming chest to chest with the champ. They keep shifting, jockeying for position. Ryan reaches up under Enson's armpits, placing his palm on his back. He then wraps Enson's arm tightly on the other side. When the coach tries to create space, Ryan feels it coming. He changes levels and executes a perfectly timed single leg takedown, a wrestling move he's worked on with Nori. This, Enson wasn't expecting, and Ryan easily dumps him to the mat.

Enson hops up, a grin on his face. He holds his hand up for a five, then claps his hands together.

"Again."

***

Enson continues to dedicate a lot of time to Ryan and his vision quest, often staying at Purebred long after everyone else has gone for the day. They work for hours in the ring, Inoue showing his American pupil ways in which he can use grappling and judo to his advantage, compensating for his blind spot.

They circle each other, always looking for the advantage, mirroring each other.

"Let's see what you've got," Enson says.

Ryan nods.

Enson shoots in for a takedown, but Ryan sprawls, kicking his legs out behind him. Coach Inoue coils like a spring, squatting, and then lunging at his student in something resembling a rugby tackle. This works, and Ryan flies onto the mat with a thud. He scrambles back up onto his feet.

They continue working until Purebred gets dark and they almost can't see each other. They clinch. Enson launches Ryan up over his hip and then falls atop him. In a swift movement, he grabs his protégé's right arm and slides into a straight arm bar. Ryan twists, hoping to relieve the pressure, but to no avail. Enson raises his hips to apply even more force. Ryan can feel the ligaments in his arm straining and taps out.

Enson lets go. Ryan sits up and rubs his elbow. Coach Inoue stands over him, kicking him gently in the side.

"At least once in your life, train with the will to die."

Enson bounces up and down on the balls of his feet.

"Your whole life is about options, choices," he says. "Life doesn't wait. You're backed into a corner, fists up, heart pounding. You either cower – or you bite down on your mouthguard and fight, right?"

He points at Ryan's elbow.

"In a choke, when it's tight and you feel the darkness creeping in, you're going to feel the urge to tap out. Most people will." Enson looks at Ryan and taps his temple. "They think it's their only choice – and they have to live with that. But that's not the Yamato Damashii way."

Ryan nods.

"Never give up," Enson continues. "Your opponent will think he has you – but that extra second might be your chance to escape. In the ring, you've got to be ready to give everything. Ninety-nine percent of fighters quit before they get there. It's the one percent who earn the strap."

He reaches down and helps Ryan up.

"We have a long couple of weeks ahead."

***

The weeks drag on. Ryan does little else besides train. Work a shift or two at Womb. Sleep. Repeat. He continues to have head-splitting migraines. When he's not at the gym or at work, he's usually in bed with the lights out, trying to allow his brain to recover. He goes through bottle after bottle of pain killers.

Despite all this, he can think of only one thing – defeating Kamikaze. Making him pay for the assault. Pay with his belt. In his mind it becomes stark, simply a matter of good versus evil. Bushido. Honor. That Tanaka would brutally attack someone in the street, including his friend Jon, was unconscionable, and the fighter was due a reckoning. He'd disgraced himself and MMA.

And he also knew his parents needed him. They would lose the house – the house he grew up in. The house they worked so hard for. The house they raised him in.

***

"You wanted to see me?"

Ryan raps gently on the door frame, doesn't wait for an answer, and plops down into the chair across from Kobayashi. She has a phone cradled in her neck and holds up her finger.

"I know," she says into the mouthpiece. "I understand it's late notice."

She breathes out heavily.

"I know there's a lot of money on the line."

Ryan can almost hear the other voice on the receiver but not quite. It's a man, for sure. And Japanese.

Kobayashi nods in the air.

"I need you to put a hold on it temporarily. I will get back to you as soon as I can. Yes, yes, I get it. Okay."

She puts her phone down on the desk and looks at Ryan with her lips pursed. She sighs, puts her elbows on the table, and looks him in the eyes.

"I've been doing a little checking," she says.

"Checking?"

"Yeah. You took a serious beating. Heads are not meant to be slammed on pavement."

"Okay. . ."

"And I found out some things."

She stands up and starts to pace.

"Things I wish you'd told me when we met."

Ryan drops his head.

I know where this is going.

"Listen. . ." he begins.

"You are putting yourself in serious danger, Ryan. Like, brain damage for the rest of your life, kind of danger. Do you want to live out your days in a dark room unable to think, basically a vegetable? Or, you know, best case, lose your sight?

"I understand the risks. . ." Ryan responds. I've been living with them my whole life."

"Yeah, well, would have been nice to know when I took you onboard and started placing you in harm's way. Now I know you. And care about your well-being. You're my responsibility, to a certain extent."

"I can take care of myself. . ."

"Can you? They scraped you up off the pavement and stuck you in jail. Is that how you take care of yourself?"

"That was Kamikaze, not me. . ."

"Yeah, well, it's Kamikaze you could be meeting in the ring if the event. . ."

Kobayashi pauses and looks out the window. She exhales heavily.

"What do you mean, *if*. . ." Ryan says.

"That was Akio." Kobayashi gestures at her phone.

"I told him to put things on hold until we figure this out."

"Put things on hold?" Ryan jumps to his feet. "You've got to be kidding. We just got it back. . . I've been training non-stop."

"I know." She paces. "But I'm not sure I can in good conscience let you fight."

"Is it your call?"

"It's my reputation. It's my bank account. I'd say that makes it my call. Christ, you're completely blind on your left. What good is a broken fighter?"

"Listen to me. . . please. . . for a minute," Ryan says. "Sit and hear me out."

Kobayashi lowers herself into her chair and clasps her fingers in front of her. She raises her eyebrows expectantly.

"It's not just about me. Yeah, you know I want this. But my family *need*s it. My parents are going to lose the house I grew up in if I can't get them the money. I *have* to fight."

Kobayashi's mouth drops open. She sits up in her seat. Starts to say something, but Ryan cuts her off.

"Plus, I've been training with Enson. He's figured out a way to compensate for my blind spot. If I get inside, I don't need to be able to see, because I can *feel*. And I'm a better grappler anyway. Those are my strengths. If I can get it to the ground, it's over. I don't care who it's against. I'll finish each and every one of them."

"Really, Enson said that?" Kobayashi asks. "He knows about your blind spot?"

She looks at him, amazed.

"And he still thinks you can fight?"

"Yeah. I told him the other day."

Kobayashi nods.

"And besides," Ryan says, "He watched me beat the Barbarian, one of the best. *You* watched me beat him too. I've had this issue my whole life, and I still got where I am."

Kobayashi bobs her head again. She turns and looks out the window. Intertwines her fingers behind her neck. The clock ticks behind her.

"Akio wants to kill me, at the moment," she says, finally. "He did not want to put this on hold. With all the press your little train escapade got, the whole world is watching."

"I can do this. And I can win it all."

Kobayashi puts her hands to her face, like she's playing peek-a-boo, and rubs her eyes. "There's a lot of money riding on this fight, Ryan. I don't really want to cancel. But. . ."

She looks at him.

"I worry about your health. Your future. Kamikaze is ruthless. He would happily kill you and think nothing of it."

Ryan raises his hand and points at his skull.

"I know," he says. "That's his MO. I'm sure there are things that chinpira's done that we don't want to know. . ."

"I don't know about *that*. . ." Kobayashi says.

"I do know. I've felt it. On the street with Eriko. And then again. Wouldn't have had to pound my head many more times on that train platform before it opened up."

Kobayashi spins in her chair and looks out the window.

"Don't take this away from me," Ryan says. "I appreciate you looking out for me, Kobayashi-san, I really do. But I'm telling you, I got this."

She doesn't say anything for a minute, staring at the city. Then she turns her gaze back to him.

"Okay. I don't really want to cancel. I'll call Akio."

Ryan stands and bows formally.

"Thank you."

***

Kamikaze thrashes the bag full force with his knee. The teardrop heavy bag sways back and forth on its tether, as if trying to break away. He repeats with the other leg, alternating strikes with each knee. Then, he steps back slightly and launches a series of punches.

"Surprised they let you train here," Akio says, walking up. "You're destroying all the equipment."

Kamikaze snorts.

"I'm the one that pays the bills. . ." He points out a couple posters of himself on the wall, his hand held up in the ring, wearing the belt over his shoulder, like a piece of golden armor.

302

"Everyone's here because of *me*."

Akio grins. He puts his hands in his suit pockets and stands there.

Kamikaze goes back to smashing the trembling target. He moves gracefully but with tremendous power, sweat making his muscular torso gleam.

"Don't let it go to a decision, Eiji" Akio says. He walks around the bag until he's facing Kamikaze.

The fighter pauses and locks eyes with him.

"End it. Finish them all. Send them packing. Let there be no mistake who the champ is. Break things if you have to. Do *whatever* you have to do."

Kamikaze stares at him. He gives Akio an abrupt nod. And then turns back to the bag, unleashing a torrent of punches and kicks with a loud *aishi*.

Chapter 19

Enson walks in to Purebred with a rail-thin man, heavily tattooed, a colorful pair of eyeglasses up on his forehead. Pedaling on the stationary bike, Ryan's on his tenth mile. He's standing up, like a kid trying to get up a hill, pushing his legs down as hard as he can.

Who's this? Has that street swagger. Except for those specs. . .

Enson waves Ryan over.

He's glad for an excuse to hop off the bike, and he walks across the gym, toweling his face and neck as he goes. The floor feels strangely solid beneath him after an hour on the bike.

"You said you wanted a trademark look," Enson says as his fighter strides up. "This is the guy for you." He pats his guest on the shoulder.

"How about a tattoo?"

Enson points at the man.

"This is Takumi, he's a tattoo artist. The best. Whatever you want, it's on me, braddah."

Ryan talks briefly with Takumi and then heads to the showers. When he returns, he finds the artist ensconced in Enson's office. They discuss some options, and Ryan sits in his typical chair while Takumi trains his rainbow-colored eyeglasses – and his slender, bamboo-handled needle – on Ryan's left arm.

"Did you do Enson and Nori's tattoos?" the fighter asks.

"Yep," Takumi says, his voice thick and raspy like scraping rocks. "Those two keep me pretty busy."

"Then I like your work already," Ryan says.

Takumi concentrates, his head down, eyes half-closed, sketching away, like a calligrapher with a quill. He periodically wipes the arm clean of blood with a paper towel. Soon, a fish begins to appear. It's a koi, swimming upstream, a Japanese symbol of perseverance.

The boss walks in to grab a piece of paper off his desk.

"Nice," he says, looking closely at Ryan's arm.

"Yea man, I love it," Ryan agrees.

Takumi looks up at Ryan over his glasses.

"Just remember the little people when you're famous," he growls. Then chuckles.

The tattoo takes a few hours and is just the beginning of Ryan's transformation.

Gotta make sure I leave a lasting impression. . .

***

Ryan walks down the street, headphones rocking Kanye and Jay Z's collab. He sings along with the beat, about how he's not a businessman but *the* business.

He pauses in front of a storefront. He looks at the slip of paper Enson had given him, confirming the address.

Must be the place.

He steps into an ultramodern salon. The subtle scent of freshly cut hair hung in the air, and chrome and mirrors cover every surface. A few beauticians stand behind chairs, styling the hair of a few young Tokyoites. In the corner, a beautiful, dark-haired Japanese woman sits under the bowl of a hair dryer. A tall, slender guy walks out from behind the desk and approaches him.

"Can I help you?"

"Hi, can you fit me in?" Ryan asks in Japanese. "I need something that will turn heads."

The hairdresser looks at his watch, then shrugs.

"I'm Naoki," he says, leading Ryan to a barber chair. "Have a seat."

The fighter plops down, and Naoki wraps a silver smock around his neck. Naoki looks at him in the mirror, considering the possibilities. When he touches the back of Ryan's head to get a closer look, his fingers land on a scab left by Kamikaze. Ryan flinches.

"Wow, what happened here?" he asks, leaning in. "Looks nasty."

Ryan tells the hairdresser about the altercation on the train, explaining that he's an MMA fighter, getting ready for battle. Naoki snaps his fingers and points at Ryan.

"I thought you looked familiar. I just got tickets to the event."

They both smile.

"When we're done, I'd like to get a picture, if that's okay," Naoki says. He hands Ryan a lookbook, and the American pages through. The styles looked great on Japanese but, he doesn't see anything that would work with his thick, coiled texture.

"Let's do something different. Can you give me a lineup and dye my hair black and yellow, like a killer bee?" he asks.

"I can do that," Naoki says, nodding. "Gonna take a while, though."

The procedure lasts a few hours, split into various phases. First is the cut and lineup with the clippers. Next, Naoki uses a trimmer to carve precise lines. When he finishes, he hands a mirror to Ryan so he can check his edges.

Next, Naoki walks his client over to another chair and has him sit under a bucket, where Ryan spends the better part of an hour scrolling through his flip phone as his hair marinates.

Naoki calls one of his co-workers over to give him a hand with the final step. The two hairstylists work in unison, crafting a black-and-yellow masterpiece.

Ryan looks at himself in the soaring mirror. He smiles.

Hell yeah. Float like a butterfly. Sting like a bee.

As he exits the salon, the gazes of passersby shift – not just because he's a foreigner this time, but because his bold new hair style demands a second look. As fight day draws closer, Ryan sees himself on billboards all over Tokyo, his hair dyed in stark black and yellow halves, with two scowling eyes in the back. With his unmistakable new look, he is stopped frequently in the street for autographs and snaps.

***

The week of the fight, competitors arrive in Tokyo from all corners of the world. Ryan has to do the usual press, Kobayashi arranging interviews. Today, he has an impromptu conference at the fight venue, Saitama Super Arena, for weigh-ins. All eight competitors make the agreed-upon weight with Ryan coming in at 70 kilos on the dot. Reporters crowd the room, thrusting microphones at him and the other fighters. Kamikaze doesn't even acknowledge him.

"Are you ready for tomorrow's event, Mr. Bow?" an older gentleman in a tie asks.

"I guess I better be," Ryan laughs.

This elicits a chuckle from the crowd. By now there are about two-dozen media people swarming, like hornets around an apple. A woman with a cameraman in tow steps over to him. She glances across the lobby at Kamikaze, who's busy answering questions of his own. Akio stands near him, lining up the reporters, cool as ever in his black suit and sunglasses.

"You and the reigning champion, Eiji "Kamikaze" Tanaka, have had some heated encounters recently, outside the ring. Care to comment?"

"With all due respect, not much to say, really. Growing up, my father always used to say that there's a time and a place for everything. Now's not the time," Ryan says, excusing himself.

"Ryan," someone else in the crowd yells, "is it true you had a fight at the train station and spent some time in jail?"

"Is there bad blood between you?" another reporter blurts out. The questions start to come fast and furious.

"Do you really think you stand a chance against the champ?"

"Think you'll last more than a round?"

"You speak such good Japanese. How long have you been here?"

"How are you going to avoid Kamikaze's vicious stand-up game?"

Ryan holds up his hands.

"I appreciate all the support. Again, with all due respect, I'm going to let my fists do the talking. In the ring. You'll see soon enough what I'm capable of."

***

Ryan shuffles down the hall of the nearby hotel. The rug beneath his feet feels about a foot thick, it's so cushy. Conch-shell wall sconces light the way. He finds the room he's searching for and knocks. The door isn't locked and opens slightly at his touch.

"Kobayashi-san," Ryan says quietly. He pushes the door and peers in. He sees Kobayashi, facing away from him, as she quickly slides on a robe. Sprawled across her back is a red-and-black dragon, its scales shimmered with a dark sheen, painstakingly detailed to reflect its strength and spirit. Its snout pushing up through chrysanthemums and cherry blossoms at her right shoulder. Ryan is struck. Not just by the graceful curves but by the image itself.

Body art like that can only mean one thing.

She turns and notices his wide eyes.

"Sorry," he says, gathering himself. "The door was open. I just wanted to know what time the photos, ah, you know, what time the photos, um. . ."

She notices his discomfort.

"Yes, tomorrow morning at nine-thirty," she says, gesturing for him to enter.

Her room, unlike the typical fighter's suite, is a penthouse, complete with a mahogany bar, plush chairs, and floor-to-ceiling windows overlooking the massive arena below. Ryan sits on a large ottoman. He fidgets with his hands and looks everywhere but at Kobayashi. She notices. They're both quiet a moment. Finally, she breaks the silence.

"You saw my tattoo?"

He nods.

She studies his face.

He doesn't say anything for a moment, glancing around her room, taking note of the king-sized bed and attendant mirrors. He turns back to her.

"You're yakuza?" It's more of a statement than a question.

"My family is, yes," she responds.

He fidgets even more, and a bead of sweat drips down his face.

"Is this something you've kept hidden?" he asks.

"Everyone who needs to know, knows. My family name has opened many doors for me. . ." She locks eyes with him. "And not just for me. For us. . ."

"Why didn't you tell me?"

She pauses, then lets out a sigh.

"You wouldn't understand. Being *Gokudo* is not just what you see on TV or in the movies. My family. . ." she trails off.

"Oh, I understand," he says. "Everyone in MMA seems to be a gangster."

"That's not fair, Ryan. I'm no gangster. I've distanced myself from that aspect of the business."

He opens his mouth to say something and thinks better of it.

That aspect of the business.

He bobs his head up and down, looking at his feet, not knowing what to say.

"Our families pretty much run MMA. I don't see you complaining when I get you fights. When I'm on the phone with Akio. When I go with you to talk to Maeda. You think Maeda's hands are clean? And Purebred? You sure it's as pure as it sounds?"

Ryan keeps his mouth shut, just continues to nod.

"You're not wrong about the sport. It has its dark side, but it's also part of the reason you're standing where you are today."

"I understand," he says, getting up to leave. He turns when he reaches the door.

"Shortly after we met, when Kamikaze and Haru attacked Eriko and I in the street, there was a phone call. Was that. . .? Did you. . .?"

He lets the question hang in the air.

She winks at him.

***

Ryan lies in his hotel room staring at the ceiling. The lights are out and everything is quiet except for the rumbling AC unit and vibration of the mini-fridge. Stretched out under the polyester bedspread, he pounds the mattress beside him. *What if Eriko got hurt? I could never have forgiven Kobayashi-san if anything had happened to her.*

His chest wells at the thought of his love. His eyelids grow heavy, and his throat tightens.

Why can't she be here? Why God? Why?

He thinks back on everything that's happened since he set foot in Japan. He built a life here – found a job, made friends. Enson took him under his wing. Kobayashi agreed to represent him. He was on the verge of becoming a champion. He fell in love. But then came the other side of it. He's been assaulted several times. He was thrown in jail. Lost the woman he loved. His mother OD'd. The looming threat of losing his family home. And now, the brutal reality that fighting – the only thing he's ever wanted – might leave him blind. Or worse.

To be fair, Kobayashi went to bat on his behalf – several times – and when she grasped the full weight of the risks, she chose his health over a payday.

But just how deep does this really go?

Ryan drifts off, unsure what to make of Kobayashi. Was he now in bed with yakuza, too?

None of it matters, though. All that matters is the house.

***

Diane has trouble moving up the walk. Amen holds her arm, keeping her upright, and they waddle toward the front door.

"Good to be home," she says.

"Good to be home," Amen repeats.

He opens the front door and walks her across the living room to her chair. He holds her hands as she sits, lowering her into it. Like an elderly person.

"Place is a mess," she says.

"A mess?" he says in feigned horror. Then he chuckles. "You should have seen it before Ryan came home." He looks around. Amen had spent hours picking up, vacuuming. Ryan had put in many more before him, bagging up trash, mowing the lawn, bringing the house and yard back to a near normal state.

"TV?" he asks.

"No, let's talk for a minute." She points to the couch, and he drops himself into it. She studies his face.

"I know this has been hard for you, Amen."

"Not as hard as it's been for you. . ."

"Let me speak."

He puts his hands up in front of his chest.

"I'm feeling better. The ECT, the therapy, the prescriptions. . . I think they're working."

"That's good news."

She looks around the room. Then returns to his eyes.

"I need you to know, none of this is your fault. . ."

"That's what you've said. . ."

"Please, just let me finish."

He nods.

"I still love you, Amen. That hasn't changed. I just stopped feeling. . . I was lost, in a haze of medication. I was angry we let him fight. Scared something could happen to him. I withdrew, from you, from everything. With Ryan gone, I wasn't sure what there was to live for."

"You're still here. That means everything."

She smiles, then continues.

"The doctors helped me understand my depression wasn't *me*. It's my brain, the way it's wired. The chemical imbalance. They helped me realize Ryan's an adult, capable of making his own decisions." She looks down at her lap. "I want things to change."

"Change?"

"Yes. I want to find a new normal. Life with you and me. I want to start playing piano again. Maybe take up gardening. I want to go back to teaching. . . There's a lot I want. You and the doctors have made me see that."

She smiles at him.

Amen bobs his head slowly.

"I'll help you however, I can," he says.

***

Diane seems better. She gets out of bed in the morning. Goes about her days. They walk together after school. Eat out a few times. Sit together on the couch, talking. He sees her smile again and laugh every once in a while. She's not the same woman he first met, but she's transformed entirely, very different from the one who inhabited their bedroom some years ago.

Diane turns her attention to the postage-stamp of yard behind the house, turning over the soil, planting seeds. She's taken up reading again, making regular trips to the local library branch and the little bookstore around the corner, where she'd get tea and peruse for hours. She has dinner ready when Amen gets home from work, and they eat at the table rather than in front of the TV.

It goes this way for weeks.

Then one day the phone rings.

Amen hops up to get it. He walks away from her, into the kitchen with the receiver at his ear. Diane bends at her waist trying to listen.

"Yeah," he says, pacing. "I understand, but I don't have it at the moment."

He walks back and forth on the linoleum.

"Yes, sir. I know," Amen says into the phone.

"But we don't have it. I can't give you what we don't have. If you can give me some time, I can try to get it. . . By when? You really think that's fair? My wife's been in the hospital. . . Ok. . . ok. . . I understand. Yeah."

He puts the phone back in its cradle, and his chin hits his chest. He takes a deep breath. Then lets it out in a long stream.

"Who was that?" Diane calls from the couch. "What's going on?" She puts her book down on the side table.

"Nothing to worry about," Amen says, walking back into the room.

"Nothing to worry about? Don't you give me that, Amen." The calmness that had been on her face a moment ago is gone, replaced by the dark he'd become used to seeing before the hospital.

"Look at me."

"It's not really any. . ."

She points at him.

"Amen, you tell me what's happening right this instant."

He sits back down, letting out another heavy breath.

"That was the mortgage company. . ."

Her eyes grow wide.

"The mortgage company?"

"Yeah, we're behind. . ."

"How'd you let us get behind?"

"It was either pay the mortgage or pay the doctors. We can find another place to live. I can't find another you."

Her head droops, and her shoulders sag. She doesn't say anything for a minute.

"This has been going on since I came home?"

He nods.

"Since before you came home."

"And you didn't think to tell your wife? You didn't think this was important?"

"I did think about it. I thought my wife's mental health was more important."

She tuts. Opens her mouth to speak then thinks better of it.

"What about our health insurance?" she asks. "I thought they were covering. . ."

"Health insurers won't cover anything else. They paid the bare minimum. It's a corporation, Diane, set up to make money. Not to help people. I've sat on the line for hours with them. Days probably. Just to listen to them make excuses. Give me reasons why they're not going to pay."

"How bad is it?" she says quietly.

He hesitates. Lets out another big breath.

"It's bad. Real bad."

She nods, surveys the room. Then says, "Tell me."

"The mortgage guy gave us four months to catch up or we're out."

She inhales sharply, her hand on her chest.

They don't speak.

Chapter 20

Spotlights sweep the crowd of more than 30,000 packed into Saitama Super Arena, one of the world's largest indoor venues, for the Rising Sun Fighting Championship. They wait for the arrival of the two fighters they're most anxious to see, necks strained as they stare up at video monitors that soar several stories into the air above the ring. Jon takes his seat with a few friends from the Gaijin House. An usher with a flashlight shows Teruo and Mutsuko to theirs, and they look around wide eyed, amazed at the spectacle, never having been to a fight.

Wearing dark suits, a pack of underworld figures walks down the concourse toward their ringside seats, and those near the aisle go quiet while they pass. Keen-eyed fans notice Haru at the head of the column, Toshi marching along beside him. They fill a row at the ground level. Akio is there, too, and confers briefly with Haru before heading backstage to see to his warrior.

The muffled sounds of the crowd flow into the locker room, where Ryan takes deep breaths, in a state of Zen-like focus. His eyes are closed as he stands shirtless, dressed only in the black-and-yellow shorts that are fast becoming a trademark. The koi fish on his arm is poised to swim.

The door to the locker room opens and a familiar face enters.

"Dr. Yuzawa-san," Ryan says, bowing.

"Ryan, glad I caught you."

"You came all the way to see me?"

"Yes, and no. I am the head physician for the tournament."

"I didn't know you were involved with the fights."

"It's new for me," the doctor says, putting a leg up on a chair and leaning forward. "Listen, Ryan, I saw your name on the roster, and I wanted to talk to you one more time about the risks you're taking."

"I understand the risks, doc."

"You think you do." He fixes Ryan with his gaze.

"You think nothing will happen. That you'll make it through because you have each time so far. But today's different. Not only is the risk always compounding – it gets higher every time you fight – but if you win, you'll face multiple opponents in the same night."

"When I win," says Ryan. "And I appreciate you coming, I do. But. . ."

"There's more, Ryan."

"What do you mean more?"

"Well, if I had to guess, your brain is still not fully healed from the beating you took in the street. And that increases your risk exponentially."

Ryan is quiet for a minute.

"I appreciate you coming," he finally says. "I appreciate your concern. But I can't stop now. Not when I'm this close."

Dr. Yuzawa bobs his head up and down.

"I assumed you would say that, but I needed to say my part. I wouldn't forgive myself if I let you go out there without fully understanding what's at stake."

"Thanks Doctor." Ryan bows. "You're a good man."

"Well, good luck."

Dr. Yuzawa exits, and as he does, Enson, Kobayashi, and Nori file in. Ryan focuses on his breath, inhaling in through his nose and exhaling out through his mouth. Beneath the steady rhythm, though, a wave of nervous energy pulses through him.

Have I trained hard enough? Will my body betray me? Did I take on too much too early? Will my head suffer any long-standing damage?

He breathes out one last time and begins to bounce up and down on the balls of his feet. He shakes his legs and torso and rotates his head around on his neck, working out all the kinks. He looks at his friends and nods at each one. Enson pats him on his back, and they push through the curtains.

***

Fans begin to scream as the spotlight sweeps across the stage, catching Ryan and the other fighters as they make their way toward the center of the arena. Flashbulbs explode from the stands. Long arrays of lights begin to strobe above them, bursts of color illuminating the crowd. Ryan notices Kamikaze and his entourage striding in the same direction. The noise grows louder and louder as the assembled masses notice Ryan and Kamikaze on the Jumbotron on both sides of the arena. Jon cheers loudly when he sees Ryan twenty-feet tall on the screen. Teruo taps Mutsuko on the arm and points up. She sees Ryan first and then the champ, and she purses her lips, unable to hide her concern.

Ryan steps out onto the platform, raised high above the crowd, and stands in a long line of fighters. Kamikaze takes his place at the other end. In the ring, a muscled man wearing a traditional *fundoshi*, a traditional Japanese loincloth, carries long drumsticks over to an enormous brown drum propped up on a stand and begins to pound on it. He almost looks like he's doing a form of martial arts himself as he pivots and spins, making long exaggerated strokes. The tribal beat echoes through the building, reverberating off the walls.

All around, the arena crackles with anticipation.

After a minute, the drummer pauses and a brunette woman wearing the black of the announcer steps into the middle of the ring with a microphone.

"Ladies and gentlemen, welcome to the Rising Sun Fighting Championship – coming to you LIVE for fight fans around the world!" She waits a moment while the crowd cheers and then raises the mic back up to her lips. "What a way to spend New Year's Eve!" More cheers.

"This will be an eight-man tournament." She gestures toward the line of fighters. "To my right is the fan favorite, the current, Impact world champion, "Eiji 'Kamikaze' Tanaka!" The arena erupts with applause. She continues to introduce each man in sequence.

"Wait, how does this work? Eight men?" Brent, who lives a few doors down from Ryan in the Gaijin House, leans in to ask Jon.

"Starts with four brackets, called quarterfinals," Jon explains. "The winners of each of those fights advance to the semifinals. The two remaining fight each other for the championship."

"So, Ryan has to win two fights before he even gets a chance at the champ?"

"Right."

Brent raises his eyebrows and settles back into his seat.

"Oh, he's good, you'll see," says Jon. He grins and looks back toward the ring, where the announcer is still doing her sales pitch.

". . .up and comer from Grand Rapids, Michigan, in the USA, Ryan Bow!"

The crowd explodes again, while the drummer resumes his rhythmic hammering. Beside Jon, Brent beams at the response to Ryan. Teruo and Mutsuko sit amazed, like parents who've just discovered their child has a precocious talent. Kobayashi clutches her hands in her lap.

"Before we begin," the announcer continues, "there are some changes to the rules. Professional-level fights are typically composed of three, five-minute rounds. But today we'll have a ten-minute round followed by two five-minute rounds."

Fans cheer. The announcer waits for them to quiet.

"Soccer-ball kicks are allowed. Elbows are not. A secondary referee will be ringside to ensure fighters remain in the ring at all times. . . And now, without further ado, in our first fight of the evening, Ryan Bow and. . ."

At Ryan's name, the arena fills with cheers and screams, and the drums resume, drowning out the announcement of his opponent.

Ryan stands in his corner with Enson behind him.

"Okay, what do we know about this guy?" Ryan turns to look at his coach.

"Small, fast, slick on his feet," Enson says locking eyes, "so it'll be good to get on the inside and grapple as soon as you can. Cut him off if he tries to circle to your left."

Ryan nods, staring at his opponent, a Japanese man with a shaved head and no ink.

***

The referee calls them both to the center of the ring and gives them the usual shpiel about fighting fair. Ryan and his opponent give one another the once over. Ryan doesn't budge. He follows his opponent's gaze left and right.

"If you're going to touch gloves, now's the time," the referee says.

Ryan puts his fist out, but his opponent just turns back toward his corner.

The bell chimes, and Ryan strides into the center of the ring. The Japanese fighter rushes in, and Ryan puts his hands up, ready to block. The guy surprises him by shooting in on Ryan's legs and dropping him onto the mat. He follows this with a savage kick toward Ryan's head, which barely misses. He then starts to repeatedly kick the American in the legs. Ryan curls into a defensive posture. Still on his back, he thrusts a kick upward towards his opponent's face. This forces the fighter back, giving Ryan time to leap to his feet, and he rushes forward, and forces the clinch. Surprised, his opponent tries to circle away. Ryan presses him up against the ropes. The Japanese fighter sidesteps and reverses the position. With his back to the ropes, Ryan takes hold of his adversary's wrist. He loops his left arm over his shoulder and back through, grabbing his own wrist, creating a perfect *Kimura* arm lock. The guy tries to spin out of it, but it only gets tighter. He gets frantic, doing everything possible to pull his arm free. The grappling contest results in the pair falling to the mat with Ryan on top in control. From side position, the American folds his opponent's arm into the crease of his lower back and steps over his head, applying maximum pressure. The Japanese contestant has no other option but to tap out.

The ref stops the fight, and Ryan jumps to his feet, arms raised above his head. The arena erupts again. The speakers come to life with the announcer's voice: "We have our first winner! RRRRRRRRRyan Bow advances to the next round!"

In the audience, Jon and Brent jump from their seats and cheer. Mutsuko and Teruo breath out, relieved. Eriko's mother had been doing some wrestling of her own, holding her husband's hand so tightly, her nails start to cut into Teruo's arm.

Fighting Blind

***

Back in the locker room, Enson applies ice to swelling around Ryan's left eye. The fighter leans back against a wall, exhaling heavily.

"You look spent already," Enson jokes, poking him in the ribs.

"Ah," Ryan says jumping.

"Yeah, I guess he got you good there. Wish you could've got him out of there sooner."

"Me too. I was trying to protect my head. If I get caught, and don't see it coming. . ."

"I get it." Enson pats him on the back.

"Ah," Ryan flinches again.

"You're going to take a lot worse than that," Enson says, chuckling.

A monitor above the lockers shows the contestants stepping into the ring for the next bout, Kamikaze's first. The underworld champ stares at his opponent, a Chinese combatant who's slightly smaller and has his head down. Wearing bright red shorts, the young fighter seems overly awed by Kamikaze right from the get go.

"This could be rough," says Ryan, gesturing up at the screen. "Guy won't even look Kamikaze in the eye."

Enson nods.

"Better him than you. Hopefully he goes long enough to tire the champ."

The referee gives the usual speech and sends the two toward their corners. As soon as the bell rings, Kamikaze sprints toward his opponent, who seems startled by his speed. He almost trips as he stumbles backward. Kamikaze leaps into the air, hurling toward him and landing a flying knee with pinpoint precision. His rival's head soars backwards, and he's out before he hits the ground, the side of his face coming down hard on the canvas. He lays still.

The crowd is quiet, stunned by the ferocity and sheer force of Kamikaze. Then they begin to cheer and rhythmically chant his name.

"Ka-mi-ka-ze, Ka-mi-ka-ze, Ka-mi-ka-ze. . ."

The champ is already leaving the ring, as if this outcome was inevitable, a foregone conclusion, and the referee has to reach over the ropes to grab his arm to hold it aloft.

"And the winner of our second bout is, in eleven seconds time, Eiji 'Kamikaze' Tanaka!"

In the locker room, Enson lets out a low whistle. He crosses his arm in front of his chest and watches the monitor.

"That didn't take long."

Ryan nods. He's almost as shocked as the crowd.

"That's gotta be a world record. Never seen such a short fight," he says, his knee bobbing up and down as he looks up at Enson.

The door opens and Nori pokes his head in.

"You see that?" he says, with a jarring chuckle.

"We saw it," Enson replies.

"He won't catch you like that," Nori says looking dead serious at Ryan.

"Thanks."

"You're up next." Nori pops back out.

"One more fight and you get your shot at him," Enson says to Ryan.

"Assuming I win," Ryan says.

Enson turns on him.

"Assuming?" Coach Inoue glares at Ryan and then shakes his head.

"How about, when? I don't see you having trouble with anyone here. . ." He pauses, pointing backward over his shoulder at the screen, ". . . except, you know. . . We fight our battles one at a time," he holds his index finger upright between his eyes.

"Stay focused."

They head for the door.

***

Fans cheer as Ryan, Enson, and Nori, make their way back to the ring. The Jumbotron picks them up, and the crowd gets even louder. Ryan tries hard to keep a poker face, taking long, shallow breaths without moving his lips. He bounces up and down as he walks, both to stay limber and to mask his emotions.

He takes his place in the appointed corner and looks across the ring to his next opponent. A chiseled Japanese fighter with a slight height advantage over Ryan stares back.

"You got this," Enson says, kneading his shoulders.

"You know exactly what you need to do. This next guy is new. Nori and I couldn't find anything on him. They call him 'Masa.' You're going to have to get your reads and do it quickly. Fast hands? Wrestler? Jiu-jitsuka? You know the drill." Enson glances over at the fighter.

"Obviously, he's got reach, and he had to be good enough to get here. . ."

When the bell rings, Ryan hesitates momentarily. He meets his opponent in the center and sends a swift kick at the guy's mid-section. The Japanese fighter easily parries it away. He fires back with a left-right combo. Ryan can't slip both of them and catches the right on the left side of his face, where it opens his swollen brow. Blood starts to flow into his left eye. Masa follows with another couple of punches and then a flurry of kicks, driving Ryan back into a corner where he is stuck, absorbing a series of blows. Masa hammers away, Ryan trying to block and shift and cover as much as he can, but he's getting swarmed.

In the audience, Jon grimaces. Brent pretends to hide his face. Mutsuko again has Teruo's hand in a death grip, her face pale with concern. Kobayashi, ringside, sits on her hands to avoid fidgeting. Haru and company look over at her, and several sneer. Haru mouths "Gaijin" and holds his own throat, pretending to choke. Kobayashi rolls her eyes at them and turns back to the ring.

Masa continues to pummel Ryan until the bell rings. Ryan shuffles over to his corner and falls heavily onto his stool. He takes his mouthguard out and breathes for a minute, gasping, before taking a drink, swishing water around and spitting.

"Take it easy," Enson says, wiping blood away from Ryan's eye.

"Now we know what we're up against. Let's regroup. Plan B."

Ryan nods.

"Clinch when you can. Get inside."

The American nods again, taking another swig from his bottle. He's still huffing.

"And calm down. No worries," Enson says. "Surprise him. You keep trading punches and kicks. He's going to win that game. Do something he's not going to expect."

Ryan puts his head down. Thinking. And then it comes to him. . .

"Ding!"

Ryan bops to his feet and meets Masa in the center of the ring. The jacked Japanese fighter instantly starts a barrage of fists and feet. Ryan counters, throwing punches that eat away at Masa's abdomen. He's able to slip inside his opponent's reach and connect with a couple of powerful punches. Masa obliges and returns fire, not giving an inch. Ryan backs away and circles, stepping to his left so that he can keep Masa in his line of view.

Masa pushes forward and delivers another succession of blows that force Ryan backward toward the corner. He's visibly tiring, moving slower, huffing through his mouth. The Japanese fighter strides toward him, growing in confidence. He's landing a few blows here and there and wants to finish the American.

In the corner, Enson looks at Nori, concerned. Nori narrows his eyes and nods. They both look back toward the ring, where Ryan continues to duck and cover.

"C'mon," Enson says under his breath.

"C'mon." He crosses his arms and lets out a long exhale.

Seeing Ryan not offering much resistance, Masa moves in closer, escalating his attack. He throws punch after punch and kick after kick. All of this aggression seems to tire him, though, and stiff strikes become sloppy haymakers. He misses as much as he connects with reckless shots that continue to sap his energy.

Ryan keeps taking backward steps, tracking his opponent. Masa follows him, eager, smelling weakness. The American steps to the side and leads his foe back toward the center of the ring.

"Keep moving!" Enson says to himself. "Don't let him corner you again."

Masa steps in to continue the onslaught. Ryan explodes into the air, bending at the waist and jumping with his torso parallel to canvas. He scissors his legs, one in front of his opponent, and the other behind his knees, taking him down with a *Kani Basami*, a flying scissor sweep. Before Masa can extricate himself from Ryan's legs, the American grabs hold of his ankle, applying a reverse heel hook. He increases the pressure until there's an audible "pop," and Masa pounds the canvas, tapping out.

The crowd screams with delight.

The bell rings. Ryan gets slowly to his feet and holds his heavy arms over his head.

***

Ryan's eye is completely closed now, an orb of swelling protruding from his brow has forced it into submission. In the locker room, Enson works his magic with the Enswell to reduce the swelling, hovering around his fighter like a watchful parent.

"You did great out there, braddah. . ." Enson says. "I didn't get your strategy right away, but it was clever."

"Got him, but it took some doing." Ryan breathes out. "That was a close one."

"A win is a win. That's all that matters. We'll get you patched up and ready for the big one."

Enson follows the eye iron with an ice pack to further manage inflammation on his pupil's face.

"Ahhh," Ryan says as he winces. He looks up at the monitor, where Kamikaze and his opponent rush at each other the moment the bell rings. The other guy fights out of Osaka, and, again, is slightly smaller than the champ. Ryan doesn't recognize him.

"Man, that guy just doesn't let up."

"Hmmmm?"

"Kamikaze, he's a machine. He still looks fresh."

"Nah, he just hasn't been tested the way you have."

Ryan breathes out. Nods.

"He is another small one. You know him?"

"Heard of him," Enson says. "Don't know much, though. Reps a gym in Umeda."

Kamikaze and his challenger trade vicious punches and kicks in a mutual onslaught, both landing heavy blows.

"Doesn't even faze him," says Ryan.

"Oh, he feels it, alright."

The Osakan fighter comes in low for a takedown, and Kamikaze stuffs it, forcing his opponent's head into the bloody canvas. Kamikaze backs off, mocks him, screaming something through his mouthguard. Just as his foe stands, the champ charges, driving him backward into the ropes. He unloads with an onslaught from all directions, battering the Osakan. The guy actually attempts to retreat through the ropes and flee the ring, but the secondary ref blocks his way.

Kamikaze explodes a right hook into the fighter's ribs and follows with an uppercut to the chin that hits like a piledriver, almost taking the guy's head off.

"Holy shit!" Ryan says leaping up to see the screen more clearly. The clock shows less than a minute has elapsed.

The blow lifts the challenger off his feet, his body goes limp, and he crashes down to the canvas like a marionette whose strings have been cut. Kamikaze stands above him, ready to end it with a soccer-ball kick. The referee grabs his shoulder and pulls him back, stopping the fight. The champ shrugs it off and steps toward his opponent, stomping on his chest. The Osakan curls into a ball. By this point the second referee, and the fallen fighter's coach have formed a protective barrier between the adversaries. Kamikaze's lips curl into a sneer, and he backs away. The referee puts his hands on the champ's chest and walks him back to the center of the ring, where he raises his hand in victory. The crowd erupts. Kamikaze pounds his own chest, walking corner to corner and staring at the fans, a tiger in a cage.

"Don't worry about it," Enson says in the locker room, where Ryan watches the action on screen, eyes wide.

"Fuck em," Inoue continues, "make him fight you at *your* fight."

"That's easy to say," says Ryan, breathing out heavily.

"Get your head right" Enson says. He fixes Ryan with a steely gaze. "You can win this!"

Ryan nods.

Nori pokes his head around the locker room door.

"You're up."

Enson puts his hand over his fist in front of his chest. "Ryan, Remember the Yamato Damashii Way. Give it all you've got, until the very end."

Ryan nods again, clapping his gloved hands together with a muffled thump.

The stage manager, a small wiry Japanese man, walks into the locker room.

"Ten seconds," he says and disappears as quickly as he appeared.

"I got something for you," Enson says, pulling a black-and-yellow satin robe out of a tailored bag. He steps up behind Ryan and slips it over his shoulders. Ryan runs his hands over the fabric and then turns his back to a mirror. His face breaks into a smile.

Raijin, the fierce and powerful God of Thunder, graces the back, pounding his *taiko* drums – each embroidered with the kanji for 'Kaminari,' the word for the thunder he controls.

"Nicknames aren't chosen. They're earned," Enson claps him on the shoulder. "You've earned yours, Kaminari."

Ryan takes a deep breath and pushes through the door.

***

The sweeping spotlights find him and light him up. He hops up and down on the balls of his feet making his way down the concourse as the sound system blasts Eminem's "Lose Yourself." Fans bob their heads and sing along to the Michigan native's anthem about getting one shot to seize a once-in-a-lifetime opportunity.

With his new robe, Enson's confidence, the song's message, and the love of the crowd, Ryan finds newfound energy. His shuffle turns into a strut, as he approaches the ring. Enson and Nori follow behind him, staying far enough back to allow him to bask in the adulation. As he reaches ringside, Ryan turns and embraces them one at a time. The crowd roars. He climbs through the ropes and his coaches take their place in his corner.

The speakers begin to pound with a techno pulse as the champ makes his way toward the ring. Kamikaze raises his arms over his head and bangs his head with the beat, a smug smile on his face. The picture of arrogance. Behind him, in trademark suit, sunglasses, and slicked back hair, is his senpai, Akio. Kamikaze climbs up onto the mat and vaults over the ropes.

The curly haired announcer walks back to the center of the ring.

"Eight men started tonight's tournament," she says, swinging her arm toward each fighter. "We are down to just two. For our final fight we have Eiji 'Kamikaze' Tanaka and Ryan 'Kaminari' Bow. For the championship of the world!" She raises her arms over her head.

The crowd comes to its feet, cheering louder than they have all night. Jon and Brent look at each other excitedly.

335

"The championship of the world?" Brent says into Jon's ear.

"I'm telling you mate. He's come a long way!"

Brent grins, impressed.

In their seats, Mutsuko and Teruo look on as they have all night. She's still sitting on her hands, motherly concern written all over her face; he's unreadable, no expression at all.

The referee waves Ryan and Kamikaze toward him in the center of the ring. The two fighters end up face to face. Kamikaze stares at the American with cold black eyes. Ryan holds his gaze. After a few seconds of this Eiji shoves Ryan backwards.

The crowd bursts into boos.

Ryan takes a step toward the champ, and the referee grabs his wrist. He does the same with Kamikaze, in an attempt to gain control of the situation. He looks at both fighters in turn and begins his brief.

"I want a clean fight," he says in Japanese. "I will not tolerate anything less and will not hesitate to stop the fight. You will listen to my instructions at all times. Defend yourself at all times. Now, touch gloves."

Ryan reaches his hands out in front of him. Kamikaze sneers, turns his back, and walks to his corner, to more jeers from the audience. Ryan stands in the center of the ring and glares at his antagonist. The bell rings.

Kamikaze bursts from his corner and charges Kaminari. They exchange blows. Ryan eats a stiff jab, followed by a question-mark kick to the head. Ryan blocks the champ's foot at the last second, amazed at the force behind it.

This guy has power.

Ryan keeps shifting to his left, always with an eye on Kamikaze. He can hear Enson shouting from the corner:

"Keep your distance."

Just as Enson says this, Kamikaze latches onto the back of Ryan's head, taking the Thai Plum clinch. He secures his hold and gets off a couple of devastating blows, his knee hitting the American's side over and over like a battering ram. Ryan struggles to break free.

"Break his grip! Pummel inside!"

Ryan works to do just that, firing a series of shots to Kamikaze's body. Then, pummels his hands up the center to gain control. His left hand sneaks through and cups the back of Kamikaze's head. A right uppercut follows up the centerline, rocking Kamikaze's head back, allowing Ryan to disengage. It's only a moment before Tanaka is on him again. The American takes a straight right to the side of his head and stumbles to the canvas.

"Scramble!" Enson screams.

Kamikaze dives in for the mount, and Ryan catches him with a thunderous upkick, which knocks him off balance. The champ staggers away, reeling like a drunk.

Just then the bell rings.

The crowd goes crazy.

Ryan drops onto his stool.

"He's better. . ."

Enson won't hear him.

"Watch out for that Thai Plum, Kamikaze loves it. You have to strike first."

He looks into Ryan's eyes.

"I don't want to see you back over here. This is it. This is your moment."

Ryan stares at him. Enson raises his eyebrows and tilts his head.

The bell summons the fighters back out.

***

Both race for the center of the ring, where Kamikaze comes in hard with an overhand right, barely missing Ryan's face. As his fist passes, the American level changes and meets him with a blast double leg down the center, sending him tumbling to the mat. Before Ryan can capitalize, the Japanese fighter pops back to his feet, and they square off again in the center of the ring. Kamikaze feints a jab and then throws a spinning back fist. This one lands – coming from the left – connecting with Ryan's jaw. His knees buckle beneath him, and he stumbles backward into the ropes. The champ grins and readies a flying knee.

"The knee," Enson yells from the corner.

Ryan throws his hands out to block the hammer he knows is coming, but Kamikaze's momentum is too great and his patella slams into Kaminari's side. Ryan lands hard on the canvas. The audience gasps. The American goes into survival mode, turning his collapse into a roll. He manages to get up onto one knee. Kamikaze leaps into the air and comes crashing down with a vicious elbow strike to the back of Ryan's head. The champ stands over the fallen fighter, ready to finish him off.

"No!" Akio screams from ringside. Kamikaze looks at him and cocks his head. His emotions cloud his judgment.

He turns back to Ryan only to find the referee standing over him.

"Foul! Striking with an elbow to the back of the head." The ref puts his hand on Kamikaze and pushes him back toward a neutral corner. Kamikaze bats his hand away.

The ref stands his ground and looks up at the champ, holding a single finger up to his face.

"One point deduction for an illegal strike." He then turns to the crowd and walks from one side of the ring to the other, making the same gesture. "One point deduction for an illegal strike!"

Ryan pulls himself up the ropes and rests a moment, trying to gather himself. His head is shrouded in fog, and he shakes it slowly back and forth. He attempts to step toward the center of the ring, but his balance is gone, and he's wobbly. He backs up against the ropes and puts his arms out wide along their length, holding himself upright. He looks across the arena, which seems hazy and quiet. He moves his jaw around and puts his hand to the back of his head.

"You can do it Ryan!" Jon screams. He's jumped up from his seat. "You got this!"

Teruo and Mutsuko crane their necks, silently. Hands clasped. Faces unreadable.

Enson and Nori exchange glances, tight-lipped, jaws clenched.

Kamikaze is trying to push past the referee to get back and finish the fight. The ref puts both of his hands on the champ's chest, like a child in a schoolyard trying to restrain a bully.

***

Ryan continues to struggle to regain his composure. Everything to his left is black – he can detect no light or shapes – and the ring seems to slant in front of him. He can hardly hear the cheers from the crowd over the ringing in his ears. He lets go of the ropes for a moment and sways like a toddler. He sweeps the arena, wondering why the fans are all silent. He sees faces that are obviously cheering and hands that are clearly clapping, but still, he can't hear. His eyes lock on an older couple, stoic, seated several rows in the distance, and he squints to get a better look. For a moment his mind clears.

They came.

Mutsuko and Teruo notice Ryan staring at them and get to their feet. They join the crowd in cheering.

Sounds begin to filter back in. Ryan continues to watch Eriko's parents for a moment and then pivots toward the corner pad. He puts his hands on his knees, pushes off, and stands. Then he arcs his back and goes fully upright. A jolt of pain pierces his side, but he remains tall. He shuffles his feet. Swings his arms in circles. Rolls his head around on his neck.

He glances over at his corner. Enson nods and bends at the waist, clapping his hands in front of him. Nori smiles and holds up a fist.

The referee lets go of Kamikaze and walks over to Ryan.

"Can you fight?"

Ryan struggles into his fighting stance. He's still unsteady on his feet, but a calm has come over him. He takes a deep breath through his nose and lets it slowly out his mouth. Thinks of Eriko. Her smile. Her voice. Her touch.

"Can you fight?" the ref asks again, staring into Ryan's eyes. He drops his chin and claps his hands together in front of himself.

The arena erupts with cheers and applause. Ryan can feel the energy rather than hear it. He's enveloped in a feeling of calm and serenity. Thousands of voices blur into nothingness, their cheers and jeers swallowed by his focus.

Akio looks on with wide eyes and open mouth as the American walks to the center of the ring. Maeda has a similar look. Kamikaze smiles, pleased he can continue the violence. He knocks his gloves together, tilts his head back, and steps away from his corner. The ref raises his hand between the two fighters and drops it, signaling the resumption of the fight.

The crowd continues cheering. Jon, Brent, and Ryan's other flatmates hop out of their seats, straining to get a closer look. Teruo and Mutsuko stand, too, clapping. Kobayashi has her hand on her cheek, her body curled forward in her seat, nervous.

Kamikaze explodes at Ryan, going straight for another Thai Plum, hoping to end the fight quickly. Using the champ's forward momentum, Ryan shucks his shoulder inward, performing a Russian tie to secure Kamikaze's right arm. Then, he suddenly drops to his knees and launches the Zainichi fighter over and onto his back on the canvas with an *ippon seoi nage*, the same throw he learned as a child in judo class. Kamikaze lands with a thud. He scrambles to his feet, but Ryan drags him back down to the ground.

Now, you're on my turf.

"Put the pedal down!" Enson yells from the corner.

Ryan unleashes a barrage of hammer fists from side position, chopping downwards like an ax cutting through wood. He connects squarely on the bridge of Kamikaze's nose, forcing him to cover his face. To free himself, Kamikaze fires an underhook, driving Ryan back, and impressively fights back to his feet. But he leaves his head hanging a bit too low, and Kaminari latches on with a vice-like guillotine choke. It's in deep. The champ is caught, a flicker of panic in his eyes. He thrashes, his hands grasping and pulling at Ryan's arm, every muscle straining, every breath a battle. His hands pry at the American's arm, searching for an opening, trying to break free. But the hold is locked in. Tight. Unforgiving. His movements grow weaker. . . slower. . . Then, stillness. His body goes limp. Ryan finally lets go. Kamikaze crumples to the canvas, motionless.

The referee steps in front of Ryan, waving his hands. "No more. No more."

Ryan leaps up onto the corner ropes, his arms raised in victory. Confetti streams down from the arena rafters, and the crowd bursts into applause and cheering.

"Ryan! Ryan! Ryan!" a chant begins to swell.

Enson vaults the ropes.

"He did it! He did it!"

Nori's wears a big grin and pumps his fists. He reaches down to help Kobayashi climb onto the apron of the ring to join in the celebration.

***

Three ring girls parade around, posing for the ecstatic crowd. One of them hands Ryan a giant check for ten million yen. Maeda clambers through the ropes, his bulk hung up briefly between them. He frees himself and walks toward Ryan with a gold-plated belt in his hand. He reaches around the American and fastens it at the back.

"Not bad for a gaijin," he says with a jolly chuckle.

Ryan drops to his knees and looks toward the sky. His arms raised over his head in victory.

The announcer steps back into the ring and hands the microphone to Ryan.

"I've been faced with a lot of challenges in my life," he begins. "When I moved to Japan, I wasn't sure this day would ever come. But with a strong team behind me. . ." he pauses, gesturing at Enson, Nori, and Kobayashi.

The crowd is loving this, Jon among them, proud of Ryan's Japanese.

"I was able to fight a strong, Japanese champion, feared by everyone in the division, in front of people who love this sport as much as I do. When I was weak. . ." he points at the crowd,

"You lifted me up with your cheers. You gave me the strength to continue." He ends with a heartfelt, "*Arigatou*

Gozaimashita!" He bows deeply in the direction he's facing. Then walks to each side of the ring, saluting all attendees. He holds his final bow for an extended period and the lights in the arena begin to fade and the iconic celebratory track fills the air.

Ryan hands the mic back to the announcer who smiles at him.

He makes his way to his corner to join his team, climbing through the ropes. On the hanamichi, the raised walkway, Ryan finds Jon, Brent, and a few others from the Gaijin House he didn't know were coming. He thanks them, bowing and shaking hands. Behind them Teruo and Mutsuko stand patiently. Ryan steps toward them. He bows deeply to each of them. Teruo gives him the hint of a smile and nods.

Afterword

Thank you for taking the time to read *Fighting Blind*. While inspired by true events, this tale blends fact with fiction to craft a compelling story – one that not only entertains but also conveys the emotional and physical challenges we all must face.

Ryan, the protagonist, is deeply flawed yet relentless, much like myself. Like all of us, he longs to achieve his dreams despite the obstacles in his way.

The path to success is fueled by those around us. Family shapes who we are, for better or worse. We tend to get swept up in the romanticized stories often displayed on social media, but the truth is, life is far more complicated than that. In Ryan's case, in addition to suffering from a prenatal stroke and having a disability, he has a loving mother battling bipolar disorder and a father whose unwavering devotion pushes him forward, even in times that would bring others to their knees. This storyline hits uncomfortably close to home because their struggles are real, their love imperfect, yet they define the foundation of his journey – and therefore, my own.

Fighting Blind

Personally, family was both a source of tremendous strength and devastating loss. My relationship with my father was tragically cut short when he passed away suddenly when I was just 21. His absence left a void I struggled to fill, so much so that I contemplated retiring from the sport soon thereafter. In many ways, this novel became my way of finally grieving – of imagining the heights I might have reached with him still by my side.

That sense of loss extended beyond family. Building a new life alone in a foreign country as a young man was a lonely road. Throughout the story, I had the chance to revisit not only the challenges of adapting to a new culture but also the realities of discrimination that we, as foreigners, face while living in Japan.

Furthermore, the novel delves into the hidden world of organized crime and its deep-rooted ties to prizefighting. It's no secret that the right connections can make or break one's career.

By the same token, in our personal lives, some bonds are stronger than others. Eriko, Ryan's love interest, is based on an actual person – a beautiful soul who entered my life when I needed her most. Unfortunately, love doesn't always work out the way we hope. The struggle to be accepted by her family was a battle we faced in reality, leaving scars that lasted long after she passed away.

Ultimately, *Fighting Blind* has been, in its truest form, a therapeutic and deeply personal endeavor to come to terms with the hand I was dealt, the unfulfilled dreams, and finally grieving the death of the woman I loved.

Because, at the end of the day, we are all searching for the same thing: acceptance. A place where we truly belong.

"Hug your Loved Ones. You never know when it will be your last."

- Ryan Bow

Let's Stay Connected

For updates, connect with us here:

Fighting Blind – The Novel

Instagram:

https://www.instagram.com/
FightingBlindTheNovel